TOM BLUEFOOT,

CHIEF TECUMSEH,

AND THE

WAR OF 1812

LLOYD HARNISHFEGER

Order this book online at www.trafford.com
or email orders@trafford.com

Most Trafford titles are also available at major online book retailers.

Print information available on the last page.

ISBN: 978-1-4907-6715-4 (sc)
ISBN: 978-1-4907-6714-7 (e)

Trafford rev. 11/12/2015

North America & international
toll-free: 1 888 232 4444 (USA & Canada)
fax: 812 355 4082

PREVIOUS BOOKS

HUNTERS OF THE BLACK SWAMP

PRISONER OF THE MOUND BUILDERS

COLLECTOR'S GUIDE TO AMERICAN INDIAN ARTIFACTS

LISTENING GAMES FOR PRE-READERS

LISTENING ACTIVITIES FOR BEGINNING READERS

BASIC PRACTICE IN LISTENING – GRADES 3 – 4

BASIC PRACTICE IN LISTENING – GRADES 5 – 8

THE KID WHO COULDN'T MISS

BLACK SWAMP WOLF

TREASURE ON BEAVER ISLAND

TOM BLUEFOOT, WYANDOT SCOUT, GENERAL "MAD ANTHONY"

WAYNE, AND THE BATTLE OF FALLEN TIMBERS

FOREWORD

"TOM BLUEFOOT, CHIEF TECUMSEH, AND THE WAR OF 1812" IS A SEQUEL TO "TOM BLUEFOOT, WYANDOT SCOUT, GENERAL 'MAD ANTHONY' WAYNE, AND THE BATTLE OF FALLEN TIMBERS". While the present narrative stands alone, readers would benefit from reading the novel about FALLEN TIMBERS first.

The following is a book of historical fiction. Dates and places are as accurate as research can establish them. Known historical figures are portrayed correctly, while conversations, dialogue, etc., are necessarily contrived.

Readers can rest assured that they have been afforded at least a glimpse into this critical time in our nation's history.

"TOM BLUEFOOT, CHIEF TECUMSEH, AND THE WAR OF 1812"

The musket ball seemed to rock the small canoe. As the sound re-echoed up and down the Ohio River, Tom Bluefoot dug his paddle deep and spun the craft directly toward the very shore from which the shot had originated. It seemed foolish to venture closer to the danger, but his only hope was to work his craft under the willows and try to escape on foot.

A finger of white smoke hanging above the bushes gave ample evidence of his attackers' location. Tom [Toom-She-chi-Kwa] rammed the birch bark canoe directly into the tangled brush lining the Ohio's north shore. He slipped into the shallows and slithered up the bank, staying as low as his small frame allowed. He heard voices. They seemed to be growing louder, and it sounded like they were angry!

With his left hand, Tom reached back and clawed up a fistful of mud. He plastered the sticky goo on his face, hoping to blend in with his surroundings. The young Wyandot forced himself to breathe as quietly as possible, but there was nothing he could do to calm the sound of his pounding heart!

"I can't stay here," he thought desperately. Footsteps were suddenly heard. They were close. Veryclose! He saw leggings and a moccasined foot touch the ground less than two paces from his head. Inch by inch he moved his right arm down toward his only weapon. Instantly a blinding pain stabbed through his skull. A war club, weighted with a band of lead, had done its job.

While Tom was knocked nearly senseless by the blow, he was not completely unconscious for he could feel the force of a vicious kick in the side. Groggily he rose to his knees and was promptly rewarded with another kick. He fell back and pretended to faint.

There were three of them. Toom-She-chi- Kwa lay very still and kept his eyes closed. Despite the awful ringing in his ears he could hear them clearly, speaking in a dialect very near to the tongue of the Shawnee. "Where did he hide the canoe?" one asked, searching back along the river trail. "As the one whose bullet allowed us to capture him, I claim his rifle and shot pouch which must still be in the canoe. It can't be far from here."

"You missed him! You have no right to his musket or anything else."

"I missed him on purpose. See how it brought him right into our hands? His gun will be mine."

"Down here!" another brave shouted, parting the willows to reveal the small craft.

"Remember the gun is mine!" the first speaker said. All three rushed down the bank to the canoe's hiding place and began pawing through Tom's small bag of possessions. "He's hidden it somewhere. Spread out and look. We'll find it!"

Tom could hear bushes breaking as the three Shawnee braves searched for the musket. Now was the time! Cautiously he rolled onto his side and crawled deeper into a thick stand of bulrushes growing at the very edge of the river. His plan was to slip into the stream and swim as quietly as possible the nearly half mile to the southern shore of the Ohio River.

"He's getting away! There he is! Grab him!"

Two Shawnees grabbed his legs and dragged him backward up the bank.

"Who are you, and what are you doing here? This is our land."

"What did you do with your musket? Tell us or we will kill you now rather than later."

Tom tried to look confused. He shook his head to indicate that he didn't understand, thinking he might have some sort of advantage if they were kept unaware that he spoke their language.

"Where is your gun?" the oldest Indian snarled, pantomiming aiming and firing a gun. "Gun?" he shouted, his face mere inches from Tom's nose.

Toom-She chi- Kwa shook his head and attempted a friendly grin. He shrugged his shoulders and glanced from one to the other.

"Are you from the camp of the big Kan-Ton?" The question came from the only brave who had not yet spoken.

"Kenton! Kenton!" Tom nodded eagerly. There was no point in claiming

Ignorance, as the famous frontiersman's name was the same in any language.

"Where is Samon Kan-Ton now?" The speaker's left earlobe was grossly elongated by a heavy brass earring. He leaned down and yanked Tom to his feet. "Kan-Ton!" he shouted, pointing in each of the four directions.

Tom shrugged his shoulders and smiled at the one he now thought of as "Earring". This attempt at friendship earned him a resounding blow across the face. Earring turned to the others and muttered angrily, unsure of what their next move should be.

"It is likely he didn't have a gun, or by now we would have found it. Also there is no bullet pouch or powder horn. He could have dropped the gun into the river but he wouldn't have abandoned his powder and shot. What should we do with him?"

"He knew of Samon Kan-Ton," one answered. "We must be careful. We are not in Shawnee lands any longer. The treacherous treaty by the 'Mad General' Wayne does not allow us to be traveling this far east."

"You speak the truth," Earring said bitterly. "If we let this ignorant traveler go he will surely alert any settlers of our presence here. He was on his way somewhere in that pitiful canoe. Who knows? He might even be heading for the fort at Chillicothe."

"The choice is clear," the one Tom thought of as 'Barefoot' nodded. "He has nothing worth taking. Only his knife and a small ax."

"There is a pouch of pemmican still in the canoe. It won't go far among the three of us, but it will be a welcome change from that tough old 'possum we've been gnawing on. Are we agreed then? We kill him now, and hide his body in the brush."

"Let's shove his canoe into the current and let it float back to the west. If anyone misses him they'll just think he drowned. That way our presence here will not be given away."

Tom had heard and understood every word. Panic threatened to overwhelm him. He prepared to leap to his feet and dive into the river, but before he could move, Earring spoke again.

"Let's have a little sport with this miserable piece of dog dirt. When he wakes up let's tie his legs together and pretend to go to sleep. If he has any brains at all, which I doubt, he will try to run. We let him get a head start, then we give chase. It shouldn't take too long."

"But if he has his legs tied . . ." Barefoot began.

"Think, you fool!" Earring growled. "Of course we will not make the knots very tight."

The one who rarely spoke, reluctantly agreed to the plan. He suggested that they not try to bring Tom out of his faint, but go ahead with the trusses while the man remained unconscious. They began, making no attempt to be gentle.

Tom groaned, shook his head, and batted his eyes. It was a fair job of deception. He tried to rise, but fell back, reaching for his ankles. Earring shoved him back with a foot on his chest. "Let us prepare to sleep," Barefoot said loudly.

"You need not shout," Earring snarled. "He cannot understand our words anyway. There is no hurry. He would not expect us to bed down this early. We should use this time to plan our next move."

Tom looked from one speaker to the other, keeping an expression of confusion on his face. "What have I gotten into now?" he thought. "These men are certainly up to no good. When they allow me to 'escape' I'll have to make it successful or I'll be filled with arrows before the sun is high tomorrow!"

Barefoot was eyeing Tom's moccasins with a wicked gleam in his eye. Suddenly he lunged downward and yanked the beaded doeskin shoes from his captive's feet. "Oho!"he gloated, but the shoes were too small for him. Unperturbed, he pulled his knife and slit the end of each one. He worked them on, paying no attention to his big, dirty toes protruding. "You see," he said proudly, "this skinny traveler does have something worth stealing!"

"If you are quite finished with such foolery, I repeat that we must make plans. Who can tell how many more enemies may be traveling on the Oh-hee-yo? And they might be well-armed settlers, or even a squad of soldiers." He looked at the silent one for a minute. "You never say much, Old Blanket, but you have more wisdom than either of us. What do you propose?"

Old Blanket still did not speak for a while, then he began. "Tecumseh himself has given us this mission. We must be successful or die in the attempt. This Kan-ton," he stopped and spat angrily, "is a traitor to our people. Granted, he survived several brutal gauntlets, and mainly because of this, he was adopted into our Shawnee tribe. But then once again he fought on the side of the Shemanese! Pah!"

"I saw him myself in the Battle of the fallen timbers near the mouth of the Maumee," Barefoot said. "He killed at least six of our people in that fight. First he shot them, then he used his rifle as a club. He even smashed the skulls of our wounded brothers as they lay in their own blood. I saw this <u>myself</u>!"

"And what were you doing while all this killing was going on? Hiding behind the biggest log you could find, I'll wager," Earring said, making no attempt to hide his contempt.

"Not true!" Barefoot exclaimed. "I fought bravely and might have done even more had my worthless musket not failed to fire."

"Enough of this!" Old Blanket growled. "Again I say we must be preparing this night. Chasing down this prisoner at first light must not be allowed to take long. We must first find the camp of Samon-Kan-ton, then find a way to kill him. Our great chief, Tecumseh, ordered this mission, and we are highly honored to be chosen to carry it out."

Earring spoke up. "Why is our War Chief so anxious to eliminate this frontiersman? And why did he not send more warriors than just we three? Of course Kanton is a turncoat, but he is only one man. "It seems to me . . ."

"More warriors would never work. They would cause suspicion immediately. Just three travelers may not. That is why he is a chief and you are not! You forget," Old Blanket continued, "that man has great influence among the Shemanese. It is said that with only a word from him, a thousand armed men are ready to march against Tecumseh's warriors. Even should the lying British actually help our cause, it is still necessary that this Kanton be eliminated before he can muster those who carry the long-shooter rifles."

Toom-She-chi- Kwa was astonished by what he was hearing. These three Shawnee warriors were on a special assignment, with explicit orders to find and kill Simon Kenton!

Evidently they did not yet know the frontiersman's whereabouts, but by feigning friendship they could soon get the information from friendly, "settled out" Indians now living along the Ohio.

Tom felt a rising sense of panic. Not only was <u>his</u> life in imminent peril, but also that of the man General "Mad Anthony" Wayne so highly respected. His mind was racing as he tried to formulate a plan.

Thankful that he had as yet not spoken aloud to his captors, an idea finally seemed to come about almost unbidden. He sat up and peered at each Shawnee in turn. Having no way to know what other languages the three knew, he could not risk using any. Motioning eagerly at Earring he began a rapid harangue in a high squeaky voice.

> "<u>Newg hata wittle bamsso</u>
>
> <u>Is sleem mus whittee seeeeef sli</u>!"

"Shut UP!" Old Blanket growled. He aimed a kick at Tom's head but the Wyandot ducked in time.

Tom began again, using elaborate gestures to enhance his "words".

> "<u>Evet tomne a mannter whens</u>
>
> <u>As twate many whens ist mooew zo tonel</u>!"

"What language is that?" Old Blanket asked of his companions. "It almost sounds like Shemanese, but I have a little knowledge of that tongue. It is not that of the whites."

"So," Tom thought, "at least one of them can understand a little English. That will help make my plan work." He looked at each brave in turn, as if expecting an answer.

"It is full dark now," Barefoot said to the others. "I think it is time to pretend to sleep. One of us must be sure to stay awake in case this underfed traveler should be foolish enough to try an escape before dawn."

"Do not worry," Earring said. "He is certainly a fool but with any brains at all he would know that thrashing around in the dark would make so much noise that he would immediately be caught. We will sleep now. Barefoot will have the first watch. Old Blanket will take over when the moon is high, then I will wait for dawn. If anyone sees him untying his ankles, let him do so. When he runs, and he surely will, don't let him get too far ahead. We have more important concerns than taking this skinny fool's scalp!"

All three wrapped themselves in ragged and dirty Hudson's Bay blankets. They had not built a fire, since they did not wish to make their presence known to those who might be traveling on the river. Tom's blanket was still in his canoe. He began to shiver almost at once. A long, cold night was facing him. Trying to forget the cold, he began to remember the recent past.

"Maybe in a week or so I'll be greeting my 'white father' again," he thought. "I sure hope he's still alive! It's been eight years since I last saw the old Quaker. A good man is Eli Miller! I owe him so much for rescuing me from my drunken father when I was little. It must have been six or seven years that he raised me." Tom's thoughts tumbled over each other as the long night slowly passed. He remembered with pleasure his service as an interpreter for General Anthony Wayne. With some pride, he recalled all he had done at the Treaty of Greenville six months before. "Sean and Chloe," he thought fondly. "My best friends! I suppose by now those two are married and living at Fort Pitt, or as some are now calling it, Pittsburgh. I hope I can get away from these assassins, and before long make it all the way there myself!"

Too cold to sleep, Tom continued thinking back. Fresh in his mind was the fighting among the twisted tree trunks near the mouth of the Maumee River, his part in inviting the many chiefs to the Council of Peace, and his experiences while attached to President George Washington's newly formed army, called "The Legion of America".

Old Blanket shifted position silently, obviously wide awake and keeping an eye on the captive. "Well here goes!" Tom told himself. Pretending to be very quiet he drew his knees up and began to work on the knotted rawhide. While he had heard them say that he would be loosely bound, his cold and shaking fingers had a hard time working the thongs off his ankles. Old Blanket lay very still and pretended to snore.

With his legs free, Toom-She-chi-Kwa began attempting to ease the cramps in his calves. He heard Earring murmur to Old Blanket that he would now keep watch, proving that morning was very near.

A sleepy night bird chirped for a moment and a hunting owl hooted overhead. False dawn was upon them. Tom gathered himself, took several deep breaths, and stumbled to his feet. He leaped completely over Barefoot and sped east down the trail.

"Aiee!" Earring shouted. "He runs!! Knock your arrows, give him a count of ten, then after him!"

Tom was small and not very strong, but he could run! He flew down the path, ignoring the bushes and branches that tore at his legs. Still not hearing their pursuit, he gave a mighty leap off the trail. A fallen tree, covered with moss was perfect for his plan. He lay prone and pressed himself as close as he could against the fallen beech. In less than a minute the Shawnee braves came thundering by, assuming he was still running east ahead of them. Tom jumped up and raced back west toward their camp. He slipped down to the river's edge.

"Why are you stopping?" Old Blanket yelled as he tried to keep up with the younger braves.

"No more footprints! He has left the path. Spread out and find him before he escapes into the forest!" Earring's words were harsh with anger. Tom could hear their shouts plainly enough, as they were as yet not that far away. With a pounding heart he put his plan into action. If it failed he would be subject to a most painful death, possibly even being scalped while still alive!

The small Wyandot picked up a fallen branch, stepped into the river and began splashing about. With the stick he began slashing at the nearby trees and bushes, making as much noise as possible. Filling his lungs and using a low voice he attempted to imitate the "parade voice" of his recent friend, Major Scott. "You there! Form up! Get in line!" Thankful that he had only spoken a word to the Shawnees, Tom tried to alter his voice and shouted, "Secure the barge. The rest of you, get ashore! Bring the baggage." He continued tramping about, using the stick as before.

"Soldiers!" Old Blanket hissed, losing his nerve at last.

"Where did they come from?" Earring's whispers sounded especially loud in the pre-dawn shadows as the three stood in a confused triangle.

"It is a bateau! There could be as many as twenty soldiers coming ashore. We must abandon our camp. The stranger's canoe is too small. We have but one choice!"

"And what is that?" Barefoot asked, using sign language.

Another loud Shemanese voice and more splashing interrupted Old Blanket's answer. "Swim! Swim as fast and silently as possible. We must be far from shore by full sunrise or we'll be shot with the soldiers' bullets. If we can

make it to the Kain-tuckee shore we should be safe for a while."

Barefoot shook his head savagely. "We have done nothing wrong. Why should we run?"

"You know as well as I that the big treaty at Green Ville says that all of the land where we now find ourselves is for whites only," Old Blanket said with disgust. "Do you trust the Shemanese? They may have lost comrades at the battle of the fallen tree trunks. No one is here to witness what they do. They will shoot us and take our scalps!" Old Blanket's words settled the issue. Each one slipped silently into the current and began swimming across the wide Ohio River, sure that at least twenty soldiers were taking aim at their retreating backs!

*   *   *

"It's an Injun!" The two young boys dropped their fish poles and scrambled up the bank in terror.

"Wait! I'll not harm thee. Call thy parents. I'll stay in my canoe until someone comes to the shore," Tom said as he rested his paddle across the thwarts. He dropped the two Hudson's Bay blankets overboard, and for the fourth time, soused them up and down. They were getting a little cleaner, but not much! He had taken them and a tomahawk the three Shawnees had left behind as they fled from the imaginary force of soldiers. The third blanket, the worst one, he had cut up to make a pair of shoes and a hat. He paddled gently, keeping the craft from drifting back with the westward current.

He had been traveling for three weeks after escaping from the assassins. Tom was slowly making his way east on the meandering Ohio River, his destination; Fort Pitt. The Wyandot's arms and shoulders no longer ached and burned from the task of propelling his canoe, but he had lost weight and found himself even skinnier than before. Food had been a constant problem. He had existed mainly on fish, pemmican, and jerked venison. Even by using a little of his remaining silver money, he'd had trouble finding settlers willing to sell food to a "thievin' redskin". The Indian wars east of the Mississippi were over, according to the Greenville Treaty of 1795, but hatred and fear still ran high among those pioneers now beginning to settle in the Ohio Territory.

"<u>There he is!</u> Right out there in that little boat, just like we said," one of the boys yelled, pointing at Tom and pulling on a tired-looking farmer's arm. A woman holding a baby on her hip was also visible, staying well behind her man.

"Shoot him Pa! You kin easy hit the varmint from here! Don't let him git us!"

"Stop it Calvin," the woman screeched. "I heered him talk our talk when you boys come a-runnin'. Ask him what's his bidness, Henry."

The man hitched up his ill-fitting homespun trousers and assumed what he considered a commanding pose.

"All right, you," he blustered, "tell me why I shouldn't shoot you dead right now."

"Well sir," Tom answered, showing off his best English, "I would merely suggest that if thy intentions are indeed murderous, thou wouldst do well to pick up the rifle ball that I distinctly saw fall out of your gun barrel!"

Red-faced, the farmer scrabbled in the dirt until he came up with it. "Quick Ma, rip off a piece of yer petticoat. I fergot to use any patchin' and the durn thing jest natcherly fell out! Now listen Injun, you may talk good but your skin's redder than our old red rooster. I'll have this here gun loaded in a minute, so yall better jest git a-goin'!"

"Thy musket must be a marvelous weapon," Toom-She-chi-Kwa said amiably. "I've never seen one that would shoot without a charge of powder!"

"Oh <u>tarnation</u> Henry! Can't you see that this little Injun don't mean no harm. If he 'd wanted to git us he could of done it while you was hitchin' up your britches. Calvin," the woman continued, "you run as fast as you kin to the Cameron's place and fetch them. They'll want to see an Injun that kin talk our lingo better than a lord!"

"But Ma, I want to see what happens with this here Injun. Besides," he whined, "it's near two mile up Hickory Crick to their place. It'll take me a hour, and another hour to git back with them Camerons. I want to <u>see</u> this! Couldn't Jacob go instead?"

"You heard your ma. Git goin' before I help you along with a sassafras switch!" The man looked at Tom as if proud of the way he handled his family problems.

Paddling a little closer to the shore, Tom called to the pouting lad. "Calvin is it? Thou seemest a promising lad. Let us palaver a bit. Do as thy mother has told thee. Should thy parents allow me to come ashore, I promise to remain until thee and thy neighbors join us here. Does that seem reasonable to thee?"

"Now wait just a durned minute there stranger. I ain't allowin' any of yer kind to come traipsin' right up to our cabin just like a white man. I've heered the stories. Lots of them! People just murdered and they scalps took by yer kind. No sir! You better jist dip yer paddle and high-tail it right on up the river. Now git!"

"You come right on to the bank," Ma said calmly. "Pay him no mind. He sees murdering Indians behind ever bush on our place. Skeered he is. Allus was! If you got guns er hatchets and such I'll thankee to leave 'em in your boat. You come on in now. Calvin, get goin'."

"I thank thee, madam. I assure you that I am not armed. I have no intention of harming anyone. I do have a tomahawk and my skinning knife, but these will remain in the canoe during the entire time of my visit."

"I don't like this," Henry growled. "You don't know these people, Ma. Why I'll bet . . ."

"Be quiet, Henry. Come on to the bank young man. What is your name?"

"I am Wyandot. My real name is Toom-She-chi-Kwa. It means 'he paints his foot'. I was a scout in General Anthony Wayne's army. The soldiers just called me Tom. Thou can do the same if thou wish."

"Who do you think you're foolin' with all that churchified kind of talk? I figger it's a trick to get such as us to let you get close."

Gravely, Tom raised his right hand in a sort of friendly salute. "I can see that thou art a man who takes care of his own. Rarely have I encountered a more stalwart and resolute citizen of the soil such as thyself. My most sincere compliments to thee, sir!"

Henry had no idea how to react to this. He didn't know the meaning of some of Tom's words, but it seemed he had been given a compliment. He scratched his head.

Mary, who'd had the benefit of a few years of schooling, laughed aloud at her husband's distress. "Gimme yer hand Tom," she said, stepping right into the shallows. She helped him ashore, not commenting on the ill-fitting bundles of wet blanket that served as Tom's shoes. "Now Henry," she ordered, "you drag that canoe of hisn high up on the bank where it'll be safe for him when he decides to leave."

Henry sniffed disgustedly, but did as he was told. Tom pretended not to notice when the man leaned into the canoe, grabbed the tomahawk, and slid it into the bushes.

"Come on to the cabin, Tom. You look like you ain't had a cooked meal in a coon's age. Is that the way of it?" Mary shifted the baby to the other hip and preceded him into the cabin. "It ain't much, but it's all ours!" she said proudly.

Once inside Tom was amazed by what he saw. It was all one room. A dry sink was attached to the west wall. A rope bed next to the table provided the only seating, but the mantle was what caught Tom's eye. Made of a single, squared black walnut log, the entire surface had been intricately carved. Birds, squirrels, and even a prancing horse were depicted so realistically that Toom-She-chi-Kwa stared in astonishment. "Why . . ." he stuttered, "who on earth did that carving?"

"My Henry, that's who! Ain't it purty though? It took him quite a while working evenings, but he got it done and now we all just look at it. Run yer fingers over them critters, Tom. See how smooth he got them?"

"Why that's the best work of that kind I've ever seen," Tom said, turning to Henry. "I saw some carvings like that in a big church at Fort Pitt when my white father, Eli Miller, took me there once. Yours is better!"

"Aw it ain't neither," Henry replied modestly. Quickly changing the subject, he asked, "How soon we gonna eat, Ma?"

"Not for a while yet Henry. See Mr. Toom ...see, . . ., whats ever yer name is, we usually eat just twice a day. Them boys of ours gets powerful hungry but we make them wait. Food goes further that way."

The younger son spoke up for the first time. "You gots two daddies then, do ya?"

Tom smiled at the lad. "I guess you could say that, Jacob. My real father and mother were Wyandot, so I'm a full Wyandot too. My Indian father was a drunkard. He was begging whiskey around Fort Pitt, and I guess he wasn't taking good care of me. Eli Miller, a Quaker man, saw what was going on. He gave my father money for drink and took me in. I was with him for six years."

"Wow," Jacob exclaimed, big-eyed.

"But what of your mother?"

"Well Mary, I don't know what ever happened to her. I guess she left my father when I was still little, probably because of his drinking." He stared into the fireplace for a minute, then continued. "When I was about ten years old my real father showed up at Eli's house and demanded that I be given back to him. I then lived mostly with his sister, my aunt, in Chief Little Turtle's village."

The talk continued. Tom learned the story of the Walkers' adventures making a home in the Ohio wilderness. They were interrupted by a booming voice signaling the arrival of Calvin and the Camerons.

"Hello the house! The Camerons are a-comin in. We got your boy with us. That kid has been worryin' us along ever since we left! Had to near hog tie him, to keep him from runnin' up ahead!"

"Come in here right now!" Mary shouted, holding the heavy oak door wide open. "Set down. I got coffee on the crane."

Matthew Cameron and his brother were dressed completely in buckskins. Matthew sported a cap of red fox fur and an enormous bearskin coat. His brother was dressed nearly the same. The woman, Matthew's wife, was small and delicate-looking. She had obviously put on her best dress for the visit. It was faded and threadbare but better than that which Mary was wearing.

"Is this him?"

"That shore is him all right," Calvin crowed.

"Calvin, you be quiet. Mind your manners around your betters," Mary snapped. Nothing was said for a minute, then the brothers strode up to Tom and looked him in the face. "What are you doing here? These ain't Indian lands no more. You ought to git a-goin' before somebody shoots you fer tresspassin'.

Leave these good folks alone, you hear?"

Mary stamped her foot. "Now Matthew you stop that kind of talk this instant! Mr. Toom . . .er . ..uh. . That is Mr. Tom, is a nice man. He's not here to harm anybody!"

"He can talk better American than any of us. And he was in the army under General, . . . General . .what's his name again?" Mary struggled.

"It's Wayne ain't it?" Henry asked.

"Yes. Some of the soldiers called him 'Mad Anthony' Wayne, but not to his face of course!" Tom said with a smile.

"Was you really in the army? Did you kill anybody? Take any scalps?" Calvin asked, his eyes popping with excitement.

"No I never killed anybody, so it follows that I didn't take any scalps either," Tom laughed. "I was just a scout for the 'Legion of America', that's all."

"A scout was you?" Matthew growled. "Probly a durned redskin spy as well!"

"Now that's about enough!" Henry snapped, surprising everybody. "This here Injun is a guest in our home, me and Ma's, so we'll all be civil here."

Mary stared at her husband in shock. "Why thankee Henry. Them's my words as well. Now Miz Cameron, I'll ask you to oblige me by helpin' me get some vittles together for all these men. How you been keepin' up there by the creek? You ain't in the family way yet are ye?"

Betsy, the Cameron woman, blushed to the roots of her black hair.

"No ma'am, I'm not," she mumbled. "What can I do to help?"

"Calvin, you and Jacob get on down to the river and dip up a bucket of clean water. Walk out on that fallen log a ways so you don't get no mud in it!"

"Aw Ma, let Jake go. I want to hear all the talk."

"You know it'll take the both of you to get it back here to the cabin so as not to spill half of it. Now git a-goin'."

Matthew's brother, Foster, spoke for the first time. "We don't mean to be bad company as to this here Indian who calls hisself Tom. But our Pa was killed in the battle at Point Pleasant. So you can see how it is with us folks. Then Matthew here, he ups and joins with the Kaintuck Volunteers in order to fight old Little Turtle's bunch up on the Maumee or some place."

"Yeah, that's true, but Foster here, he was too skeered to jine with me."

"Was _not_ skeered!" Foster yelled. "You know as well as me that Ma wouldn't _let_ me go. 'I already lost one good man', she said, 'and I don't aim to lose two more!' That's erzackly what she said, and you know it too!" Foster said, scowling at his older brother.

"Aw don't take on so. I was just funnin' you a little. Simmer down!"

"So you were in the battle they are calling 'Fallen Timbers' were you?" Tom asked, surprised.

"Well I was, shore enough. I was one of the Kaintuckee Volunteers. Had my own horse and everything. I'm proud to say that us from Kaintuck just about won that fracas all by ourselves!"

Tom nodded, but failed to mention that the volunteers from south of the Ohio had indeed led the charge, but turned and ran as soon as the firing began! It was all General Wayne and his officers could do to drive them back before their poor conduct could start a disastrous rout.

"I was there too," Tom stated, watching Matthew's face as he said it.

"I lost my best friend in that war," Matthew said, anxious to change the subject.

"So did I." Tom stared at the mantle for a few minutes, then added, "He was one of Wayne's special sharp-shooter squad."

Matthew punched his brother, Foster, and said gruffly, "come on you two. We need to git a-goin' before full dark. We ain't got no time to eat nothing here." He wanted nothing more to be said about his part in the Battle of Fallen Timbers, certainly not by someone who obviously had been there!

"Betsy," Mary said, holding the young woman's hand, "you come on back here real soon, you hear? You and me can have some real girl talk while the menfolks is foolin' around outside."

"Oh I will. I will!" she replied eagerly, as her husband literally pulled her out of the door.

"Ifn I was you," Matthew yelled as they left the clearing, "I'd put that Injun outside all night and be sure to bar the door. You hear me?"

No one answered.

"Well Tom, it's gettin' on to our bedtime. We got a lantern, but no oil fer it, and we're saving our last two candles for emergencies." Mary was embarrassed.

"We ain't got much room as you can see," Henry apologized. "Things gets pretty crowdy in here of a night. Me and Ma and little Lizabeth sleeps in the bed and the boys underneath of it."

Calvin spoke up quickly. "You could stretch out on the floor, right in front of the fireplace. You'd get along jest fine as long as a spark don't pop out and light on you!"

"No thanks. I'll sleep outside like I have been doing for about three weeks now." He paused a moment, then spoke to Mary. "How old is your little one?" he asked, watching the sleeping child.

"lizabeth's about a year and a half now. She never seems to grow much, and I reckon you've heard that bad cough she's got. I'm real worried about her Tom."

"That little gal's doin' poorly, and that's a fact. I was lucky to find a bee tree up on the hill and Ma's been dosin' her with honey mixed with a little mush. It helps some."

Tom felt real pity as he observed the infant. It was obvious that she was very sick. He had seen this before. Some of the "camp followers" in General Wayne's army had families. Many of the smaller children got sick from the harsh conditions prevalent in the army camps. Many died before they reached the age of three. "Is there any way you can get some milk for the little one?"

"Not anymore," Mary said, dabbing at a tear on her cheek.

"Them Meekers, upriver from here," Henry began, "got a cow, but their place is a long ways from here, and anyway we got no money nor anything to trade. They say there's herbs and such in the woods that can heal, but we don't know which ones they are. Do you, Tom?"

"No. Wish I did. Tell you what; just turn your backs a minute." He lowered his trousers a little and untied the neck of a small pouch strapped under his thigh. He pulled the drawstring tight after extracting a circlet of Spanish silver. Only two remained.

"Here," he said handing the coin to Henry. "Lay this on a log and use you ax to cut it in half. Have your boys go to the Meekers' every day. Give that family one of the halves if they'll fill a jug or something with milk every day for a week. Tell the Meekers they'll get the other half after another week. Better heat the milk a little each time you give her some."

Mary was crying silently. "Bless you, Toom . . .uh, . . .er . . . Blue Shoes! Bless you!"

"Many thanks Tom," Henry agreed. "Ifn you ever come back this way you're to stop and visit with us, and no mistake on that!"

"I will," Tom promised. "Now Calvin you listen to me. If you're up early, I'll give you a ride upriver to the Meekers' place. My Canoe's pretty small, but if you sit real still we can make it all right. I'm sorry I can't take you, Jacob, but I promise I'll bring you a present when I come back west."

Jacob was not happy with that arrangement. He refused to look at Tom again. "I'll be down by the river, wrapped up in my blanket. Sleep well, all of you, and remember to bar the door!" Tom said, laughing.

The night passed quickly enough. Dawn had hardly broken when Calvin, fully dressed, came racing down the path, Matthew following. Tom suspected that the boy had hardly slept during the night.

"Mornin'! Mornin'. Here, let me help you get your canoe in the water. Well i'll be," Matthew said. "I don't see your tomyhawk. I'll betcha it jest naturally fell out when I was beachin' yer boat!" He poked around for a minute then exclaimed, "Yessir, I was right! Here it is, under these bushes. Lucky I could find it fer ya."

"It sure is. Thanks Matthew," said Tom, hiding a huge grin.

"Wait! Wait up you two!" Mary came hurrying down to the river, carrying a small doeskin pouch. "Here's some Johnny cake for your journey. Mind you don't let that Calvin get at it or it'll be all gone long before noon!"

Matthew waded a few steps and pushed them into the current, Tom paddling and Calvin sitting on the bottom, still as a stone.

*   *

Three more weeks of fighting the Ohio's increasing current found Tom greatly relieved to finally see the Fort Pitt blockhouse showing above the trees. He cut across the river and beached his canoe on the Pennsylvania shore. For a few minutes he simply sat and rested as a crowd began to gather, their expressions anything but friendly.

"Keep moving Redskin! We don't allow no savages near the fort!" a big man shouted, advancing on the canoe.

"Shut your trap, Oliver. I'll handle this. That varmint can't understand good English anyhow." The second speaker was dressed in what appeared to be a sort of homemade military uniform. He had a star pinned to his coat that said "sheriff", but it looked like it was homemade. "You there, Isaiah, see kin you find that Indian who's always hanging around the livery. He can do sign language. Most all of these varmints understand that. We'll just stay right here and keep this savage from coming any closer to the fort." He took another step toward Tom, who had remained sitting silently in his canoe, watching the crowd. The man squared his shoulders, took another step forward, and extended both hands, palm-forward in an obvious order for the Indian to come no closer.

Apparently the man Isaiah could not find the Indian who was to do some sign language. The crowd shifted nervously, the cold wind off the river causing them to huddle together. Not a one would leave however, curious about the outcome of this situation.

"You better listen to me!" the speaker growled. "I don't care if you can understand civilized talk or not, but I reckon you <u>can</u> understand <u>this</u>!" he whipped his overcoat open, drew a derringer from a pocket, and took careful aim at Toom-She-chi-Kwa.

"Good afternoon Captain," Tom said politely. "There is no need for a weapon. As thou can plainly see I am unarmed."

Someone in the crowd laughed. "State your business right now!" he roared, anxious to regain his authority. "I ain't fooled. You probably got a murderin' hatchet too. If you got such as that, you just throw them out on the bank right now."

Obediently Tom drew his knife and tossed it into the grass. The tomahawk he'd taken from the abandoned Shawnees' camp came next. He sat back down and waited, feeling almost naked without his only weapons.

"See there? I told yall he'd have some weapons. I know just how to handle his kind, by jingo!" He looked around triumphantly, feeling that now he had carried the day. "Somebody pick up them things of hisn. I'll just keep my pistol handy in case he tries to make a break for it!" No one, including Tom, had any idea where he might try to go!

"I don't mean to trouble anyone Captain. I'm here to find the man who raised me."

"Don't listen to him," Isaiah yelled. He hadn't found the Indian who knew sign language, but it was now obvious that signing would not be necessary. "That's how they do, Jameson. They get you to talking and the first thing you know they're taking your scalp!"

"I <u>know</u> all of that, Isaiah. I've fought more of them red devils than you could dream about. What this smart aleck with all his fancy talk needs is some time in the lock-up until he learns his place. Now some of you men come along and we'll just get this savage under lock and key."

Captain Jameson's "jail" was actually the guardhouse inside the fort. Two prisoners were already incarcerated in the small square room, both sleeping off a drunken night of revelry. "What the . . . who's this, Captain? We don't aim to share our cell with the likes of a stinkin' <u>Indian</u>!"

Tom couldn't help but notice that the two men themselves were the cause of the bad odors in the place. "I'm not happy to be here either, gentlemen, but until my case is settled we might as well get along, don't you think?"

"That corner over there is yourn," the bearded man pronounced. "Me and my brother here will take the only bench in this place. You stay over there. You hear?"

Tom leaned back and let himself slide down to a sitting position in the corner. He hadn't eaten anything in two days and he was starving! "Do they bring food to you here?" he asked, politely enough.

"Hey Captain," the bearded prisoner yelled, "your Indian friend wants to be fed! You still got plenty of steak and sweet taters? I reckon he'd like a slab of pie, and maybe a cup of hot coffee. He'd like to have that <u>right away</u> too!"

Toom-She-chi-Kwa knew it was nothing but a cruel joke, but the mention of food set his mouth watering.

"Pipe down in there Jefferson. I can't see no need to feed a man who'll be dangling from a rope come sundown! Ha ha."

Tom's copper-colored face turned an ashen gray. Joking or not, he knew that such "instant justice" occurred far too often on the frontier. "Captain," he called out, "could someone just send for Mr. Eli Miller? He's the Quaker who runs a grist mill about three miles north of here. He could tell you that I've done no mischief and am not planning any. If he could get here it would save a lot of trouble for all of us. Please sir?"

"A Miller who's a miller, eh?" The jailer laughed loudly at his own wit, but did not agree to locate the man. "Wal, wal!" he exclaimed, as at that moment the heavy jail door creaked open. "Why Miz Jefferson, I'll bet you brought my dinner didn't you?"

"Now Captain you know as well as I do that these vittles is for my man Lige Jefferson and his no-account brother. Don't know why I bother with them. What did they do this time?"

"Got liquored up they did, then tried to bust all the winders outn the church building. If they promise to behave themselves in the future," he had raised his voice for the brothers' benefit, "I just might turn 'em loose about sundown. Now Miz Jefferson, you know I got to examine whatever you got in that basket. Have to make sure there's no contraband in there, you see!"

"I know what you're up to Captain Jameson. Well go ahead and take something, but I'll thank you to leave enough for them boys."

"What's fer supper today, Miz Jefferson?" her brother-in-law yelled. "Hope the Johnny cake's got lots of honey onto it!"

"What in the world . . ." she began, "who's that in there with you? Don't tell me you've taken up with the likes of <u>him</u>!"

"He's my prisoner Ma'am. I captured him myself and never had to fire a shot. He claims he was a scout for General Wayne, but you know what liars they all are."

"What you gonna do with him? Hang him?"

"I've done nothing wrong, madam. I've come to Fort Pitt to find the Quaker man who raised me. If someone would only fetch him I would very soon be exonerated."

"What's 'exonerated' mean?" she asked.

"For him it means hung by the neck! Haw haw!" The Captain guffawed.

"Land sakes, he can sure talk good can't he? Sure enough he can. Kind of scrawny-like though, ain't he?"

"My name is Toom-She-chi-Kwa. The soldiers called me Tom. I'm a Wyandot Indian, and I haven't eaten in two days. Is there any way I could get some food?"

"Shore! Shore there is. Regular prison food will be coming in about an hour, so just hold your horses."

"Pardon my familiarity Miss, but I can't help but admire your bonnet. It's French isn't it?" Tom asked, peering through the bars.

"Why . . .why. . . no it ain't. Made it myself, I did! These here ribbons were give to me by my man hisself. He's the bigger one in there with you."

"My congratulations, Mrs. Jefferson. Your creation is the very image of one I saw at a Frenchman's trading post back there at Fort Green Ville. He said it had come directly from Paris, France this very year."

"Well Tom, or whatever your name is, that's awful nice of you to say. Lige, you got more than you two need. Give this nice man a pone of bread. And dribble a little molasses on it too. He's got more sense and better manners than a lot of white folks I could name!" She looked at each of them, including Captain Jameson. "Now somebody better find this Quaker feller and get him down here! Oh never mind, I'll go myself. Now Mr. Indian Tom, do you have any idea where this mill happens to be?"

"I am very sorry, but I have forgotten exactly. However, Dr. Friederiech , whom I knew as General Wayne's army surgeon, might know. That is if he is located here at Fort Pitt."

"Doctor Friederiech?" the woman exclaimed. "Why he has an office just a few miles south of this fort. I wanted to go to him myself just last month to ask him about . . .about . . .well you men don't need to know why I wanted to see him. Anyway, Lige here wouldn't let me go."

"Heck fire, woman! What was we supposed to pay him with, sour apples?"

"Alright! Alright! I've heard enough of this. I'll get Jonas, the little colored boy who works at the livery, to go down there and see if the sawbones is willing to come," the jailer said. "That kid can ride one of the nags he's supposed to be taking care of. Now Mrs. Jefferson, you get on home and get your chores done, 'cause these men of yours won't get loose until after dark. Go on now."

"Here you are, Indian," Lige said as he threw a piece of cornbread in Tom's direction. "You wouldn't have got that if you hadn't sweet-talked my woman like you done. I can see you're mighty slick with them 'thees' and 'thous'. Makes a person wonder what else he's been up to, don't it Hal?"

"Aw let him alone Lige. Let's just wait and see what the doc has to say about him. That is if the doctor even comes up here. I'm beginning to think maybe he did do some scouting for old 'Mad Anthony". Otherwise, why would he try to get Captain Friederiech, the sawbones, to come to the jail? 'Course I reckon he'd try <u>anything</u> to keep from doing a 'rope dance'! I know I would!"

Tom had wolfed the bread down in less than a minute, and was busy licking the crumbs off his fingers. "I thank thee kindly Mrs. Jefferson," he smiled. "I hope the time may come when I might return the favor."

"You better figger a way to get yourself out of this lock-up first," Lige drawled as he and his brother tried to arrange themselves for a nap on the hard bench.

Tom was dozing in his corner when after nearly two hours the big door creaked open. "Well, where's he at?"

Toom-She-chi-Kwa leaped up, overjoyed to hear the familiar gravelly voice of the surgeon. "Captain Friedereich, is that you?" he shouted.

"Shut your mouth in there, Indian!" Jameson roared. "Here's the man you been a-clammerin' to see. Well he's one of them anyway. Come on in doctor. I thank you for leaving your work long enough to help us decide what to do with this here little Indian. I captured him myself, and didn't have no weapon but this here little double-barreled derringer. Course my military training taught me how to handle the likes of him! You see I was . . ."

"Tom, my boy! It's so good to see you again. But why are you locked up like this?"

"I can't tell you how glad I am to see <u>you</u>, Captain! I assure thee that I've done nothing wrong. I came by canoe all the way from Greenville. I was hoping that thou would be here. And I hoped you could direct me to my white father, Eli Miller. You see . . ."

"That's enough for now," the doctor stated gruffly. He turned to the jailer expectantly. "What is necessary to obtain this man's release?" he demanded.

Jameson came to attention and actually saluted the doctor. "Well sir, if you're willing to take him into your personal custody I reckon . . .that is I don't see why . . ." He saluted again.

"Forget all that saluting!" Friedereich snapped. "Neither one of us is in the army anymore. I accept your conditions. Let him out!"

"You can't know how glad I am to see you and to arrange for my release. How can I thank you? You may very well have saved my life!" Tom cried.

The doctor waited while Jameson fussed with some of the papers strewn across his small desk. "I'll need you sign this here paper, Captain Friedereich," the jailer said, shoving a rather ragged piece of parchment in the doctor's direction.

"Mr. Jameson sir," Tom spoke up, "would it be possible for you to use your influence to release these two men as well? It would take someone of your authority to do so, of course." Lige and Hal stared at Tom in astonishment.

The man puffed out his chest and assumed an air of dignified importance. "Wal now," he said grandly, "I think I have such authority, but why do you, just an Indian, ask me this?"

Tom and the two brothers hurried through the barred gate, all anxious to get going in case the jailer changed his mind. "I have been thinking of this man's young wife. It will be dark soon and snow is coming. She should not have to be concerned with heavy work in her condition."

"By golly I never thought I'd say it, but fer a Injun you're alright! I was some worried about my Catherine too. Come on Hal, we'll have to hoof it to get home before full dark."

"Just one durned <u>minute</u> now," Captain Jameson growled, "I'm telling you boys right now that you better be high-tailin' it right out to your place . If you figger on stopping at the tavern I'll soon know about it and you'll be right back in here for a lot longer stay!" Pushing and jostling each other, the brothers burst out of the door. Everyone, even Captain Jameson laughed at their eager departure.

The snow was coming fast and heavy, making the doctor's horse stamp its feet and shake its mane. "Get in! Get in!" he cried. His surrey had a roof, but it was doing little good as the wind continued to rise. They headed south, jouncing along on the frozen, rutted road. Even by shouting they could hardly hear each other.

Tom was wrapped in the doctor's buffalo robe, thankful for its warmth. His few warmer clothes had doubtless been stolen after his arrest. "Have you seen Sean and Chloe lately?" Tom yelled.

"What's that you're asking?"

"Sean O'Casey and his woman, Chloe. Have you seen them?"

"Yeah, I've seen them both, just about two hours ago," he chuckled.

"When I came to get you, Sean was just finishing up with an operation on a woman's appendix. Chloe was getting ready to sew her up."

"They're both with you then!" Tom shouted joyfully. "How are they doing?"

"You'll see them yourself in about half an hour. They're getting quite a reputation these days, even though there's some complaint about a woman's place being in the home. Almost half the people they operate on live to tell about it! Poor Chloe though. The work's hard for her, mainly because she can't get close to the operating table anymore! Ha Ha!"

"You mean they are going to have a child?" Tom asked, delighted.

"At least one, but I'm thinking maybe two!"

*   *   *

The reunion had been a happy one. Tom and his army friend spent most of the night telling each other what had gone on during the year-and-a-half that they had been apart. The small room Sean and his wife lived in had often been noisy with laughter. Poor Chloe attempted to share in the revelry but it was obvious that the mother-to- be was not feeling well. She crawled into bed early.

Tom was comfortable sleeping on the floor, even though he had been awakened several times when Sean's wife had to leave the little room. Although still not feeling well, Chloe managed to make breakfast for the men.

"Going to be a cold day," Sean said, peering out of the single small window. "Looks like there are drifts out there too. Wish I could go to Eli's place with you, but I've got to relieve the doctor at my patient's bedside. He'd probably loan you the shay. It's three or four miles out to Boulder Creek and the mill."

"No, I'm used to walking. It's sure good to see you and Chloe doing so well, Sean. After I spend some time with my 'white father', Eli, I'll come and have a real visit with you two. It's getting light out now, so I'm anxious to get started. Thanks for the breakfast, Chloe. You'd better rest some today." She tried to smile, but wasn't very successful at it.

"Tom," Sean began hesitantly, "maybe you ought to think about some different clothes. Those buckskins will surely draw attention here at the fort."

"They're all I've got. Anyway, as soon as anybody sees my long hair and red skin, they'll know what I am. The Indian wars are over. I'm not afraid." Sean was not so sure.

Once out in the weather, Toom-She-chi-Kwa had no trouble remembering the way to the place where he'd spent over six years of his childhood. Even before the grist mill was in sight he could hear the familiar clicking of the wooden gears that turned the grindstones. Assuming that the Quaker would be at work, he entered the mill as soon as he arrived.

He was met by a tall, handsome man who appeared to be too well dressed for work in the dusty building.

"We give no handouts to Indians!" the man growled, raising his voice to be heard above the noise of the machinery. "Get out before I use this club on you!" He had picked up a four foot filling pole, and pointed it in Tom's face.

Tom was taken aback. "Where is Eli?" he asked, taking a step toward the door. "Is he still alive? I've come a long way to see him again."

"Aha!" the man exclaimed. "I know who you are now! You're the Indian kid my uncle raised for a while, ain't you?"

"Yes, I am. My Indian father came here and reclaimed me so I had to go with him. I've been gone for over six years. Has Eli passed on then?"

"I saw you one time when mother and I were here for a visit. She wanted to see her brother. I'm John Grant from Virginia. What do you really want here?" He had not lowered the club and his brows were knitted angrily.

"I only wish to . . ."

"Never mind, Indian. I know what you're up to. You've been hanging around the fort and heard that old man Miller is bad off. Well I'm running the mill now and I intend to keep on running it. No good-for-nothing redskin is going to try to take what's legally mine. So get away from here. Don't go near the house or I'll fix you good! I could break you in two with my bare hands. Now leave and don't let me see your face around here again! He suddenly dropped the club and drew a beautiful double-barreled pistol from his front pocket. He cocked the piece and took deliberate aim. "Now I'll be watching you, so stay away from my house!"

Frightened an confused by this tirade, Tom backed out of the mill, keeping his eyes on the pistol. That the man, John Grant, would actually do as he threatened there could be no doubt.

"I meant no harm sir, I just . . ."

Crack! The ball whizzed past Tom's head and clipped a twig from a nearby tree. "If I have to shoot again I'll kill you! Now git!"

Tom ran south along the creek. He did not look back, but he was sure that Grant was still watching. The Wyandot kept on going until he was well-hidden in the forest. He sat down, breathing hard, his hands trembling. "I'm going to get into the house and see Eli," he told himself. "As soon as he gets busy in the mill I'll sneak around to the back of the house and see if I can get in. My white father will soon tell me what's going on here, but I'll have to be mighty careful. That man acts like he wants me dead!"

Tom knew that waiting for darkness wouldn't work. Apparently John was living in the house, and would be going there at the end of the day. The best time was right now while Grant was still at work in the mill. He waded the shallow creek and circled through the woods until he was well behind the millpond. After spending several minutes watching and listening, he approached the house. He saw no tracks in the snow around the building, so he sprinted to the lean-to near the back door. A lump was forming in his throat as the familiar building brought back so many memories.

The snow was undisturbed near the door, which surprised him. "Why hasn't he come out here for wood?" he wondered. "It's really cold today, and there seems to be plenty of firewood stacked right here." Taking a deep breath he stepped up and knocked on the door. There was no response, so he knocked again, louder this time.

"Who's out there?" a woman's voice asked, but the door was only opened a few inches.

"I am Tom Bluefoot. I've come back to see my white father, Eli Miller. Please let me in."

"There's an <u>Indian</u> out here!" Tom heard, still standing in the snow. "Says his name is Tom. I'm not opening this door for any savage!"

The door burst open and there in the doorway was a very old man. He was seated in a straight chair which had been fitted with wooden wheels. "<u>Toomie</u>! <u>Toomie</u>!" he cried. "Is it really you? Come in! Come in!"

Tom entered, sliding past the rolling chair. The house was a mess. The fire was nearly out and the kitchen was cold. Standing uncertainly by the fireplace was a young woman whom Tom correctly assumed was Mrs. John Grant. "Who is that man?" she cried, pointing at Tom. "He's an <u>Indian</u> Eli. A real red Indian! What does he want with us? You shouldn't have let him in the house. He'll kill us. I'll go get John."

"Now Martha we have nothing to fear. He's the very one I've told thee about. He is like a son to me. He lived here for a long time. I thought he was dead, but now, glory be, here he is alive and all grown up! Oh Toomie, sit down here and tell me all that has befallen thee. Hast thou had anything to eat? Martha, make some porridge right away!" he said, too excited to get his thoughts in order. "There's bread right there on the table. Cut off a slice. It's burned a little but still good." He pushed the loaf toward Tom, sliding the bread knife along with it.

"Oh my father, my <u>father</u>! How I have missed thee! Before I tell you my story, I need to know what is happening at the mill. Hast thou decided to retire from that work? And why is your nephew running the mill?"

Eli's face clouded. He glanced at the young woman he had called Martha, as if afraid to speak in her presence. For the first time Tom observed the girl. She was tall, thin, and very pretty. What was troubling to notice however were several bruises on her jaw and cheek, as well as a cracked lip. She kept her left arm in the folds of her apron. It appeared to have been broken and improperly set.

"Go ahead Eli, tell him the truth. John means nothing to me anymore. Nothing but trouble I mean," she stated bitterly. "This Indian is the one you told me about then? Maybe he can help us somehow."

Eli cleared his throat repeatedly, but when he finally began, his words seemed to tumble over each other. "I don't know if thou ever met him. My sister's son, he came from Virginia to visit me. He was newly married and seemed to be all an uncle could hope for. The mill was becoming too hard for me, so for a time John worked along with me to learn the business. I couldn't pay him much, but allowed the newlyweds room and board here in my home."

"You mean thou and they shared this little cabin?" Tom interrupted. The Quaker method of speaking was appearing almost automatically.

"That is correct. At first all went well, but before a year was out, Martha's husband began to feel that he knew more about operating a grist mill than I, who had spent a lifetime at that business. He began raising prices, and even giving short weights to those who came to have their grain made into flour. Many of our customers were my friends, which made his actions even harder to bear."

"Why didn't you just fire him, Father?"

"I wanted to of course but couldn't do it for two reasons. First, I really needed his help. My joints were becoming very painful, and lifting a full sack of grain was nearly impossible. He was a quick learner and could do the work well enough. The second reason I had to tolerate the young man is she who is sitting right here." He smiled at Martha and patted her hand. "She takes care of me and the house, but that's not the main reason I allow them to stay."

"Eli protects me," the girl blurted out. "John has a terrible temper. He hates running the mill and when he comes home tired and angry he takes his frustrations out on me. You can plainly see the results of some of his tantrums." She pointed at her bruises.

"I am very sorry for both thee and Eli," Toom-She-chi-Kwa said. "Perhaps I can be of help, but I've been ordered off the property. The man threatened to shoot me if I came back."

"I heard the gunshot," Eli said.

"But why," Tom asked, turning to Martha, "dost thy husband not leave here if he hates operating the mill?"

Martha shot a quick glance at Eli before answering. "I'm sure that Eli knows that John wants to <u>own</u> the mill. He has told me that he is the only heir so the property will go to him when . . ." She glanced at the old man in the wheeled chair again. "Well I mean when this good man is gone." Upon hearing these words Eli showed no emotion at all. He was quite old and practically unable to walk, but his mind remained clear. He had known of his nephew's plans for some time. Martha had told him that her husband had three brothers, so actually John was not the only heir. The man was assuming that none of his brothers back in Virginia would want any part of this small business in the wilderness.

Nothing was said for a few minutes. Finally Martha began to speak, her voice barely above a whisper. "John was not always this way," she said. "His family had a plantation in Virginia. The youngest of four brothers, he never had to work. He spent his time attending parties and gambling at cards. He was handsome! I fell in love with him and we were married. All went well for a year, but his older brothers were each successful, two as lawyers and the eldest in charge of the plantation. I think John was jealous, so when we visited here he immediately saw a chance to make something of himself. So here we are, none of us happy!"

"Dost thou have a will?"

"I do," Eli replied. "The mill is to be sold. John is to obtain one-third, another third to be sent to headquarters of the Society of Friends Church in Philadelphia. The final third," and here Eli smiled proudly, placing a trembling hand on Tom's arm, "plus the house and all property, is to be thine, providing thou could be found. And, thank our God, thou hast been found indeed! Welcome home, my son!"

Tom was troubled by this news. "I thank thee, Eli. I am not worthy of such consideration, but I do thank thee from my heart!"

"He talked about you all the time," Martha said shyly. "I should have known you when you came to the door. Mr. Miller's kindness toward John and me will be more than enough for us to . . .well . . .to try to make a new start somewhere else. Of course we don't want our kind and loving uncle to need a will any time soon!" She patted his hand.

Tom stared into the fire for a minute, then turned to Eli. "Thou sayest that all of these plans are written down in thy will?"

"Yes, Toomie. I made sure that everything was in good order. Joshua Meekam, the lawyer who comes to Fort Pitt three months out of each year, helped me write it out. It's all properly signed, witnessed, and everything. How thankful I am that thou hast come back to me at just the right time. I know that my days are limited now. God is good!"

"Oh no, Eli! You have many years yet ahead of you. Don't say such things." Eli smiled at Martha's words but did not reply.

The entire scenario was becoming clear. Tom considered the hatred he had encountered from John Grant the moment they had met. It was obvious that the nephew had expected to gain not only one third of the mill's sale price, but if Toom-She-chi-Kwa could not be found he would inherit all the rest of the property and the sale price, except for the amount for the Quaker headquarters. Tom could see that his return at this critical time was crucial. Steps must be taken immediately, not only for his own welfare but for that of Eli and Martha as well.

"Does Mr. Grant know the terms of thy will, Eli?" Tom asked, a look of concern on his face.

"Oh no! Until this moment, no one except myself and Joshua Meekam, the lawyer, knew the contents of my last will and testament. I was especially careful that John didn't learn what the paper contained," Eli said proudly. He looked at Martha but she showed no emotion. Then without looking at her uncle she began to speak.

"Dear Eli," she murmured, "but he <u>does</u> know. He knows <u>all</u> <u>about</u> <u>it</u>!"

"<u>What</u>? Are thee sure? But I . . . the lawyer promised . . .how could he know?" the old man cried.

"Maybe thy husband has been only guessing about his uncle's plans," Tom said, much concerned. "I can see no way John Grant could have learned what the will specified."

"He knows alright," Martha asserted bitterly. "He learned it from the lawyer himself!"

"But that is impossible!" Eli groaned. "It is my understanding that lawyers cannot give out such information. That was agreed to by both of us."

Martha suddenly jumped to her feet. She grabbed a dirty cup from the table and dipped water from the bucket. Eli was trembling noticeably and his face had turned beet red. She held the cup to his lips but most of the water spilled down his chest.

Tom was up and standing over the old man. "Why would thy lawyer break his promise like that?" he asked, gently massaging Eli's neck and shoulders.

Martha answered. "John told me all about it months ago. He goes to the tavern every Saturday night. A bunch of men meet there and spend the evening drinking and gambling. One night lawyer Meekam was losing at the cards. That man got deeper and deeper into debt. With no way to pay, he asked my husband to step outside. When they were alone he offered to provide critical information contained in Eli's will in return for cancellation of his gambling debts. That's how my man learned all of it." She suddenly showed a rather pitiful look of pride. "My John is good at cards," she said.

Eli was having trouble breathing. His gasps and tremors alarmed both Martha and Tom. "We must get him to his bed right away!" the young woman exclaimed.

Between the two of them they managed to move the sick old man onto his bed in the tiny room off the kitchen. It was not apparent if he was conscious or not. Tom felt sure that he must get an answer to the most critical problem facing him. "Where is the lawyer man now?" he asked Martha. "We must make sure he has the copy of Eli's will. Your husband may have the lawyer's copy already. John will surely try to get his hands on the one Eli has hidden. If he can get both copies and destroy them he would have legal right to everything my 'white father' owns, even the share that was to go to the Quaker headquarters."

"The lawyer has gone back East," she said sadly. "As far as anyone knows he won't be back until next summer when he can travel on the rivers."

"So that's how it is," Tom moaned. He knew that if Eli did not recover and produce the remaining copy of the will, "frontier justice" would be swift, and one young Wyandot would be left with nothing. Even worse, Eli's wishes would have been lost forever. He leaned down until his lips were almost touching Eli's ear. "Canst thou hear me, my father?" he asked softly. "If so, raise your hand a little."

The old man did not move, but suddenly he took a breath and tried to speak. The words came out as a ragged, whispering sound. "It's . . . it's hid real good . . .in . . .in the . . ." He could not continue. His eyelids fluttered, then finally remained closed. Martha laid her head on his chest and was finally relieved to hear a faint but definite heartbeat.

"We must let him rest now," Martha whispered. "He's had these spells before but never this bad. I think he needs a doctor, John says . . ."

The front door sprang open with a crash that shook the whole house. "Don't nobody move!" Grant yelled. He barged into the room, bringing a fog of swirling snow with him. He held his right arm straight out, the double-barrel aimed directly at Tom's face. "Caught you, didn't I, you red devil! Invading my home, assaulting my wife, and trying to murder my uncle! Well Indian I'm taking you to the fort, and I'll see that you're locked up. Get the rope that's hanging next to that old harness out in the shed. And you," he motioned with the gun, "you just lay down right on the floor. If you move a muscle I'll shoot you dead. I ought to anyway. It'd save the cost of locking you up!"

Martha, back from the shed, white-faced and cold, started to approach him with the rope. "Stop!" he yelled. "Just throw it to me. I don't trust you any more than I do him! Stay back by the wall. Where's the old man?"

"Don't bother him, John. He's resting right now."

"Your wife's right Mr. Grant. He . . ."

"He's unconscious," Tom said out of the corner of his mouth.

"You shut up!" John roared. I'll just go in there and see for myself. If you try anything you'll be one 'good Indian' in less than a second!" Keeping his pistol trained on the man on the floor, he backed into Eli's bedroom. Satisfied that Eli was indeed unresponsive he came back and carefully picked up the rope. "Martha," he commanded, "hold this gun on him while I tie him up. If he moves, shoot him. And," he said fiercely, "be danged sure it's him and not me! I know you'd be glad to get rid of me, but I'm not going to allow that to happen. Here." He handed the heavy gun over, butt first.

Tom was terrified. He knew that if Grant managed to get him trussed up and taken to jail there would be no justice for him. Any number of charges could be trumped up and the Indian haters would believe every one. These thoughts blazed through his mind in less than a second. It was time to move! He rolled to his left and tried to get up. Grant planted a heavy boot on Bluefoot's middle but the Indian twisted away, grabbed the man's leg and pulled him over.

"Gimme the gun!" Grant screamed, leaping to his feet. Tom jumped up at the same moment and wrapped his arms around the bigger man's middle. Locked together, they struggled across the small kitchen and crashed into the table. Quick as a cat John Grant yanked the gun from Martha's outstretched hand and fired. Tom would never know if the young wife had helped him, but suddenly he found himself clutching the long-bladed bread knife. As John brought the second barrel into firing position, Tom thrust the knife hard into the big man's stomach. It was only then that Tom began to feel the pain in the side of his neck.

"Oh . . .Aiee!" Grant screamed, the smoking pistol falling to the floor.

He crumpled up and fell, knees drawn up to his chest, blood already soaking the front of his shirt. Tom stood staring in terror, the bloody knife still in his hand.

"Tom! Oh <u>Tom</u>! Is he dead?"

"I don't know if he is or not. What's wrong with my neck?"

"You're bleeding some, but I don't think it's too bad. Here." She handed him the dish towel. He wrapped it tight around his neck, then knelt beside Grant, who was moaning and crying at the same time.

"Let me see where you're hurt," he told the man.

"Stay away from me damn you! You tried to <u>kill</u> <u>me</u>! I'm dying but . . ." he groaned, "I'll live long enough to see you get hanged! Martha, . . . Martha, honey, get a doctor! Hurry! Oh it hurts awful! I can't . . .I can't . . .He seemed to pass out but remained curled up, blood starting to drip onto the floor.

"Does anyone have a wagon around here?" the Indian asked desperately. "He needs a doctor! We've got to get him to the surgeon's office south of the fort!"

"Masons have a hay wagon and a team. Their place is only about a mile north. Maybe I could go over there and . . ."

"That would take too long. I'll go. I can run all the way. You get a towel or something and press it against his wound. Try to tie a belt or a piece of rope around him to hold the towel in place. I'll be back as soon as I can. Keep him warm."

John was waking up. "Martha, Martha," he gasped, "don't let him go, he'll just run away! He's not going to . . . going to get the Masons, the lying devil. You'll have to . . . in the mill . . . the little sled . . . it's . . . it's . . ." His voice faded again.

"John says," she shouted, "that I . . ."

"Forget that! I'll be back as soon as I can get the Masons to bring their wagon. We'll get your man to Doctor Friedereich's office. It's not far from the blockhouse. You need to stay here to take care of Eli." He rushed outdoors and sped north, running as if his life depended on it. It probably did!

The wind tore at his braids, and his moccasins were too thin for this much snow. "Fool! Fool!" A voice in his head seemed to be shouting with every step. "I should run away right now!" he thought. "If that man dies, they'll hang me! Nobody will believe that it was self-defense. An Indian like me will never get justice. Run away, you fool!" the voice insisted.

Where the snow was blown clear he ran. When snow crossed his path he plowed ahead as fast as he could. "White man's God," he prayed aloud, "help me find the Masons. Keep that man alive." Hardly had the words left his lips than in the distance he saw a team and wagon heading directly toward him.

"Where you heading, Indian?" the oldest Mason boy shouted, hauling back on the reins.

"I'm Tom Bluefoot," the Wyandot yelled, gasping for breath. "There's been a bad accident at Eli's mill. John Grant is hurt bad. Can you take him to the doctor in your wagon?"

"Shore I can! I remember you now. You used to live with the miller didn't you?"

"Yes," Tom answered shortly. "Can you get the horses to trot?"

"I could," he growled, "but I won't! It's pretty hard going for them in this snow. If they founder, then where will you be? It's mighty lucky that I was out for wood when you came. Just let me do the driving, you hear?"

Grant was awake once more when they arrived. Martha surprised Tom and the Mason boy by having things ready and taking charge of settling her husband in the wagon. John was crying and cursing all the time, screaming threats at Tom whenever he found enough breath to do so. Alan Mason soon figured out what had happened but he didn't ask Tom anything about it.

Grant's cries and curses soon died away as pain from the jolting wagon caused him to lose consciousness. Alan had kept the horses moving as fast as conditions allowed, but still it took over an hour to make the trip.

"What's all this? That you out there Tom?" Friedereich bellowed, standing in the open door.

"Yes, Captain, it's me. John Grant's in the wagon hurt bad. Can we bring him in?"

Tom's friend, Sean O'Casey, appeared in the doorway beside the doctor. "What happened to him? And it looks like something happened to you too! Your neck is bleeding. Come on in, all of you!"

They lifted John onto the operating table. While the doctor examined and cleaned the knife wound, Sean bandaged the bloody gash where the bulled had creased the side of Tom Bluefoot's neck. Grant suddenly moaned and tried to sit up. "Lay still there son," the surgeon said soothingly. "You drink this potion down as quick as you can."

"Where is he? Where's the dirty Indian who tried to kill me"? Painfully he turned his head until he could see Tom sitting on a bench within arm's reach.
"That's him! Don't let him leave or he'll run for it! He . . . he . . . tried to kill me with a knife! Is that you, Alan?" he gasped, swiveling his head until he could see the young Mason boy standing nervously by the door. "Go and get the major. Tell him this here Tom Bluefoot should be . . . should be . . . locked up. He tried to murder me! Get going kid!"

As the laudanum started to take effect, Grant began to relax. "That looks like a bullet wound on your neck, Tom. What happened? Did you two get into a fight?" Sean asked, wiping his bloody hands on a rag.

"Sean, you've got to help me!" Tom pleaded. "He's going to charge me with attempted murder. I was only trying to defend myself. We fought. He shot at me and I grabbed a bread knife off Eli's table [actually he wasn't sure if Martha had put the knife in his hand, but he wasn't going to cast suspicion on her] and . . .and . . .nobody's going to believe me. He'll say it was all my fault. What am I going to do, Sean?"

The door burst open. Major Maxwell, Commandant at Fort Pitt, charged into the room, Alan following. "That the Indian?" he asked, glowering at Tom.

"This is Tom Bluefoot, Major," Sean answered quickly. "He's the one who used to live with Eli Miller. He's a really good man."

"Well did he use a knife on that man lying there? Say, ain't that John Grant, the one who runs the grist mill these days? Why me and some of the boys plays cards with him just about every Saturday night. Is he gonna die, Friedereich?"

"It's a very bad wound Major. He needs an immediate operation, but he may pull through. The sooner we can operate the better will be his chances. I'll ask both of you to leave now so we can get started."

"That Indian hurt bad? I see he's got a bandage on his neck."

"It's just a crease from John Grant's bullet. I'll take care of him," Sean said, moving quickly toward the operating table.

"Oh you will, will you?" Maxwell growled. "Well I don't think so! That varmint needs to be locked up till we can hold a trial and hang him. Tried to knife the new owner of the only grist mill we got in these parts, did he? He'll soon see how the law takes care of these no-account redskins, always hanging around the fort and causing all kinds of trouble."

"John Grant doesn't own the mill," Tom began, "he's just running it for his uncle, Eli Miller. He <u>wants</u> to own it though. That's why he tried to kill me. He knew . . ."

"<u>That's</u> <u>enough</u>!" The Commandant roared. "No more lies out of you! You'll get your say at the trial, that is if we wait long enough to even bother with one. Now you come with me. We're going to wake up that lazy jailer who thinks he's the sheriff, and get you inside. Alan, you're one of them Mason boys ain't you? You get hold of one of his arms and I'll take the other'n. He ain't very big but all of his kind can be mighty tricky. We can handle him!"

Sean spoke up quickly. "He's going to need more care, Commandant. You'll have to leave him here with the doctor and me. He's a friend of mine. I'll be responsible for him."

"Ha! I reckon you're a friend all right. 'Don't send a fox to guard the henhouse' my old ma always said. No sir, he goes to jail. Come on Alan, grab hold of the slippery devil."

The jail was almost as cold inside as the night outside. Tom had wet feet from running through the snow, but luckily there were no other prisoners. The jailer surprised him by throwing a blanket into the cell, so Bluefoot removed his wet moccasins and curled up on the only bench. He had little hope for the future. Despite the throbbing of his neck wound and the completely unfair accusations, the young Wyandot soon fell asleep.

Hardly had Tom been dragged from the room than the doctor and his assistant, Sean O'Casey, were standing over the wounded man.

"We'll have to go in," Friedereich said brusquely. "No telling what has been severed inside of him. You go ahead and get ready Sean. I'll see if I can get a better edge on the scalpel."

"I'll sharpen the instrument Doctor. You can wash up. I'll get the clean towels ready. Should I tie him down"?

"As usual, you're not listening young man. I'm not doing the cutting, you are!"

"But . . .but . . . I ain't never done anything like this before! You do it. I'll help."

Captain Friedereich suddenly held out his hands. "Take a look son. Take a good look!" The trembling was obvious. "If I got a knife in that wound I'd likely carve him up like Job's turkey. You've got the job!"

There was no use arguing. His mentor's mind was made up. Sean washed his hands in the pail that rested under the operating table. Working together they secured the heavy straps that would keep their patient as still as possible, thankful that he had not regained consciousness.

Sean's mind was working overtime, but his hands were steady. "I sure wish Chloe was here," he thought. She had been a fine helper during the Battle of Fallen Timbers, but he would not call her. Their baby was due any time.

"Better open that wound a couple inches," Friedereich said quietly. "That'll give you more room to work." Sean did so, although he had absolutely no idea what he was to do once he had exposed the extent of the damage. The truth was the doctor had no idea either!

Sean probed carefully until he could see what was needed. A sudden thought ran through him like a lightning bolt. "It wouldn't take much," he thought. "All I'd need to do is let the knife slip an inch or so. This guy would never wake up to accuse Tom of attempted murder!" But then Captain Friedereich's words from two years ago came clearly. 'First do no harm' the Captain had often repeated. Apparently the knife had missed the liver, but there was a neat gash in the wall of Grant's stomach. He stitched it up, feeling much more confident now. He'd done lots of sewing on the many wounded soldiers in General Wayne's army. Then he quickly used the needle and cat gut to close the entrance wound.

A long moan, followed by a racking cough signaled that Grant was waking up.

"Oh! . . .Oh!! . . . It <u>hurts</u>! Oh the <u>pain</u>! I can't stand it!" Sean forced a few drops of laudanum between Grant's lips. In a few minutes he passed out again.

*   *   *

"This is <u>awful</u>! Can't you even bake a potato and get it right?" John snapped, shoving his plate away. "It's been three weeks since that dirty Indian stabbed me, and all you do is fuss over that old man in there!" He jabbed a thumb at Eli's bedroom.

"I know I'm no good at cooking," she said, a tear making a shiny path down one cheek. "No one ever taught me. Proper girls didn't prepare meals at Rocky Hill plantation. You knew that when you married me."

"I wish I'd never come out to this God-forsaken place. I should have stayed right on our plantation and took you in there. We had plenty of slaves to do the cooking, and everything else as well. What's going on with my precious uncle?" he asked, changing the subject.

"Sometimes I think he hears me when I talk to him, but so far he hasn't moved a muscle. I could use some help dealing with him. He's almost more than I can lift. He is <u>your</u> uncle after all!"

"<u>Not me</u>!" he shouted. "You take care of him! If he ever does wake up, you know what your job is don't you?"

"I'll try to get him to tell where he hid the other copy of his will, but so far there's been no chance." She sneaked a look at her husband as he stared moodily into the fire. "Are you having much pain today?" she asked softly.

"<u>Pain</u>?" he shouted at her. "It hurts all the time and it hurts mighty bad too. You know what I think? I think that young O'Casey, the one who helps old Friedereich, tried to finish me off. It was him, not the Captain who operated on me. They say that Irishman's a friend of the murderin' redskin. Them Irish are just about as bad as the Indians. They ought to hang <u>both</u> of them!"

"But John," Martha began timidly, "the Indian man ran all the way to the Mason's to fetch the wagon. He could have just run off in the woods. You'd have died right here on the floor if he . . ."

Crack! John backhanded his wife so hard she was nearly knocked out of her chair. "You say one more word about that fiend as call himself Tom Bluefoot and I'll break your <u>other</u> arm for you! You hear?"

Crying softly, Martha retreated into Eli's bedroom, closing the door behind her.

"Get back out here!" John shouted. The words were followed by a cry of pain. He had been told to avoid loud talk, and he was rapidly finding out why. "See if you've got enough sense to make me a cup of coffee if there's any left."

She re-entered the kitchen, dabbing at a trickle of blood on her cheek. "I'll make some but the doctor said you shouldn't drink anything hot until your stomach is all healed up. Don't you remember?"

"A pox on all doctors!" he growled, this time being careful not to shout.

As she busied herself with the hot water she attempted to change the subject. "When do you think your brother will get here?"

"Who knows?" he complained. "His letter said it might take two weeks for the trip. Well it's going on four now. You can't count on the weather in this blasted place. First it was all the snow, then it warms up and the trails turn to mud. No wonder it's taking him so long. As soon as I take ownership of the mill I'm selling this whole thing and going back to Virginia where I belong."

"That will be a whole lot better for both of us, John. I can't wait to . . ."

"Both? Did you say <u>both</u>? <u>You</u> ain't going! Soon as the mill's sold and I can get around without somebody helping me, I'm leaving you. You never were any kind of a wife."

"But John," she cried, "what could I do? Where could I go? It's not fair It just isn't!"

"Maybe that old man will finally die and get it over with. I hope he does!" Grant said cruelly. "Now if you ever get that coffee done, pour me a cup then go out to the mill. Bring in my pen and the ledger book. See if you can do that right."

"Oh John, you're not going to work on the accounts and such are you? I think you should just try to rest like the doctor told you."

"No, I'm not going to 'work on the accounts,'" he mocked her, in a high whining voice. "I intend to write down everything the very way it went on. If Lucius ever gets here I'll have the story on paper just like it happened. That ought to speed up the time it'll take to get that conniving Indian on the end of a rope. Now get out there and do like I told you."

Obediently Martha began to put on a coat, but Grant stuck out his foot to block her path. "You don't need to bundle up like a durned Eskimo just to get to the mill. Go on, it's not that cold out."

"Well finally!" he sniffed when Martha, cold and shivering, arrived with the ledger book. "Don't give it to me," he stated. "You write a decent hand. Just mind that you put down everything exactly like I say." He wriggled around on the kitchen chair, trying to find a way to ease the pain in his stomach. "Wait! Wait!" he suddenly cried, cocking his head to one side. "Somebody's coming!"

Martha hurried to the tiny window, wiped away the frost and peered out. "I think it's your brother. There are some others with him too. I've got to change my dress!"

"No you don't. I can't get up. You'll have to let them in. Forget looking pretty for my brother, the lawyer."

Lucius Grant Esquire, Attorney At Law, seemed to fill the entire door frame as he entered the cabin. "Ho, Little brother, how you doing? Martha," he said with a small bow, "it's good to see you 'way out here in the wilderness. Sorry it took me so long to get here. What a trip!" he sighed.

"Ask your friends to come in too, "Martha said.

"<u>Friends</u>? Haw haw! That's a good one. That's Simon and Lymon, two of Ma's house slaves that she insisted I take along to see to my needs. She was a great one for rhyming things, Ma was. But it's caused no end of trouble. When you call one of 'em they both come or neither of 'em does! You remember them John?"

"Of course I do. I haven't been gone that long."

"Those boys are seeing to the horses. I told them to put them in the shed. Is that all right?" Lucius asked.

"Of course," Martha answered. "It's too cold to stay outside long."

"It sure is," Lucius agreed. "I don't want my horses to suffer if I can help it."

"What about the two slaves?" Martha asked.

"Oh they'll be fine. The horses are the main thing."

"How long do you plan to stay, Lucius?" John had managed to stand, holding onto the chair back. "Since I had to close the mill, Martha and me, we're just not too burdened with money."

"Why little brother I'll be here until your Indian is hung and you've got clear title to all of this." He looked around wryly, obviously unimpressed with Eli's holdings.

Martha suddenly stood up and opened the door. "You boys come on in here," she shouted, holding the door open. Seeing both John's and Lucius' looks of surprise, she amazed them by saying, "We do things a little differently out here in the wilderness!"

Lymon, the younger brother, slipped in and immediately sat against the wall. Simon stood for a moment, keen eyes taking in the entire scene. "Masa John," he said bowing. "Miz Martha." He snatched the hat of his younger brother's head and sat down on the floor beside him.

"They'll be fine," Lucius said, grinning. "They're trained almost as well as my prize fox hounds. Now John, you and Martha just listen to me. I got everything all worked out. I stopped at the tavern on my way out here. We're all going to stay right there till all of this is settled. Well, all of us will stay there except these boys of course. They've got plenty of rooms and the food ain't bad at all."

John panicked. "Lucius we just can't afford to do that. I told you the mill's closed and . . ."

"Don't worry about it. I'm paying for the whole shebang. I hired the tavern matron to take care of Uncle Eli until he gets better, if he ever does. They've got a little room next to the chimney flu that'll be just right for him. So like I said, it's all settled."

"But Lucius, there's no way I can ever pay you back," John said, perplexed.

"There's no way now John, but after we get all of this property in your name and sold, <u>then</u> we'll talk about my fee. Haw, haw!"

Martha had found a piece of bread that wasn't too moldy. She cut it in two and held out a portion to each of the slaves. They eyed it hungrily but shook their heads without saying a word. Raised on a plantation next to that of her husband, she was used to all sorts of drama and intrigue among brothers, sisters, and cousins. It had made her a quick and accurate judge of others. As she watched the two black youngsters she became immediately aware of the older one's obvious intelligence. Well-mannered, he was not intimidated by his white master. For some reason, instinct seemed to tell her that Simon might be a possible ally in whatever was to happen to her during the coming days and weeks. It was plain enough that she was going to need all the help she could get.

"John, you should have studied for the law like me and your other brother did. Do you know how much cash money I made when we beat old Lester Morris out of that hard-scrabble farm of hisn? Six hundred and twenty nine dollars, haw haw! Now you boys get back out there and hitch up the team again. Martha, get all the quilts and such you got and wrap old Eli up like a cocoon. We're going to get to the tavern and eat a big meal. Then, Brother John, you and me will set at the table and not get up till we've got our case sewed up tighter than a widder's purse. Let's go!"

"Look at Lymon there," the older brother said, shaking his head. "That boy can sleep <u>anywhere</u>!"

Toom-she-chi-Kwa nodded through the bars. "I'm sure glad you two came in here," he said. "It gets mighty lonesome in this cell all by myself. Still I'm glad there're no other prisoners right now."

"We're glad too, Tom. They didn't know what to do with us. That old tavern-keeper made it mighty plain that our kind wasn't welcome to sleep there with the Grants and them, even on the floor. 'Course we could clean up the place, empty the night jars, and do things like that," Simon said bitterly. "So our master, Lucius Grant, suggested the jail and here we are. It's warm in here, two meals a day and hardly any work to do. That's easy livin' for the likes of us!"

"Yes, jail's not too bad, especially since you're not locked in a cell. You're lucky that way."

"They know me and Lymon won't run. Where would we go in all this forest? We don't mind a little sweeping up, keeping the fire going and such. Hope it lasts for a while yet."

"Can I ask you a question? What's it like being a slave?"

Simon slid off the bench, walked to the door, and stood listening for a moment. Then he approached Tom's cell, looked around once more, and answered the question. "For some of us it ain't too bad. Like Lymon there. He bows and scrapes, grins a lot, and tries to get out of all the work he can. I don't think it bothers him much, 'course he's still pretty young. "

"How is it for you then, Simon?"

"For me it's the worst thing you can imagine. It's like I'm not even <u>human</u>. They treat me as if I'm little more than their work horses. I'm not lazy, Tom. Really I'm not. I know how to work, and if the white folks would just let me, I'd be the best man on the plantation. I know I'm smarter than a lot of the men on the place, but they sure won't give me a chance to show it. You know what? I've been learning the stone mason trade. Got pretty good at it too, building chimneys and such." He leaned forward gripping the bars of Tom's cell, and listened again. Finally convinced that no one was coming to the jail, he began to whisper. "Now I'm going to tell you something that if you told anyone else it would be the end of me!"

Tom found himself whispering too. "What is it Simon? Did you kill somebody? Steal something? Kiss a white girl?"

"I can <u>read</u>!"

"What's so bad about that? I can read a little myself. My white father taught me. It's nothing to be ashamed of."

"I ain't ashamed. Teaching a slave to read is against the law. Want to know how I did it?"

"Sure."

Before answering he tiptoed over to the bench where Lymon lay curled up, snoring softly. "Just look at that kid," he grinned, dropping his jacket over his sleeping brother. "Like I told you, he can sleep anywhere! Sometimes I wish I could be more like him. Anyway," he was whispering again, "it was my sister who taught me. She was a nanny to Miz Tatlow's little girl. Them Grants just gave their young'uns anything they wanted. Little Imogene had a whole box of little books. They had nice pictures and almost all of them had some words across the bottom of the pages. Well Cocoa, that's my sister, every chance she got she'd slip one of the little books under her apron, keep it hid until night when she'd show me the words. Next day she'd put it back in the box. It didn't take long till both of us could figure out what the words were saying. Later on, when Lymon was given the job of burning the trash, he'd sneak me a piece of newspaper or something else with writing on it. I'd practice reading with that."

"Weren't you scared your little brother would get caught doing that?"

"Of course I was. He <u>did</u> get caught once too, but that little dickens, he just started sniffling and hacking really hard, pulled the paper out from under his shirt, and blew his nose on it! The Master just walked away. Naturally I didn't want that little bit of writing. It had snot all over it!" Both men laughed so hard that Lymon woke up and nearly fell off the bench.

"Well that's a little bit about being a slave. Now you've got to tell how it is being an Indian."

Lymon stood up, yawning mightily. "What you boys talkin' about?" he asked, coming to the bars.

"Nothing as concerns you, little brother. Throw another log on the fire and go back to sleep. It must be near midnight by now."

The jail door opened, letting a blast of cold air come in with the jailer. He was obviously drunk. The man looked around owlishly, pulled Simon back from the bars, looked around again and left without a word.

"Like I said, I can read too. The one who raised me was a Quaker man. From what I've heard those Quakers, whatever that means, believed that us Indians ought to be treated better. I wanted to go to school but he said that wouldn't be a good idea. He taught me himself. I'm not good at reading but I know my numbers and can even do a little figuring when I have to."

"How'd you end up being raised by a white man?"

Toom-She-chi-Kwa's explanation of how Eli Miller had "bought" him from a drunken father, took a long time. Lymon was asleep again, sitting against the wall next to the fire.

"So we're both just 'no-goods' for the white folks. At least you can go and come as you, please."

"Oh yes, I can just walk out of this jail and run around in the forest, can I? You know better than that, Simon! They'll keep me locked up until the visiting judge stops by here. They'll put me on trial for trying to murder John Grant. It'll be <u>some trial</u> I can tell you! The judge will probably bring the hangman's rope right to the trial with him!"

"But you said John, he's my Master's brother, tried to shoot you first. Can't you tell the judge that?"

Tom laughed bitterly. "Sure, I can tell him, and I will, but do you really think those Shemanese will pay any attention?"

"I reckon not," Simon answered sadly. "What's 'Shemanese'?"

"I guess it means white people. That's what my people always call them anyway. Lean up close to the bars, Simon. Is Lymon still asleep? I've got something to tell you."

The slave pressed his face against the iron and waited to hear what Tom had to say.

"This is for you alone, Simon! Don't even tell your little brother, you hear?"

"Of course I won't tell anybody, but I think I know what's on your mind even before you tell me. You're going to try to figure a way to escape ain't you?"

"That's it! What other choice do I have? If I can get out of here somehow, even a bullet in the back would be a whole lot better than <u>hanging</u>! If only Eli would wake up and be able to talk, he could speak for me and maybe the judge would listen to him."

"If he saw the whole fight, I'd think they would have to listen, Tom."

"That's the sad part. He <u>didn't</u> see it. He had fainted or something and we had put him to bed in a room off the kitchen. The only other witness was Martha, John's wife."

"I know Miz Martha. She's always been a good woman as far as us slaves is concerned. Old Massa John beat her sometimes. At least that's what the kitchen slaves told us. I'll bet she'd tell the truth to the judge."

"That's no good either. I heard your Master tell John that the law says a wife can't testify against her own husband. Lucius will see to it that she's not allowed to say anything at the trial."

"I' m sure sorry about this Tom. I'm one who can really know what you're up against. If I was in your kind of trouble it would be the same for me. This whole thing reminds me of Old Toby. He must have been about eighty years old. Had white hair, white whiskers, and wrinkles all over. He used to tell stories to us pickininnies in the evenings. Sometimes the white children would come down to the quarter and listen too. They thought it was all just for fun but our black parents told us that these yarns were a way of secretly teaching us how to get along in the white man's world. You want to hear one of 'em? I've heard it so often I can tell it by heart."

"Go ahead. Maybe it'll give me an idea of how to get out of this mess I'm in."

Simon shook his head at Tom's remark, knowing the fable was hardly good news for the oppressed. A natural-born mimic, the slave began:

"They was this here goose, ya see. That ere goose had got hisself

accused of bein' uppity with the white farmer. Well sir, he jest ups

says right out, 'This here shore ain't right! Not atall it ain't!' Turns

out this pertikler goose was smartern most of 'em in the pen so he

sez to hisself 'I'll jest take this to the court. Then we'uns will see

who has the right of this here.' So he goes and does it. At the

co'thouse he sees that the judge, he is a _fox_! So he looks at the jury

and alla them was foxes too! So there's no hope for old Mr. Goose!"

Simon looked away. He was not willing to face the Indian, for the parable perfectly illustrated the plight that both red man and black had to face.

"He must have been a pretty smart man," Tom said, shaking his head. "That story explains the whole thing better than if it was written in a book!" He leaned forward once more and whispered. "If I get any chance at all I'm going to run. Who could blame me? Sean o'Casey, the doctor here at the fort is my best friend. He might be able to help me get away, but I'm not telling him. He could get in bad trouble if they found out he helped me escape. He already saved me once, back in the war, and got whipped so hard it blinded him in one eye! No, I can't let him know a thing about it."

"You've got another friend, Tom."

"Well I sure don't know of any."

"Lookee here, Indian man. You're looking at a friend right now!"

Toom-She-chi-Kwa was shocked. "What are you saying? You mean you're willing to help me?"

"More'n that there. I'm planning to run too! That is if you'll have me."

"Simon, you don't know what you're saying. If we got caught, and it's pretty likely we would, both of us will hang! Don't even think that way!"

They stood staring at each other, dumbfounded at what they were considering. Tom was about to speak again when the jail door opened. Lucius and Jameson the jailer, entered, stamping snow off their boots. Lymon jumped up and made a show of dusting off the bench he'd been sleeping on.

"Mistah Lucius, sir" the smaller slave said respectfully, "You jest set right down right cheer and I'll pull off them wet boots. You can put your feets right up next to the fire. You too, Mr. Jailer Man." He put on his best grin and bobbed his head repeatedly at both men.

"You do that boy," Lucius said, rubbing Lymon's kinky head. "I sure wish somebody around here could give me something for this damnable headache I've got! I wish it would either stay winter or get on to spring. I get this way every time the weather changes, but it's worse out here in the wilderness. Now Simon, you come on back to the tavern with me. My clothes are in terrible shape. They need cleaning and brushing. Get your coat."

"I'll stay here with our prisoner," the jailer said importantly. "I'll keep an eye on him you can bet!"

"Good idea." Lucius said, but his sarcasm was lost on the jailer. "Lymon, you stay and help out here. I'll send your brother back in a few days, soon as he gets my clothes in good shape." Almost talking to himself, he muttered, "That Martha, she don't know how to do anything but look pretty. But," he elbowed the jailer and winked, "she sure is good at doing that! Haw haw."

As they trudged the short distance through the melting snow, Simon had a sudden attack of fear. "What," he asked himself, "am I thinking of? Sure I'd like to be free, but free to do what? And go where? The whole idea is crazy. Just crazy!"

"I told you, counselor," the innkeeper whined, "his kind's got no bidness in this establishment, slave or free, so I'll thank you to get him gone." He glared at Simon.

"My, oh my," Lucius said mildly. "I guess if that's the way it has to be we'll all just pack up our things and go elsewhere. Let's see, there's old Eli, Martha, John Grant, this young slave, his little brother, and me. That's uh . . . I think that makes six of us at two bits a day plus what you charge for meals. It must amount to quite a sum for you, and who knows how many more days we'll have to stay until that judge finally arrives. Well sir, business is business, so I'll tell the others and . . ."

"Hold on! Hold <u>on</u> there! I just thought of something. There's that mop and broom closet under the stairs right over there. Your slave boys could sleep in there just fine. That way all of your party could just stay right where you're at, 'snug as a bug in a rug' like my woman says."

"Well that would be fine!" Lucius remarked, taking no trouble to hide his contempt. "Mr. Proprietor, do you have any of those powders that some say help a headache? I've got a bad one, and it won't seem to let up at all."

"No Counselor I don't, but my woman swears by a poultice of salt, lard, and vinegar. Want me to have her make some up?"

"No thanks. That sounds worse than the headache. Now Simon you go up to my room and get busy on my clothes. Be sure to brush my hat too. I want to look my best when the circuit judge arrives."

Two weeks passed with everyone getting very tired of the inactivity. Everybody that is, except the tavern-keeper. He was making more money than he ever had before.

With all the work on his master's wardrobe finished, Simon was allowed to go back to the jail and relieve his little brother.

As soon as they were alone Simon looked all around, then pressed his face tight against the bars. "If you can get loose," he whispered, "how will we go? Will we run through the woods? Try to get to Kentucky? Or what?"

"Running won't work! They'd track us down in no time. Practically every man around here has a hunting dog or two. They'd sic them on to us. No, there's only one way. We've got to get on the river and float on west."

"What river?"

"The Ohieeo. We're practically living on the bank of it here at Fort Pitt. Simon, if you're really serious about running away, maybe you can scout around for a boat we could steal. Even if you decide you don't want to take the chance you could tell me what you come up with."

"Sure I will, but as of now I'm planning to go right along with you. What we gonna eat, Tom? I'm used to pretty good food, even for us slaves at Rocky Hill plantation. Will you shoot deers and rabbits and such for us?"

"All that sort of stuff we'll have to decide as we go. The first thing is a boat. See what you can find. If there is . . ."

Lucius suddenly opened the door and strode into the room. "Simon," he growled, "get away from that red devil! Don't you know he could grab you and choke the miserable life right out of your body? Then who could take care of my clothes until the judge gets here?" Tom thought the lawyer was making a joke. He was not! It was no wonder Simon would be willing to risk his very life to try for freedom!

"Did yall hurt your head Massa?" Simon asked, eyeing a not too clean piece of cloth tied around Lucius' forehead.

"No I did <u>not</u>!" he growled. "That fool tavern-keeper's woman put this on me. It stinks like the very devil, and the vinegar in it keeps running into my eyes!"

"I sho' does hope it helps yall," Simon said.

Tom was not surprised to hear how quickly the slave could revert to a sort of subservient mode of speech. He was learning a lot about the life of a slave in the early eighteen hundreds.

"Do it make yo' headache better, Massa?" Tom thought that maybe Simon was overdoing it a little but his master did not seem to notice.

"No it doesn't! I've had this headache ever since I got to this awful place. How do people stand to live with such privation? Why, you can't even get a glass of decent wine anywhere around here. 'Pittsburgh' they're calling it. Well it's some burgh all right, nothing but a half-abandoned fort, and a bunch of shacks. Some burgh," he repeated. "I can't wait to get this Indian hung so me and mine can get back to the real world."

Tom had heard this, of course and his heart leaped in fear. There was little doubt that Lucius' sentiments were shared by all his accusers.

"Well, there's one piece of good news at least. John got a letter from Circuit Judge Lewis Collarin. He says he'll be here by Friday, next. <u>Finally</u>! Come on Simon, I need you."

As sometimes happens to persons in desperate straits, inspiration seemed to fill young Simon's head in an instant. He acted immediately.

"Massa Lucius, Suh, I'm shore mighty sorry 'bout your achin' head. I been doin' some powerful thinkin' and cogitatin' as to how I could help you git over this triberlation, 'specially since the judge be a-comin' fore long now. So I says to myself, I says . . ."

"Blast you! If you've got something to say, <u>say</u> it! This cold jail is making my headache worse. I'll try anything. That is if you ever stop yammering and tell me what your idea is."

"Oh I's so sorry, Massa Lucius! I'll just hurry right up and tell you 'bout what I been 'memberin' these last days. Does yall 'member that old Mammy on the Packard Plantation, name of Lilly Red?"

"Well, what about her?" Lucius shouted in exasperation.

"Well Suh, she once showed me a little fern-like of a thing that she'd bile up in crick water to make a potion fer them as has the headache. You drink about a pint of that stuff and by jingoes yo' headache's <u>gone</u>!"

Lucius stared at Simon in astonishment. "It really does help, you say?"

"Oh yassuh it shorely do. Old Toby, he drunk it whenever the headache come on him, and <u>poof</u>, ol' headache's gone, gone, <u>gone</u>!"

Tom's spirits were lifting like mist off the river. It was plain enough that Simon had come up with a plan, and any plan was a reason to hope. He listened carefully.

"You say you <u>saw</u> this plant, Simon? Maybe it would grow around here somewhere. Everything else sure does!"

"Why don't you get out in the woods and see if you can find some. This thing," he ripped off the bandage and threw it into the fireplace, "sure isn't doing a thing for me."

"Now I rekoleks even more 'bout that plant. Lilly Red, she'd go along that little crick what runs right along the edge of your property with her gatherin' bag and the walkin' stick she allus carried. Wore a old green bonnet, she did. Why she jest . . ."

"Carnsarn it!" Lucius exploded. "Will you just get on with it? I want you out there finding those greens as soon as you can! Is that Clear?"

"Yassuh. That's clear all right. Sho' 'nuff. But sir I ain't got hardly no warm clothes atall, only this here rag of linsey-woolsey. It's mighty cold way out here next to nowhere!"

"All right, all right, you little beggar. I'll send Lymon down here with my good hunting coat. I'll even let you wear my wool cap. Just get that cure, and as soon as you can, too."

"I'll jest 'bout run all the way, Massa Lucius ifn I only knowed which way to run! I don't know if there's cricks or rivers and such anywhere around these parts."

"May heaven give me patience," Lucius sighed. "You good-for-nothing! The fort's built right on the river! Get on down there!"

Simon looked down at his feet, as if in alarm. "Right on the river, Suh? What keeps us from just floatin' away?"

"Watch it, Simon," Tom thought. "Don't overplay the 'ignorant pickininny' role. Lucius is no fool."

Evidently Simon also realized he had allowed himself to get carried away in his attempt to make a fool of his master. He quickly changed his course. "I'll find that river sho' enough, Mass Lucius, soon as I gets them warm clothes."

When the jailer entered, Lucius left, holding his head. Simon turned toward Tom and sneaked a wink. He'd have to wait to tell the Indian what he planned to do.

*   *   *

"The Honorable Judge Lewis Collarin! All rise," the tavern-keeper intoned.

The frontiersmen in the tavern grinned and nudged each other. Two laughed outright. They were not impressed with the slave-holding country gentlemen's attempts to impress them. Four off-duty recruits did stand up, their military discipline much in evidence.

Nonplussed, the judge took his seat behind a small table next to the bar. He cast a critical eye on those who had come to witness an event most unusual here on the border between Pennsylvania and Ohio Territory. "Welcome friends," he began. "As we begin these proceedings let me remind you that serious harm has been done to an upstanding citizen of this community, one who is also the proprietor of a valued service. We should also remain cognizant of the fact that the life of a young man, even if he is an Indian, is in jeopardy here."

"What's 'cogerzant' mean, Judge?" The ragtag listeners laughed and swigged their watered ale.

Without raising his voice, the judge said, "This is the only warning. The next person who speaks aloud will be escorted from these premises. If more than one decide to misbehave in such a crude and ungentlemanly manner I will clear the room."

They glanced at one another sheepishly and a few grinned, but not a voice was heard. After all it was a cold and rainy early spring day outside, but nice and warm in the tavern!

"Now who represents the plaintiff?" the judge asked, settling a pair of glasses on his nose.

"I do your honor." Lucius had a practiced courtroom voice that was impressive indeed. "I've come all the way from Great Notch, Virginia to provide legal counsel for Mr. John Grant, an outstanding citizen of Pittsburgh." He nodded to his brother, who stood up, making a pitiful show of terrible pain from his wound.

"Thank you. The plaintiff may remain seated during these proceedings, as it is obvious that you are still suffering from you injury. Now will there be anyone acting in behalf of the Indian man, Tom Bluefoot I think he is called, who stands before you as the accused?"

"Well I aim to do what I can, Judge." Heads swiveled until all could see the small red-haired Irishman standing near the far door. Tom's head snapped up as he saw his best [and only] friend who'd come to defend him.

"And who are you young man? You don't look old enough to have read the law, let alone passed the bar."

"Them Irish don't pass up _many_ bars! Haw haw." One of the ruffians hooted. The judge said nothing but simply pointed an accusing finger at the man, who was quickly hustled out of the room before the judge could make them all leave.

"What credentials do you have that will allow you to take part in this court of law?"

"Well your Honor, the truth is I ain't got any. But I've known this Indian for quite a few years. We served together in the American army under General Anthony Wayne. He's a good man, and I want to say right now . . ."

"That will do. No more at this time. You'll get your chance to speak later. Now I would like a complete accounting of the incident which brings us together here this day." He turned to the scared-looking young woman seated at the next table. "Are you getting this down, Mrs. Blythe?" She nodded, the quill in her hand scratching away.

"Permit me Your Honor," Lucius intoned, bowing to the magistrate. "I will speak for my client, who is still in much pain from being knifed <u>by that Indian</u>!" His voice had risen in the accusation, but the judge seemed unimpressed. "According to my client, Mr. John J. Grant, an honorable and respected business man of this community . . ."

"OH get on with it counselor. We're not in Boston you know. Just the facts if you please." The judge shook his head in disgust.

"Sorry Your Honor. Knowing of your august reputation in the law, I only felt it proper to follow accepted courtroom procedure, even here in this . . .this . . wilderness, so I . . ."

"What in tarnation happened out there at the grist mill?" the judge thundered. "That's all I want to hear from you, or anybody <u>else</u>!"

"Certainly! Certainly." Lucius stated hurriedly. "It happened like this," he cleared his throat, began to survey the listeners, thought better of it, and quickly continued. "My client was busy doing an honest day's work at the mill, where I must add he had come all the way from Virginia to help his aging uncle, when this <u>Indian</u>," he jabbed a finger at Tom, "showed up there, uninvited. The rascal claimed that Eli Miller, the original owner of the establishment, had raised him, and therefore at the death of Mr. Miller, he should inherit the property. A preposterous and absolutely unfounded claim, especially in light of the fact that my client is the nephew, the nearest blood relative of the owner."

"That's not right at all, judge!" Sean O'Casey had jumped up and taken a few steps toward the front.

"He's out of order Judge Collarin!" Lucius shouted, pounding the table.

"Thank you Counselor for informing me of the proper protocol in a court of law. How could I have missed such an important point after only twenty-nine years on the bench?"

The onlookers laughed uproariously, glad to see the pompous Virginian get his 'comeuppance'. The judge gave them a little more time, then tapped his gavel for order. "Mr. O'Casey is it? I've already informed you that you will be given a chance to speak, even though it is highly irregular. In view of the remoteness of this place I will allow it later. Please proceed, Mr. Grant," he said calmly.

Feeling justified, Lucius began. "Thank you Judge Collarin. Naturally John Grant was deeply concerned. Think about it. A full-blooded Indian man suddenly appears, making a claim on the property itself. Furthermore, John's wife," here he paused and bowed toward Martha, who was sitting primly among the onlookers, "and his bedridden uncle were unprotected in the nearby cabin. My client politely asked the Indian to leave the premises, but this <u>sneaky</u>, <u>dangerous</u> native . . ."

"That will be quite enough of that, Counselor! You know better. Proceed, but do not dishonor your profession with such inappropriate and slanderous remarks again!"

"I <u>am</u> sorry Your Honor. It's just that I was carried away by remembering the terrible predicament in which my client found himself. Well Sir, the defendant did not leave as requested but sneaked into the cabin and menaced the uncle and the young niece." Again he bowed in Martha's direction. The judge gave a great sigh and rolled his eyes, but allowed Lucius to go on. "By cleverly tracking the redskin through the snow he found the defendant right in the cabin! Having armed himself against the intruder, he drew the pistol from his coat but the Indian pulled a knife and stabbed him in the stomach. He tried to defend himself by firing a shot at the attacker, but understandably due to the severity of his wound, his aim was not good. So traumatic was the event that it caused our . . . I mean John's sick uncle to suffer some sort of a spell from which he may never recover. Those are the facts of the case, Judge Collarin." He sat down, beaming proudly at everyone in the room.

"Now," Judge Collarin said, nodding at Sean, "you may have a short time to speak. You must keep in mind however that your contribution may not be relevant, due to your lack of legal documentation."

"Thank you your Judge . . . I mean Honor," Sean floundered. "I been talking to Mr. Tom Bluefoot ever since he's been put in jail. He told me just what happened out there, and I believe him too! What that there John Grant's been saying is not . . ."

"Objection!" Lucius yelled jumping to his feet. "That's plainly just hearsay Your Honor. It's not admissible."

"Sustained," Collarin said wearily.

"Stained? What's that mean?" Sean asked, bewildered. "Everybody here should know that Tom could have just run away, but he ran all the way to a neighbor for a wagon to fetch Grant to the doctor. That doctor is me, and . . ."

"Oh for heaven's sake Judge," Lucius growled, his face getting red, "hasn't this farce gone on long enough? I'm, a patient man, but this is ridiculous!"

Sean cleared his throat but before he could begin again a boy of about ten years burst into the room and pushed his way to the Irishman. "It's my <u>brother</u>!" he sobbed. "Near cut his foot off with a ax! You gotta come right now! He's bleedin' bad. <u>Real</u> <u>bad</u>!" Sean gave a hopeless look in Tom's direction and grabbed his coat.

"That does it!" the Judge growled. "Court's adjourned until this afternoon, or as soon as everybody's had a good lunch." Cheers broke out at this announcement, but the disgusted magistrate did not even attempt to stop them.

Simon, who had been ordered to help out in the kitchen, was appalled at the chaos, as those who'd had to stand around the walls at the trial fought for seats. Such bad manners would never have been seen on the plantation, but the young slave was getting a lesson in how different life was on the frontier. The duty in the warm kitchen had been wonderful. As they worked, the cooks and maids plied him with questions about life on a Virginia plantation. What were people wearing? Especially the women! They also raised many questions about the life of a slave, curious to know if it was as bad as some had heard. Smiling constantly, Simon kept them enthralled so that when none was looking his way he could snitch a potato or a piece of turkey. As soon as he could, he hid each one at the bottom of the bucket of dry corncobs which were meant for the big iron cookstove.

Lymon had been sent to the kitchen as well. As usual he was managing to charm everyone in the room. So much so that he did virtually no work! Once he even improvised a little "soft shoe" shuffle, which brought shouts of appreciation and laughter. "That kid," thought Simon, "could sell a bucket of ice to a Exkimo!" He didn't know what an "Exkimo" was but he'd heard the expression somewhere.

Simon was thinking ahead! His mind now totally made up, he was looking for anything that would help as he and Toom-She-chi-Kwa made their escape. He kept his eye on one young girl as she attempted to cut slices off a large slab of bacon. "'Scuse me ma'am," he said in his best plantation voice, "I believe that your knife is a little dull for that work, if you don't mind me sayin' so. Let me take it to the sharpening stone out back and I'll have it sharper than a hound dog's tooth." He picked a smaller utensil out of the box and said, "Here, use this one. Better cut off most of the rind first. I'll be back soon." He wrapped the blade in a napkin and when she was not looking slid it into his ragged stocking.

"Simon! Where you at boy?" Lucius' appearance in the kitchen shocked everyone, but they all kept their eyes down and tried to appear very busy.

"I'se right cheer, Massa Lucius. Is they somethin' I kin do for yall? I reckon the ladies can get along without me for a while."

"Don't get uppity with me you insolent devil!"

"But Lucius Suh, I'se only sayin' the truth! I shorely didn't mean no . . "

"Forget that! Get down to the river and hunt up some of those ferns you told me about. My head feels like it's going to explode!"

"I'll shorely do my bestus to find some Massa Lucius, but it's still mighty cold and raw outside. My old coat's only got about two threads holding it together anymore. Be awful hard huntin' them special ferns and tryin' to keep warm at the same time. So you see . . ."

"Blast you! We've been over this before. Find the innkeeper and tell him I'm loaning you my hunting coat. Might as well take the hat and boots too while you're at it. There's still a couple hours of daylight left, get going! If you come back without those greens I'll whip the hide right off your back! Now git!" He stalked out of the kitchen without another word.

"Well that was slicker than goose grease," Lymon thought to himself, "but he ain't as good at it as me!" Hiding a grin he went back to pretending to make hominy.

*   *   *

"Hello Tom. I brought you a little food." Martha passed a towel through the bars as Captain Jameson, the jailer, watched carefully. Bluefoot looked at the man, not sure if he would be allowed to accept the package.

"Go ahead, Injun. I already examined the parcel. I didn't find a gun, a file or nothin'. Haw haw!" He stepped close to the bars, checked the lock, then turned to Martha. I'll be going to my supper now, but I'm right across the street if this redskin should try to excape." Laughing, he put on his coat and left the jail.

"How are you doing Toomie?" she asked, using Eli's favorite name for the Wyandot he'd helped to raise.

"I'm afraid, Martha. I've never been so afraid! Even during the war I was not as scared as I am now. They're going to hang me, I'm sure of it."

Martha made no attempt to dissuade him. They both knew he was probably right, but still she tried to comfort him, even a little. "But Toomie, even if they convict you it can't be for murder. My husband is still alive and he's getting well!"

"I know that Martha, but there's still something the jailer talked about called <u>attempted</u> murder. They might send me . . .send me . . .you know. . . lock me up!" Tears streamed down his face but he made no sound. Martha cried too.

"I'm so sorry! I'm ashamed of my husband! I saw everything. He's a liar, but according to my brother-in-law Lucius, a wife cannot testify against her husband. Still I'm going to try before all of this is over." She stepped to the door and listened a moment. Back at Tom's cell she turned her back, raised her skirt above her right knee, withdrew a small object, and thrust it into Tom's hand. "This may be of help, "she whispered and with a rustle of her long skirts left the jail.

Tom stared in amazement. It was a tiny steel "strike-a-light" used with flint for making fire. "So she suspects what I'm planning to do," he thought with the first smile he'd had in a long time.

The jailer soon came back from his supper. He checked the lock again, threw another log on the fire, and lit his pipe. "It don't look good for you, Injun," he said, not unkindly. "That Virginny lawyer is one big blowhard. The judge put him in his place a couple times though, ha ha. He's the brother of John Grant, the one you tried to murder ain't he?" Tom said nothing but the Captain continued, almost as if he was talking to himself. "They been saying at the tavern that some redskins is at it again. You ever know a Injun name of Tecusperah or something like that?"

Tom did not react, but he was instantly alert. The jailer was undoubtedly referring to Tecumseh, whose Indian name meant "Shooting Star". Head hanging, Tom tried to look uninterested but his mind was whirling. He most certainly <u>did</u> know the young chief, and it was very possible that Shawnee would remember <u>him</u> as the interpreter at the Greenville Treaty. If he and Simon could somehow make their escape, they might be able to find the famous native and possibly join his band. There was also the plot on Simon Kenton's life that he'd heard about. Could he find him and warn him? He could if . . . If . . .If . . .If!" Tom knew there was very little chance he could even get away, much less find Kenton or join Tecumseh. Still he now had a glimmer of hope. That feeling was shattered by the jailer's next comment however.

"I suppose you heard already that the judge, his name is Collarin, he's going to make his decision on Wednesday, 'right after dinner' he says. That man can sure put away a passel of food. Says the tavern cookin's the best he's had since he left Philadelphy! I reckon . . ."

"What day is it?" Tom suddenly interrupted.

"Why I thought you was asleep. It's Sunday, of course. I reckon 'The Lord's Day' don't mean nothing to a heathen like you though. Now I'm gonna go and get that slave, the older one, and send him down here for a couple hours." He patted his ample stomach and yawned mightily. "I intend to take a nice nap on this fine Sunday afternoon."

They were back in only a few minutes. "But Suh, I don't want to stay in this old jail with that Indian man. I's sposed to be helpin' in the kitchen, and keepin'

Massa Lucius' clothes clean, and all like that, Suh!"

"Mind your tongue, <u>darkie</u>! You stay right here like you're told. Sweep up and empty the slop bucket too. No, you better not open the cell door till I get back. That there Injun," he pointed at Tom, "would sure try to excape, cause he knows that judge is gonna find him guilty! You go ahead and clean up in here. I'll just take the keys with me so there's nothing going wrong in my lock-up." He looked all around once more, then ambled out the door.

Tom got a little angry when he saw Simon pick up the broom and start sweeping the floor. "Why don't you . . ." the door opened quickly. The Captain stepped inside, watched Simon for a minute then left, this time for good. "How'd you know he'd come back like that?" Tom asked incredulously.

"After you've been a slave all your life you learn how to keep out of trouble. You've <u>got</u> to! White folks is always trying to catch us coloreds at <u>something</u>," he added bitterly.

"They hate us Indians too, Simon. Let's forget that and see what we can do about getting me out of here."

Simon approached the bars, lips stretched in a big grin. He was whispering again. "Tom," he began, "I didn't find any of those imaginary headache ferns, but I found us <u>a boat</u>!"

"Oh man that's wonderful! Where is it? How big? Come on Simon tell me!"

"It's not very big is the only thing. It's got a flat bottom and it's not pointed on either end. It's lying upside down by a little shed, not too far, maybe fifty steps from the edge of the big river."

"That sounds like it could work. Of course that's if I can get out of here <u>first</u>! We'll have to hurry because I learned the judge is going to make his decision on Wednesday. Martha says they can't hang me, since her man ain't dead. But it could mean life in some prison, and as far as I'm concerned that's even worse!"

Simon suddenly seemed reluctant to meet the Indian's eye. Finally he spoke. "It won't be Wednesday, Tom. My master talked the judge into movin' things along a couple days sooner."

"What do you <u>mean</u>?" Tom cried.

"I hates to say it, but old Judge Collarin says now he'll give his decision on Monday, right after dinner."

"<u>Monday</u>? You mean <u>tomorrow</u>?"

"That's right Tom. I hated to tell you, but we have to know how much time we've got."

"How much time we <u>haven't</u> got!" Tom replied bitterly.

"Don't give up yet. Let me tell you what I've been doing to get us ready. First off I stole a knife from the kitchen, and I talked Lucius into loaning me his coat and boots so I could hunt for them greens for his headache. I got a little food too from the dirty plates coming back to the kitchen. It's wrapped in a old gunny sack that I hid under the back porch of the tavern. About the best thing I took was a piece of bacon as big as my hand, and a hunk of bacon rind."

"I sure appreciate all you're doing, Simon, but what good is it if I'm still locked up in here?" he asked glumly.

Simon shook his head at Tom. "I'm sorry to tell you <u>this</u> <u>too</u> my friend, but there's another problem."

"Well what is it? It can't be much worse than the way everything else is going right now!"

"The fact is there's a big dog chained up pretty close to that boat I found. He'll likely bark if we start messin' around that boat in the night."

"We might as well forget the whole thing, Simon," Tom moaned. "There's too many things that could go wrong. You don't have any jail time facing <u>you</u>. Just go on back to being a slave with your brother. If Lymon can take it you can too."

"I know about dogs," Simon said. "Lookee here what I got wrapped around my middle." He pulled up his shirt. The long strip of bacon rind circled almost half way around his skinny stomach, grease still running from it. "We just sneaks up and throws this piece of sow belly to that hound and he'll be too busy chewin' on it too bark hardly at all!"

"You've surely been doing some powerful planning. Did you get clear down to the river at any time?"

"I did all right. What folks calls the 'spring breakup' must have come about a week ago. There's lots of big pieces of ice floating along, but the water's running good and fast. If we can get the boat on the river we ought to be able to travel a good ways before full light."

"How heavy is it? The boat. How heavy would you say it is?"

"I didn't get too close on account of that old hound dog, but I reckon it's pretty heavy. Also it's laying there upside down. We'll have to turn it over and slide it down to the river. I expect it'll take about all we can do to launch the thing, but once we're on the river we should be able to leave all of this behind us! I've been thinking about letting Lymon in on our plans, then he could help us move the boat. That way . . ."

"No! I'll not have your little brother involved in any of this! Don't you tell him a thing, you hear?"

"Yassuh Massa! Oh yas Suh! Yall kin count on ol Simon. Sho yall kin!"

For the first time in weeks they laughed aloud at his antics. "Simon, I'll say it again. Thank you for all you're doing to help me try to escape! But none of this will amount to a thing unless I can get out of this cell somehow."

"I got a plan for that too, but we better quit talking now. I think I hear the Captain coming back." He picked up the broom, but instead of sweeping, he leaned up against the chimney flue and pretended to be asleep. Tom hurried back to the bench.

"Wake up!" the jailer yelled. Simon jumped so hard he nearly fell down. "You lazy darkey! You ain't swept a lick have you? Been sleepin' standin' up all this time I'll wager. Well you're to get back and help out at the tavern. I'll mind this convict now. Where'd you get that good coat and them boots?" Simon grabbed the articles and made for the door. "Come back here you! I ast you a question!"

"I'se shore sorry , Suh. Massa Lucius loaned 'em to me Suh. I's to gather some greens for his headache, but so far I've had trouble findin' jest the right kind. You see, this early spring weather just ain't proper for . . ."

"Oh go <u>on</u>! I swear I don't see how decent white folks can stand bein' around the likes of you. You hike yourself over to the tavern and no lingerin' on the way!"

*   *   *

Sean hurried in, still fastening his heavy surgical apron. "Tom, my good friend," he began, "I'm sure sorry I ain't been to see you more lately. I suppose you've heard about all the whooping cough that's going around. Me and the Captain have been about run ragged lately! There's hardly a cabin that doesn't have somebody down with it. Even some of the soldiers here in the fort are whoopin' and coughin'! So how are you doing?"

"I'm trying to keep my spirits up but I don't sleep much in this jail cell. I'd like to talk to you some, but I know how busy you are. You must be quite a doctor already. How's Chloe and the baby?"

"Stay back from them <u>bars</u>!" the jailer growled, peering at Sean over a pair of thick glasses. "I've kept that redskin locked up all these weeks and I don't aim to have anything happen to him the night before the judge says his piece."

Sean moved back a step but otherwise ignored the jailer. "They're both fine, Tom. Chloe would like to come and see you, but her <u>doctor</u>," here Sean grinned self-consciously, "won't let her out till the epidemic is over. Little Becky's trying to walk already, but mostly she just falls on her bottom!"

Nothing was said for a while. What was there to say? Both men were well aware that Tom's chances were practically hopeless. Nearly everyone around the tiny hamlet of Pittsburgh had lost a loved one or two in the late Indian wars, or knew someone who had. Also, reports of torture and mutilations were still fresh in their minds. Revenge on an Indian, any Indian, was almost to be expected. John Grant was taking full advantage of the local sentiment. He knew that he had little to fear from the law. This was true even if Eli Miller did recover, since the old man had been unconscious in another room when the fight took place. John and his attorney brother strutted about the village taking opportunity to show off their fine clothes and polished boots.

"You been here long enough O'Casey. Better forget this Injun and get back to your doctorin'. By the way, stop off at my place on your way back. My old woman's got the misery again. She wants some more of that brown medicine Doctor Friedereich gives her. Seems like she needs more of that all the time! Go on now."

"I'll do what I can for you," Sean said to Tom on his way out. Neither man knew what that could be.

Another late morning hour dragged by, Tom sitting morosely on the bench in his cell. He had not slept at all during the long night. The jailer, nearly asleep behind his desk, suddenly woke up with an oath. "Where in tarnation is that darkey? He was supposed to have been here an hour ago. If I don't get over to the tavern pretty soon I won't have time to eat before I escort you over there for the verdict."

As if on cue Simon entered the jail, still dressed in the hunting coat and boots Lucius had loaned him. "It's about time, blast you! Where you been anyhow?"

"Oh I's sorry Suh, real sorry, but old Wiggins, she had me warshin' them good dishes till they almost lost the flowers on 'em, Suh! Yassuh that's erzackly whar I been all this hyar time. That old woman tryin' to show off in front of them Virginny gennelmens. It's just what she be doin', sho enough. Well Suh I jest . . ."

"Will you shut up for once? Now you listen to me and you listen good! I'll be back for him," he jerked a thumb in Tom's direction, "before long. I want this jail swept till it shines. I'm taking the keys with me," he patted a bulge in his vest pocket, "so you won't be able to empty the slops. Stay away from the bars too. There's not going to be any funny business until this Injun is brought to justice! You got all of that?"

"Yassuh! I's just gonna do all of that. Yawl gonna see one mighty clean jail when you gits back. I do declare that when I cleans a room . . ."

The jailer left, slamming the door behind him. As before Simon pretended to sweep for a few minutes but this time the jailer did not slip back. Evidently he was too hungry for such games.

Still holding the broom, just in case, Simon began immediately. "It's got to be tonight, Tom. They'll probably be sending you off tomorrow with a squad of soldiers. There won't be any chance then."

"Do you know where they'll send me?"

"The kitchen ladies been talking. They know more about what's happening than most of the men do! I heard them say that six soldiers have orders to go to Philadelphia. There's a big prison there at a town called Red Bluffs. It's only half a day's journey from the big town. I'm sorry Tom, but they've got it all planned out. The verdict is just for show. That's why it's tonight or <u>never</u>!"

"You sure you want to be part of this Simon? You could help me, then claim that I knocked you out or something."

"I'm <u>going</u>! That's that!"

"I really appreciate all you've done to get us ready, but I ask it again, what can we do to get me out of this cell?"

"I've got a good plan for that, Tom. I'm sure it will work, but if it don't maybe we could try something when they take you to Philadelphia."

"No Simon, that's no good. With six soldiers there'd be no chance for anything then. Also, you'd probably be back in Virginia. It's tonight or never, just like you said."

"Trust me Tom. By this time tomorrow we'll both be free! I'm getting more stuff ready all the time, but I'll have to be careful now or I'll get caught. Here," he pulled a heavy brown sack from under Lucius' coat, "you keep this sack, Tom. We'll need it."

"How can that help? The jailer will see it. Besides, what do we need an old sack for?"

"Just fold it up and sit on it. It's almost the same color as that dirty bench in there. The old jailer's nearsighted anyway. No pickaninny ever goes anywhere without his tow sack! Now I got to get to the kitchen. I'll be back some time in the middle of the night."

Another hour passed until the jailer returned. "<u>Where</u> is <u>he</u>?" he raged. "Blast him, he's left you unguarded. When I catch up with him he's gonna wish he'd never been borned!" He checked the lock carefully until he was satisfied that all was well. Either he didn't see the old sack Tom was sitting on, or he didn't care.

An hour slowly passed, Two hours. Then Tom had another visitor. "Good afternoon, sheriff." Martha gave him a dazzling smile.

"Well howdy-do Miz Martha. The fact is I ain't ezackly the sheriff yet, but I sure aim to be, soon as the Major can organize some kind of an election. Did you know we're calling this place Pittsburgh now? As you can see the old fort's about served its time."

"Well I'm going to call you 'sheriff' anyway. It's obvious that you are already doing that work. I have a favor to ask of you."

"And what might that be, Mrs. Grant?"

Martha held out a folded blanket. It was rather tattered, but fairly clean. "I know that Eli, my husband's uncle, was fond of that young Indian," she nodded at Toom-She-chi-Kwa. "I can see that he's cold in that cell, so I'm asking you permission to give it to him to use tonight." She smiled at the jailer, then shook out the blanket, turning it so both sides were in his view. She held it by the corners.

He adjusted his glasses and made quite a show of inspecting the cloth. "Why shore. He can use it tonight, but you'd better come back for it tomorrow, 'cause I'm afraid them soldier boys would conferscape it on their way to Philadelphy. Haw haw!"

She pushed it through the bars, being careful to place one corner directly into Tom's hand. She talked to the jailer for a few minutes, said goodbye to Tom, and left.

The Indian drew the blanket around his shoulders and sat back down, careful to fold the corner under his knee. There was something there alright, but to see what it was he'd have to wait until the jailer left.

*   *   *

Lucius Grant, Attorney at Law, had waited until Judge Collarin was getting noticeably impatient before helping his brother into the big room in the tavern. John groaned pitifully as he limped to a waiting bench and eased himself into a sitting position. Lucius hovered over him like a hen over her chicks, making sure all the spectators could not miss how serious the stab wound was. Actually it was almost healed.

Sitting on a straight chair to the judge's left, Toom-She-chi-Kwa watched the ridiculous drama with disgust. Even the judge seemed unimpressed. An explosive belch from one of the settlers proved that one of the onlookers had added substantially to his tavern bill. There was a titter of laughter, but the judge silenced it with a tap of his gavel. His Honor secretly wished he could relieve himself like that. "I should never have had that second plate of sauerkraut!" he thought. But there was nothing that could be done about it now.

"Good afternoon Judge," Lucius said, smiling at His Honor.

"Good afternoon to you, Counselor. Is the plaintiff's case ready?"

"Ready and <u>eager</u> Your Honor!"

The judge peered at Tom over a pair of tiny round glasses. "The prisoner will rise." He used his admittedly effective courtroom voice. "State your name for the record."

"My name is Toom-She-chi-Kwa. I am a Wyandot from Chief Roundhead's sept."

A low growl could be heard from the crowd, but again the judge was in charge. "Thank you. Is there a name you use when in the company of white folks?"

"Yes sir. Most call me Tom. Tom Bluefoot."

"Are you able to get this down Miss Blythe? And is your child doing well so far?"

The young schoolteacher turned proudly toward the homemade crib at her elbow. "Thankee kindly sir. My little honey is just fine, but if she does start fussing, Mrs. Jenkins there," she pointed at a large lady seated nearby, "will see to her in the other room."

Judge Collarin was intrigued. "You are the local school teacher are you not? How do you manage, with a child so young? I presume your husband takes over when you are in the schoolhouse."

"My husband is <u>dead</u>!" she said angrily. "He was killed by the Indians in one of them battles." She shot a look of pure hatred at Tom Bluefoot. "So I take my young'un right along to school with me. She mostly sleeps in her crib next to the stove. When she gets hungry of course she cries some, but I just take her into the cloak room and . . .and . . . well, feed her." There were some grins but no one laughed aloud. They were learning how things were done in Judge Collarin's court. "The older girls help with the baby. They're learning lots more than arithmetic! I got another good helper too. He's Amil, back there. She looked fondly at a young man whose muscular frame seemed about to destroy his homespun shirt. "He comes to school when all the crops are in. He just <u>loves</u> my little one! Carries her around ever chance he gets. He's a real good man, Judge, and I . . ."

Lucius stood up from his chair on the judge's right. He risked an audible groan. "How <u>long</u>, Your Honor, must we be afflicted with this frontier drivel? Can we not finally get on with the <u>sentencing</u>?"

"The point is well taken, Counselor. State your case for the record."

Lucius hooked both thumbs in his vest and began. He gave a lurid account of his brother's version of the fight, making certain that Tom was portrayed as a vile, marauding Indian who was intent upon harming an unprotected wife and a bedridden old man. By the time he finally finished everyone present, including the judge, was convinced that the young Wyandot was deserving of the absolute worst punishment the law would allow. Lucius was an excellent lawyer!

Even though his mind was completely made up, Judge Collarin followed the usual procedure and asked the prisoner if he had anything to say in his own behalf. Tom merely shook his head without looking up.

"This court finds the defendant, one Tom Bluefoot, guilty of attempted murder, and is therefore sentenced to life in the Territorial Prison near Philadelphia, Pennsylvania. Court is adjourned."

*   *   *

"Well Injun, I reckon you'll be on your way tomorrow, soon as the detachment of soldiers is ready to leave. I suppose they'll be taking a horse and wagon, so you'll get to ride in it whenever the trail's fitten to travel on. 'Course they may decide to make you walk all the way! Them moccasins of yourn in good shape are they? They better be! Haw haw!"

Tom said nothing, so the jailer finally gave up the game and began shuffling through the papers on his desk. "Now where," he grumbled, "is that confounded darkey? Off sleeping somewhere I'll wager. Well if he don't show up purty soon I'll have to go and fetch him. I don't aim to spend the night alone with the likes of you!" He jerked a thumb in Tom's direction. "With the two of us on guard it ain't likely you'll try anything. Wouldn't work if you did. I'm keeping your hands tied all night. Not even a decent pair of handcuffs in the whole fort! Oh well, it don't matter none. Them soldiers will probly jest leave 'em tied like that. Save them a lot of trouble."

About an hour later the door opened and Simon stuck his head inside. "I'se been a-rushin' right over here Mr. Sheriff, Suh. Yessir I been a-doin' jest that there, and I'se shore happy to be here and help you on account of . . ."

"Oh hush up! Take off that nice coat the lawyer man loaned you. The hat too. You better not get them boots of hisn dirty. Looks like somebody took a long time shinin' them up. Did you <u>hear me</u>? I said take off that coat!"

Simon turned his back on the man and began slowly removing the coat. It was clear that the slave was concealing something. The jailer's suspicions were realized when a soft "clink" was heard. "What you got hid in there, darkey?" He grabbed the coat and managed to catch the small cut-glass jug that was falling out. "So! Thought you'd get away with stealing this fine little demijohn did you? This handsome bottle looks like it came right off the table at Lucius Grant's plantation. Wait till I tell him what you've done!"

"But Mistah Jailer, Suh, you got it all wrong. This here's a gift for <u>you</u>! Massa Lucius sent me right over with it, so here it is!"

"You lying rascal! You stole that flask and meant to drink it all up yourself! I know your kind. Now I'll just have a little sample of that, just to make sure it's fit for human consumption. Haw haw!" He grabbed the bottle, twisted out the cork, and took a drink.

"Oh no, Massa. You mustn't drink that so fast. Massa Lucius says he's the only one alive kin drink more'n a couple swallers of that kind of liquor."

"He does, does he? Well I'm here to tell you I can out-drink, out shoot, and out-rassel anybody in these parts, <u>including</u> your 'Massa Lucius'. Watch this." He raised the cut-glass decanter and poured half a cup of the fiery stuff down his gullet. He coughed, choked, and gasped for breath.

"Oh Mistah Sheriff, Suh. You shorely can drink! Better not take any more though. Massa Lucius says he's the only one . . ."

"Gimme that bottle!" he shouted, peering around with a sort of dazed expression. "Give it to me, I said!" he yelled, wiping his mouth on his sleeve.

"I cain't. Beggin' your pardon Suh, 'cause you're a-holdin' it your own self!"

For the first time in a long while Tom Bluefoot's lips spread in a huge grin. "He is something!" he thought as he finally realized how Simon was manipulating the jailer. "I can see that it's just like he said. Slaves have to use a lot of guile to outwit their white owners without them catching on. What would I do without Simon's help?" he asked himself gratefully.

The jailer sat down rather suddenly, and so hard his chair nearly tipped over with him on it. He sat there, staring into space, a silly grin raising his mustache. He held the bottle clutched to his chest for a minute then raised it to his lips and drank the last few swallows. "Told ya! I told ya I could . . .I could . . . ol' Lucius couldn't . . . he . . . Why is it so blasted hot in this jail house all to onct? You, Mison . . . you stop throwin' all them logs on the fire! Get the andirons and drag one of 'em out of that pireflace, you hear? Now yall just get busy doin' . . .doin' what I tole you. I'll have me a little nap, then I'll take over watchin' that ere Imdiam there . . ." He was asleep in minutes, draped over his desk, head on his arms.

Tom motioned for Simon to approach the bars, but the slave shook his head violently, pointing at the sleeping jailer. Tom nodded, eager to allow Simon to dictate what had to be done and how to do it. Holding one black hand aloft, fingers crossed, he tapped the sleeping man lightly on the shoulder, then immediately knelt down behind the chair. The jailer grunted, lifted his head a few inches, then fell to snoring again. Simon grinned at Tom, but held one cautious finger to his lips. They conversed in whispers. Outside it was beginning to rain.

"Can you get the key, Simon?"

"I think so, but it may take a couple of tries. Let's get everything together and be ready to run as soon as I can get you loose. He slipped the small kitchen knife he'd stolen through the bars and quickly slashed Tom's bonds.

They prepared as best they could without making noise. Simon silently removed Lucius' coat from a hook behind the desk. He could not risk the boots or hat, for fear of making enough noise to wake the sleeper.

Tom was draping Martha's blanket around his shoulders when he remembered the tiny folded corner. It was lightly stitched, and soon came open. He motioned excitedly to Simon, who came close to see. There was a Spanish dollar and two heart-shaped earrings of heavy gold. "She's given me everything of value her nasty husband allowed her to have!" he though gravely. "Somehow, some way, I'll pay her back for this kindness," he vowed.

Simon took the tow sack from Tom and piled everything they had beside the door. Tiptoeing noiselessly about, he considered several items but rejected them for various reasons. Tom motioned impatiently at the jailer, but Simon shook his head. He knew that everything depended upon the man sleeping soundly enough that he could not feel slim fingers searching his vest pocket!

Nearly an hour passed. Jameson did not waken, so both red man and black knew they must make their attempt now in order to have the advantage of darkness and rain. Shaking with fear, Simon knelt directly behind the sleeping lawman. With infinite caution he reached around the man's waist until his fingers found the flap of the jailer's vest pocket. Inch by inch he inserted two fingers. When he touched the large keyring he began to tug, rivers of sweat nearly blinding him. Suddenly the entire set of keys popped out, making a jingling sound that to the terrified listeners sounded as loud as a gunshot!

Simon waited several more minutes, the keys tight against the jailer's stomach. "If he wakes up now," Simon thought, "I'll shove these back in his pocket and run out the door!"

"Gitchie Manetou," Tom prayed silently, "I'm asking you to get me out of this jail and away from this place. Oh, and White Man's God, I'm asking you too!" Evidently one or both of the deities was willing. The keys were secure in Simon's quaking hands!

Fortunately the lock was well oiled. No sound was heard as Simon gingerly turned the key. The door hinges were another matter however. The slightest motion resulted in the beginning of a high-pitched squeal. Thinking fast, Tom pressed Martha's blanket against the metal, and the door opened almost silently.

Never had two young men moved so quietly and so fast! Tom shrugged into the jailer's coat. He checked the pockets. All but one were empty. At the very bottom of the inside left he found Jameson's homemade sheriff's badge. It was ready if and when he got the job! Simon, already dressed in Lucius' hunting jacket, carried the borrowed boots and paused by the door. He was about to open it when Tom held up a finger. The Wyandot slipped back into his cell and used one foot to silently upset the stinking slops bucket. As the vile mess spread across the floor, Tom smiled in satisfaction.

As quietly as two cats, they slipped out into one of the first heavy spring rains. They were <u>free</u>! [For the moment at least!]

Both men knew they would be pursued as soon as the jailer woke up. Tom thought of some of the tricks his uncle, Black Pipe, had taught him when he was still a lad. None of these would be of any help on this wet and windy night. Their first objective would have to be the boat. Progress was necessarily slow, as the night was black as ink, and they needed to be very quiet. Simon remembered the way to the shack where the boat lay, but everything looked different from his trip in daylight. At last they heard a dog bark. Simon was sure they had arrived at their first destination. He held Tom back and unwound the strip of bacon rind from his middle. Almost feeling his way, he approached the shack, holding the strip of side meat in an outstretched hand. The hound charged out of the half barrel which served as his doghouse. Simon threw the rind in front of the dog. The animal ignored the offering and barked louder. Frozen in terror the two escapees had no plan for this, but Tom saved the day. Harkening back to his days with Eli and the grist mill, he threw back his head and gave a respectable imitation of a tomcat.

A feeble light suddenly appeared through the chinks in the old cabin. The door cracked open and a man's voice split the darkness. "Shut up, Schooner!" he yelled. A thrown stick of kindling wood hit the dog. Finally picking the strip of meat out of the mud, he crept back into his barrel, out of the rain.

They backed up against a nearby shed and stood unmoving, hating the delay. The darkness was what they needed and there was not much left.

Still it would be disastrous to try for the boat until it was likely the dog's owner was back to sleep.

The boat turned out to be much heavier than they had expected. Luckily, the owner had turned it upside down on two fence rails, so it was not mired in the mud. Working together they managed to turn it right side up. A sudden flash of lightning lit the area bright as noonday. Terrified, the fugitives forgot being silent and dragged the heavy craft through the mud, heading for the big river. Fear gave them strength that neither one ever had before. The punt slid across grass, weeds, and the occasional cobble, until it finally slid down the wet river bank on its own.

"Tom," Simon hissed, "we ain't got no paddles, do we?"

"No. Won't need any for a while. The river's running high, so it'll take us right on west, the way we want to go. Later on maybe we can make some paddles or use some sticks or something. What's the matter? Why aren't you getting in? I can't hold this boat much longer. The current's getting hold of it."

"I just remembered. I can't swim! What if this old tub dumps us out in all this water and hunks of ice? I'll be drownded like a old rat!"

"Don't worry about it. Soon as it's light we'll get on shore, hide the boat, and fix you some logs or something to hold onto if we go over."

"How will we get to shore with no paddles? This river's likely to take us right out in the middle of it. Anybody onshore will see us plain as day! Oh Tom, we're sure to get caught!"

"You're right! We've got to find a couple of branches or poles or something.

Every time the lightning flashes look hard for anything strong enough to push the ice floes out of the way. Grab anything that could help. You go that way and I'll go this way."

Tom made sure the boat was secure, then slipped and slid his way along the shore in search of anything that could be used. There was quite a bit of brush and flotsam at the river's edge, but he found nothing strong enough to be useful. The search was taking too much time. They must be far down the river by first light. He hurried back to the boat, but was amazed to see Simon standing there holding a thick pole at least eight feet long. "Where'd you get <u>that</u>?" Tom whispered.

"Come on, let's go!" Simon said aloud. "Some old woman is gonna be missing the pole that holds up her clothesline!" His white teeth flashed in a wide grin as the whole scene was lighted by a brilliant flash of lightning.

"One more thing," Tom whispered. He cocked his arm and threw the keyring far out into the river.

*   *   *

Even though the rain continued and thick clouds were lowering, it was plain that dawn was nearly upon them. In spite of their stolen coats, both were freezing. The cold rain seemed like trickles of ice as it continued to soak their sodden clothing. Taking turns "paddling", and pushing ice blocks with the pole had warmed them some, but not much! Simon's misery was exacerbated by his fear of the water.

"Tom, we got to get <u>ashore</u> somewhere! Don't you see how close the water is up on the sides of this boat? If any kind of wind comes up we'll sink for sure. I can't swim, and even if I could, how would we get around all these big chunks of ice that's all around us? Oh Tom, I'm mighty <u>scared</u>!"

"I know you're scared. To tell the truth I'm pretty scared myself. All right, we'll make for shore. I'd wanted to cross the river and land on the Ohio side, but with no paddles, and people surely after us, there's no way to get over there today. Maybe in a couple of days."

"Why go way over there? Let's just get ourselves on <u>land</u>! It don't seem to matter which side of this awful river."

"I'll tell you why, Simon," Tom said pushing on every piece of ice that could move them closer to shore. "The north side is Ohio Territory, and so far as I know settlers over there don't allow any slavery. You'd be a lot safer there. Also I know several Indian tribes in the Territory. One of them might take us in. We can't survive in this wilderness without help. We've got to get over there as soon as we can."

Finally close to shore, they watched for a place where there was not much of a bank. They would have to pull the boat out of sight, and it was a heavy old tub. Gliding along sideways with the current, the bow suddenly struck bottom. Tom, using the pole to hold them steady, was about to tell Simon to jump out and pull them ashore, but the slave was already in the water, dragging the boat behind him! He was happier than he'd been for several days just to feel the mud under his feet. Tom stepped out too, lightening the boat. Between the two of them they soon had it well above the river and hidden in a thick clump of cattails.

Tom broke off a branch and quickly altered their tracks, as well as the ruts made when they pulled the boat up the bank. The rain had about stopped but the fugitives were still nearly freezing in their dripping clothes. "Kin we get a fire going Tom?" Simon asked, his teeth chattering so hard he could hardly be understood.

"I'm sure going to try, but first we'll have to get deeper into the forest."

"Why is that, Tom? Let's get some heat going right <u>here</u> and right <u>now</u>!"

"Can't do it Simon. Any smoke would give our pursuers a beacon they couldn't miss. Now this here," from deep in his pocket he pulled the tiny steel "strike-a-light" Martha had given him, "will sure help, but it won't work without a piece of flint . Do you know how this thing is used?"

"Of course I do," Simon said disgustedly. "I had to make the fire near every day back on Lucius' plantation. Let's hunt us up some flint and get that fire going!"

Carrying their few possessions in Simon's tow sack, they hurried inland, looking for a likely spot to make some kind of camp. "<u>Lookee here, Tom</u>!" Simon cried, pointing to a bit of feathers protruding from the base of a rotten stump. He yanked it out, elated to see an arrow, its flint tip broken, but half of it still attached.

"Gitchie Maneto is helping us!" Tom said, almost in tears. "That little piece of an arrowhead is just what we need! I know how to get a fire going, even when everything's wet like it is today. Come on, friend. Watch for a thick clump of trees."

They crossed a small hill. On the other side was an old paper birch tree, just what Tom was looking for. "Gather up all the sticks you can find, Simon. Use the knife to shave off the wet bark. Keep scraping until you can see dry wood, then get some bigger sticks and do the same. We can make a camp under those hickory trees down there."

"How'd you learn all this kind of stuff, Tom?"

"My uncle, Black Pipe, showed me, but I didn't learn near as much as most boys. I was still living with my 'white father' during the time I would have been taught how to hunt, use a bow, find edible plants, stuff like that."

"That reminds me, Tom, what we gonna <u>eat</u> out here in all these woods, once what I stole is gone?"

"I don't know. That's why we've got to get to the Ohio side and try to find a settler or some friendly Indians."

"What if we find some Indians and they <u>ain't</u> friendly though?"

"I suppose they'd either kill us or we'd both become slaves for them. But let's hope for the best."

It took nearly an hour to get a blaze large enough to partially dry their clothes. The sun was above the trees, but still hidden by low-lying clouds. "I think we probably ought to keep an eye on the river, don't you Tom? If they've figured out where we run to they might smell smoke or somehow find us."

"You're right Simon! One of us should get up on that little hill and watch the river. If we see anybody and they head in to shore where we did, we'll have to make a run for it. I'll go first. You keep the fire going, and don't let it make much smoke."

"Yassuh, Massa! Oh yassuh! I'll do it jest like yawl said, and I'll do it right quick too! I knows . . ."

"Stop that!" Tom laughed as he headed up the hill.

It is a fact of life that good planning is essential for success in any endeavor. It is also a certainty however, that those charged with the execution of such plans often fail to carry them out.

Although very hungry and still chilled, Tom sat down against an oak tree to watch, but within minutes he was fast asleep. An hour later he was awakened by voices and the rattle of oars. Terrified, he peered out from a screen of bushes to see a large bateau with six men aboard making directly for the exact landing spot he and Simon had used that morning! Hardly breathing, he slid partway down the hill, then dashed to their camp. The fire was out! Simon lay curled up under Martha's blanket, which was nearly dry. Tom knelt, clamped one hand over his friend's mouth, and shook him violently. Simon's eyes were rolling in fright, but he made no sound when Tom removed his hand. Casting a quick glance up the hill they could not see anyone coming, but voices could plainly be heard.

Simon gestured wildly toward the forest, and started to run. Tom grabbed his arm, then very carefully pressed his moccasins into the soft earth next to the cold ashes. With sudden inspiration he grabbed up the arrow they'd used in fire making and jammed it upright into the ground just beyond several partly burned sticks. Simon was not about to be delayed a minute longer. He dashed away, heading for the thickest underbrush in sight. Breathing hard and trembling, Tom forced himself to follow the slave at a walk, being careful to leave a moccasin track in every open area. Then he too ran!

"Somebody's been here and not very long ago neither." It was Lucius' voice. The posse had not yet left the river, but were maneuvering their boat in order to allow the jailer and lawyer to get ashore without wading. "Look there!" Lucius exclaimed. "Somebody, maybe the ones we're after, walked up that little hill. They didn't even have enough sense to wipe out their footprints." The two men moved on to the top of the knoll.

"Coulda been Injuns," the jailer said, peering all around. "They wouldn't have had no reason to hide their tracks. Accordin' to the Treaty, them red devils is supposed to be friendly, but maybe they don't hold with no treaties!" He moved on down the hill. "What's <u>that</u>?" he hissed, pointing to the arrow which was sticking up in plain sight before them. "Ain't that a Injun arrer? And that right there's another moccasin track ain't it?"

"It certainly is," Lucius whispered, "and you can see where they had a fire right there too. That arrow probably means they're coming back. I don't like this. Let's get out pf here!"

*   *   *

No longer afraid of immediate pursuit, the pair had had a good night's sleep, curled up under their overturned boat. Using Simon's stolen knife they cut the clothesline pole in two. Tom fastened two slabs of elm bark to the poles, using strips off Martha's blanket, to make crude but effective paddles. They slept during the rest of the day, and when darkness came, made the long voyage across the river to the shore of the Ohio Territory. The occasional ice floe posed no problem but Simon's lack of experience with a paddle sometimes did.

Once again they dragged the flat-bottomed boat into the brush, well out of sight of anyone moving on the river. Simon suggested that they sink the boat or just let it float away down the river. Tom suspected that his friend just wanted to make sure he'd never have to go on the water again!

"You as hungry as I am Tom? All the stuff I stole from the kitchen has been gone for days!"

"I think I'm <u>hungrier</u>! I've got an idea but it means we won't eat for a while yet. When I left Green Ville all those months ago I met a family of homesteaders by the name of Walker. Their place is along the river somewhere west of here. If we can find them I'm pretty sure they'd help us. That alright with you, partner?"

"If there's food there I'm for it! All I can think of is the sowbelly and hominy we had plenty of on old Lucius' plantation."

"You thinking of going back, Simon?"

The former slave shrugged his shoulders and looked sadly into the distance. "There's no going back for either of us is there Tom? I got to ask you something that's been bothering me for all this time. Why'd you empty that slops bucket all over the jail cell? That will sure make them madder than before. I can see no reason for you to do that."

Tom stared at the ground for a minute, then replied. "I did it to make them mad. Mad enough to shoot me on sight if they caught up with us. I'd rather be dead than rotting away all my life in that federal prison! That's why!"

"But what about <u>me</u>? I don't want no musket ball rippin' up <u>my</u> guts!" He was angry and made no attempt to hide it.

"Don't worry Simon. If we do get caught they won't shoot <u>you</u>. You're worth maybe a hundred dollars on the slave market. I've seen enough of Lucius Grant to tell me he knows the value of a dollar. That's why he came along with that gang that's been hunting for us. He wants to make sure nothing lethal happens to one of his slaves. You'd probably get a flogging but you could stand it. I have. Now let's get headed west. Maybe we can find those settlers and get us some vittles!"

The fugitives spent the next two days walking west, the boat turned upside-down and set adrift. Tom figured that when it was found all would think that they were drowned in the river. They were careful to stay well back from the water. Twice they heard voices of travelers and the sound of oars scraping the gunwales. Peering out from hiding, it was apparent that they were merely more settlers heading into the Ohio country. Because of the Indians' defeat at the Battle of Fallen Timbers, they now felt safe to homestead in this beautiful and as yet unoccupied country. The great "Treaty of Greenville" which followed the victory opened the Northwest Territory for settlement. Tom was justifiably proud of the part he had played in these momentous events.

"We must be getting close to the Walkers' place," Tom said. "I'm pretty sure I recognize this little crick. Their cabin should show up just beyond that next hill."

"I sure hope so, Tom. I ain't never been so hungry in all my borned days! I'll say this much for slavery; we was never too hungry!"

As they climbed up yet another of the seemingly endless hills bordering the Ohio's shore, Tom broached a subject he'd kept from the slave ever since their escape. "Simon," he began, "if we don't get caught by Lucius and his gang, and we avoid capture by any Indians who ain't supposed to be here anymore, there's something I've got to do."

"I hope it has something to do with food! What is it?"

"There's a frontiersman by the name of Kenton, Simon Kenton. I heard the Indians, the ones I got away from, say they had orders from their chief to find him and kill him."

"Well, what's that got to do with us? Does this Kenton guy have anything to eat with him?"

"I've got to warn him! It looks like Tecumseh, and maybe Blue Jacket too, are planning to go to war with the Shemanese again. They know that Simon Kenton could raise an army of volunteers in no time. So they have to get rid of him before they start the war."

"You go right on and find this Kenton man, but I ain't coming along. What I'm gonna do is find me some rich folks and work for my keep. If I got plenty to eat and a warm place to sleep, I don't give a rat's tail for whatever war is going on. And another thing . . ."

"Look!" Tom hissed, "There's their rail fence. We're <u>there</u>, Simon! <u>Hello the cabin</u>!"

"Stay right on top of that hill, you! Show yourself, but don't come no closer. I got my rifle trained on you, and my finger on the trigger. Now come out of them bushes so I can see you. Don't try nothing or I'll shore enough shoot!"

"Hello Walkers. That you, Henry? It's me, Tom Bluefoot. I've come back. I've got a friend with me. Can we come on down now?"

"Is that really you, Toom . . . Cha . . . or whatever your name is? You come on down here right now. You're shore more than welcome. We're mighty obliged to ya and that's the truth."

"Say, who's that with you, Tom?" Mary asked as the two fugitives hurried to the cabin. "Come in and get warm, you two. I'll bet you're hungry too and . . ."

"Let them boys get a word in, Ma," Henry said, grinning. "I'm goanna call our boys. They'll shore be happy to see you again, Indian Tom, and . . . and . . . you too I guess," he added lamely, staring at Simon's dark skin. "<u>Calvin</u>! <u>Jacob</u>! Come on to the cabin. We got company!"

"Now Tom, our little Jacob caught a catfish this morning that's near as big as him! I was gonna fry that up for supper, but you look like you're about starved to death, so we'll just have us a fish fry soon as I can get the fire going." She looked uncertainly at Simon for a moment. "You kin have some too if you want, but I reckon you'd feel better eatin' it out on that stump yonder."

Tom was outraged. "Simon here is my <u>friend</u>! He saved me from life in prison. If he's not welcome to eat in your house, then Toom-She-chi-Kwa isn't either! Come on Simon. We've seen enough of this kind of thing back there in Pittsburgh. I'll not tolerate any more of it!"

"Aw come on Tom. I ain't offended. Heck's fire, they're no different than my old masters back in Virginny was. I couldn't eat with them white folks either. I'm just about starved. That fish will taste just as good on a stump as it does in here!"

"Pa! Ma! Who's here? Where are they?" Calvin yelled, bursting into the cabin. "Why . . . why . . . is that you, Indian Tom? I'm glad you come back here to our place. Hey, who you got with you? He's a darkey ain't he? What's he doing here? Jake! Jake! Look who come. It's the Indian what got milk for little Lizabeth and give me a real nice canoe ride too. How you been keepin' Indian Tom?"

Mary aimed a quick slap at her older son's head, but he easily avoided it. "Mind your manners, youngun'! You set down there and get the fire going right. We're gonna have an early supper. Now, 'children should be seen and not heard,'" she quoted, glaring at Calvin. "See how nice your little brother is behaving? He knows his place. We're gonna have that big catfish he caught for our supper. It'll be enough to feed all of us, and mind you save a piece for Tom's black friend here too."

Jake hadn't said a word yet but all at once he blurted out, "Reckon you forgot yer promise didn't you Tom?"

"Promise? Promise? What promise was that, Jacob?" Tom teased.

"About bringin' me a present when you come back. You said . . ."

"Oh, that promise. No Jacob, I didn't forget. Close your eyes and hold out your hand. He plopped the shiny, homemade sheriff's badge into Jake's palm. The boy was speechless!

With the fire burning nicely, Mary broiled the fish one slab at a time. Using the "tine tubby" she soon had them all enjoying the early meal. "Here Tom," she said handing him a wooden plate with a good-sized filet of smoking, broiled catfish on it. "You go on now and take this out to your friend."

"I thought things might be different 'way out here in all this wilderness," Simon said between huge mouthfuls of fish. "Why does it have to be this way, Tom? I ain't no different than them folks in there. If I cut my finger I bleed red just like they do."

"I don't know Simon. I get treated the same way just because my skin's red. You saw how it was with me back there at Fort Pitt. That's the main reason I ran. Same as you."

"I know that, but what I'm asking is why . . ."

"Well Simon, I can say this much. The Indians, some of them anyway, keep slaves too. Mostly they capture them in battle or on a raid. The thing I noticed though, was that the lowest, most shiftless in the tribe, were always the ones who abused the slaves the worst. I figure that by mistreating those poor souls it made them feel a lot bigger. Do you think that might be it?" Simon was too busy eating catfish to answer!

The Camerons came the next day, bringing a haunch of venison. Everyone, even the ladies, pitched in to help work up the garden. Mary took charge, proud of a poke of precious seeds; corn, beans, and squash. They would have to wait until warmer weather before the actual planting, of course, but with the extra help the soil would be ready. "You better get busy splittin' rails," Foster Cameron said, rinsing the mud off his fingers. "You don't, the deer'll have everything et up soon as it comes outn the ground."

"I know it, Foster," Henry said, "I been working at it, but without a saw it's been mighty slow work. I got a little done on the east side."

"Lookee, Lookee!" Calvin was yelling as he dashed into the clearing. "Jake thinks he's so smart, ketchin' that old catfish. Look at this!" He was struggling with a pike so big its flopping tail was almost dragging the ground. Everyone praised the boy, and he finally felt exonerated.

Toward the end of the second week, relations were becoming somewhat strained. Too many people, too little food, and three different ethnic groups was almost more than any of them could tolerate. The Camerons had been gone for a week. Tom and Simon had discussed leaving, but the truth was they didn't know where to go. Their situation was about to be resolved however.

"Pa! Ma! Everbody! "There's Injuns paddlin' right up to our bank! Three canoes, two Injuns in each one! Here they come!" Calvin dashed into the cabin.

Henry, off in the woods splitting rails, heard the commotion. Still carrying his ax, he came running. Tom and Simon left the stump they'd been trying to move and peered fearfully toward the river. Calvin reappeared carrying his pa's musket, but looking mighty scared. Mary had scooped up little Lizabeth and slipped behind the cabin and into the forest. Simon was right behind her!

Tom caught Calvin's arm. "Easy, son. Lay that gun on the ground," he whispered. "Get a big smile on your face, but stay behind me. Try not to look too afraid. Come on."

The Indians advanced steadily, their eyes roving over the buildings and the clearing, missing nothing. "Who this is?" one of the braves asked in broken English. "Who is?" he demanded. Still no one answered.

"What are you all doin' here?" Henry shouted, still gripping the ax. "This here's American land. You got no . . ."

The Indian speaker strode directly up to the settler and knocked the ax to the ground. Having done so, he contemptuously turned his back and rejoined his companions.

Tom stepped up, arm raised and palm forward. "Aho, brothers. What is it that you want? Perhaps you need food. We have some. Not much."

"So you speak our tongue. Who are you and why are you here with these Shemanese?"

"I am but a traveler on the river. These white people gave me food and shelter, so I stayed to help them. Now, how can we serve you fine gentlemen?" As he spoke, Tom was assessing the situation. Immediately he noticed that one of the Indians, a tall, handsome man who appeared to be in his thirties, hung back from the rest. Wearing a sort of buckskin hood, he kept it pulled low on his forehead, almost over his eyes. Tom was careful to let his gaze glide on past this mysterious visitor without paying him undue attention.

Henry had picked up the rifle. Pushing Calvin behind him he advanced on the Indians. Before he could speak a word however, Tom stopped him. "Lower the musket to the ground Henry! Smile and raise your hand in a greeting. We don't know if these Shawnee mean to harm us or not, but let me see what I can get out of them. Stay near your gun though!"

"So! You also speak the Shemanese tongue do you? Perhaps the rest of what you told us is a lie. Do you live here with these white people? And where is the black man we saw running away when we first landed our canoes? Is he hiding in order to shoot at us from the forest? We would speak to him."

"You six braves are welcome here. We will share what food we have, although it is very little." Tom was talking fast, keeping Henry by his side. "This man is the father of three. His woman and baby girl have run into the forest, afraid of so many stalwart warriors. His sons were fishing somewhere along the river. As to the black man, he is my slave. I shall call him back, although he speaks only the Shemanese language. Is that acceptable to you fine visitors?"

"Bring them back. All of them!" The one who made this command seemed to be in charge, but Tom noticed that before he spoke, the Shawnee brave had looked for approval at the mysterious hooded figure who was still hanging back.

Tom filled his lungs and shouted. "Simon! Mary! Jake! Come back right now!" He pretended to be angry as he gave them instructions. "Be polite. Offer food. Smile!" Mary appeared first, Lizabeth tight in her arms. The younger son then showed up, clutching a thick branch of wood like a weapon, and juggling two fish poles. Simon did not appear.

"Where is the black one?"

"My apologies great chief. As I said that one is my slave. He is afraid of everything! Allow me to call again. <u>Simon</u>! Come on back. I told them you were my slave, so be sure to act like it! You might even do a little dance for these savages, like Lymon would do if he was here."

"What is all this <u>talk</u>? Are you giving them instructions? Say no more in Shemanese!"

Simon trotted up then not stopping until he was right in front of the Indian leader. His white teeth were flashing in a huge grin. "Bless you Simon!" Tom thought as he watched the young black go into his act. Certainly it was an easy role for him, having perfected it after nearly twenty years as a plantation slave. Simon bobbed his head, shuffled his feet, did a little dance, then finished by bowing repeatedly to each of the six silent watchers. While the Indians' faces showed no emotion at all, Tom could tell they had relaxed somewhat.

Mary came boldly forward to stand by her silent husband. "Food?" she asked pointing to her open mouth. "Food?" The universal gesture was not lost on the savages. Without a word they marched into the cabin, grabbed portions of the venison stew right from the cold kettle, sat on the floor and ate.

For the first time they began to converse with one another in low tones, well aware that Tom could understand what they were saying.

Mary handed the baby to her husband, motioned for Calvin to build up the fire, gave Jacob the water pail, and pushed him toward the river. There being no more meat in the kettle, one of the braves lifted it from the crane, brought it to his lips and drank some of the cold broth. He passed it on and several others also drank. When it was empty the one who didn't get any angrily threw the kettle into the corner. Mary picked it up, confronted the Indian and raged at him. Two of the Indians looked at each other and grinned. They admired courage!

"Sai-ga! More!"they growled. The wife and mother lifted her hands and shrugged. There was nothing left. Accepting this, the Shawnees filed outside, started a small fire, and sat down. One grabbed Simon and pulled him toward the fire. With motions and signs they made the former slave understand that they wanted to see him dance again. Simon was quick to seize the opportunity, but he planned his own sort of entertainment. One that he thought might help their situation. Clapping his hands and stamping his feet, he appeared to be accompanying his own performance. Tom was watching with a knowing look.

> *What do ya suppose? ha ha*
>
> *What's they gonna do? Ho ho*
>
> *Should we run, run, run, er not? Haha*
>
> *We could grab a canoe, and paddle paddle paddle Ho ho*
>
> *On down that big, big river Ho Ho. Should we? Ha ha*

He gave a big leap, kicked up his heels, and fell down exhausted.

"Sai-ga! Sai-ga" Two braves shouted, but Simon shook his head and exaggerated labored breathing. After a few minutes

Tom was shocked when the brave who'd tried to hide his face suddenly stood up, threw back his hood and advanced on Toom-She-chi-Kwa. Like a flash of lightning from the west, Tom knew who the man was! But he gave no indication of it. He needed any information that might give him and the settlers an advantage in this perilous predicament. The brave was none other than Tecumseh himself!

"Do you know who I am?" he demanded, almost in Tom's face.

"No, I am sorry but I have never seen you before, or if I have it has gone from my memory. I am a Wyandot, you are Shawnee. There's little reason that I should know you. Wait a minute! Are you Shell Rider, he of many horses?" One of the other braves laughed, but Tecumseh silenced him with a look.

"I am not that one, but merely his uncle. My name is Gol-si-gan. I am told that I look like Shell Rider, so that may explain your mistake." Tecumseh walked back to the fire, looking much relieved. He made no further attempt to cover his face.

Tom had to smother a grim smile. What was going on was clear enough. Tecumseh was trespassing on "Treaty Land," undoubtedly in order to find Simon Kenton and kill him. The Shawnee chief did not want anyone to know that he and his squad were in the area. His reputation as a warrior was becoming known. If word got out that he was in this forbidden territory, soldiers would certainly be dispatched to hunt him down.

"What do you Shawnee warriors plan to do with this settler and his family?" Tom asked boldly. "They say they have a legal right to live here by the river."

"What right?" Tecumseh demanded angrily. "This is land of the Miami. It has been so for more years than anyone living can remember. The Miamis of today have always granted those of other tribes the right to live and hunt on their holdings, so how does this miserable half-starved man and his family think he has <u>any</u> right to be here?"

"He has told me that some great treaty was recently made and signed by many chiefs from many tribes. Perhaps he was lying. He did not know the name of the treaty. You, Gol-si-gan, may know if such a paper ever existed. You look to be one of much wisdom who will soon become a great chief of the Shawnee."

The man gave Tom such a look of contempt that it was instantly clear that flattery and manipulation would not work on this intelligent and resolute Indian. Toom-She-chi-Kwa would have to be on his guard! "You should understand, Wyandot, that these settlers must die. We need to keep our movements secret as we travel along the Ohieeio. We will kill them and burn their log house. You and your slave boy may need to die as well. We shall see."

"No, Great One! This would be a mistake. There are many more Shemanese starting to clear land very near here. They will see what has happened and will undoubtedly hurry to report the raid to the soldiers. You and your men would be hunted down, your mission, whatever it is, ended!"

Tecumseh stared at Tom for a minute, his expression unreadable. Finally he motioned to his companions and they moved a short distance away from their fire. Tom could see them arguing, but was unable to hear what was being said. After a time it appeared that a decision had been reached. Simon jumped up and moved to Tom's side. "Man oh <u>man</u>!" he whispered, "They're going to kill us! I seen one of them checking the charge on his rifle. Another one has his hatchet out of its case! What we gonna <u>do</u>, Tom? What we gonna <u>do</u>?"

"Gol-si –gan," Tom called. "I have an idea you may wish to consider. Let us reason together."

"What is in your mind Wyandot?"

"Let the Shemanese live. My man and I will become slaves for you, and will go where you go and do what you do. These whites will think little of your visit here if you leave them in peace. They would then have no reason to report your presence in this place. As for me and my slave, the settlers will be glad we are leaving with you. They have hardly enough food for themselves. Two less mouths to feed would be seen as a good thing!"

"Do not listen to him who speaks the Shemanese tongue," one of the six said. "I do not trust him."

"His words make sense," Tecumseh replied. But still he seemed undecided.

"Let me present you with a special gift," Tom said, trying to help make his offer be accepted. He pulled what was left of the blanket given to him by Martha Grant from his shoulders. Turning his back, he worked the stitches loose on the corner. The two heart-shaped earrings flashed in the light. He turned, motioned for Tecumseh, and handed them to the Shawnee leader. "These bergulia are of solid gold. They will not tarnish. Not like the cheap ones given to us by the traders. Also, the one who presented them to me was a great healer. They have certain magic powers that will keep the wearer safe, especially during travel over water!"

Tecumseh, no fool, gave a derisive snort. He obviously did not believe a word of this, but he liked the ear bobs. He snatched them from Tom's outstretched hand and dropped them into the squirrel skin pouch he wore around his neck.

"What's going on, Tom?" Simon asked. "Look at them poor folks. They're just naturally skeered to death!" He pointed at the family, lined up behind Henry, just inside the open door.

"Well the leader there," he pointed his chin at Tecumseh, "was going to kill all of them, and maybe you and me too. But I sold the two of us into slavery under him. I know his real name, but I won't tell you what it is. He's trying to keep anyone from knowing they're in these parts. I didn't know what else to do, Simon. We're lucky he accepted my 'trade' for the lives of these people."

"So, I'm a slave again am I?" Simon muttered angrily. "All our plans and all this starving and I'm right back where I started from. Is that it?"

"I'm afraid so my friend, but now there's two of us sold into slavery. At least you'll find it a lot easier than it was back on the plantation. One thing I can tell you is if you keep on dancing and acting like a fool, you'll be able to get along fine with them. My people love this sort of thing! Think about Lymon. He has this method down to an art. You can do it too! The 'singing' you did was clever. We can use that sometimes if we think that maybe one of the braves knows some English. Now I better go and tell the family what's going on."

*   *   *

"Oh <u>Massa</u>! Oh Lordy sakes alive!" Simon moaned. He was lying in the bottom of the lead canoe as they rocked and pitched with the growing waves. They were almost halfway to the Kain-tuck-kee shore, but battling a strong headwind from the south made progress difficult. The Indians, strong swimmers all, grinned at the black man's fears. Only a part of his cries was an act. He was truly terrified! "Lordy, Lordy, have mercy!" he cried again. Owl Nest, the largest of the Shawnees, smacked him on the rear with a wet paddle, but not very hard. As Tom had said, they enjoyed any sort of a performance, whether it was real or not.

Tom had been put to work as soon as they saw his ability with a canoe paddle. As the dugout bounced and slewed about, he could not help noticing the fairly new-looking kettle rolling about near their feet. One side and the bail showed unmistakable evidence of dried blood. A shovel and a garden hoe had been lashed to the thwarts. These items gave mute evidence of what certainly must indicate a family of settlers, killed, butchered, and left unburied for the wolves. If they had been scalped, the Shawnees were not foolish enough to hang these trophies on their belts. No doubt the scalp locks had been left in some secret place to be picked up on the return trip. All of this was sobering evidence of the very real danger in which Tom and Simon found themselves!

They landed without incident on the Kain-Tuck-Kee shore, Simon doing a joyous dance which Tom suspected was only partly faked. The Indians showed little emotion at the black man's performance, but Toom-She-chi-Kwa noticed that Tecumseh himself handed the dancer a choice piece of venison heart.

After hiding the canoes the travelers headed inland, following a small creek. Tecumseh, or Gol-si-gan, as Tom reminded himself to think of him, seemed much relieved. He had sent a runner on ahead, telling no one what his plans were, but on the second day, Owl Nest walked back into their camp, looking pleased.

"I found them Tec . . .er . .Gol-si-gan, about where you expected but further east. We are welcome at their camp, but Macton warns us that those settlers in this wilderness will shoot any warriors on sight, whether friendly or not."

"Let us camp here, then in the morning we will go to Macton's camp. Did he know anything of Symond Kan-ton?"

"He is not sure, but one of his people claims that the frontiersman and his companions have been seen at what is called 'Big Bone Lick'. Perhaps they are making salt. But there is some doubt about this."

"Will Macton and his braves join with us and be of help in our mission?"

"No. He insists that he has no intention of involvement in <u>any</u> such plans. He is tired of fighting, and also suffers much from a bullet wound in his ankle. It appears that neither Macton nor any of those with him will be of help."

"It is well," Tecumseh grunted. "I am sick of those who are so quick to give up the fight for our lands and our ways. We will go to Macton's camp but will not spend many days there. Kan-Ton must die, or my plans will go nowhere!"

Tom was careful not to mention his capture and eventual escape from the three assassins who were also intent upon the death of Simon Kenton. "Perhaps," he thought, "Tecumseh himself had sent them!"

He and Simon were put to work preparing food for the evening meal. Both considered merely slaves, they were kept busy doing every job the rest found unpleasant or beneath their dignity. The work was not hard, and both tolerated it well. Therefore Tom was shocked when Tecumseh suddenly gave a quick command and Owl Nest seized him in a choke hold. Sputtering and gasping, Tom struggled for breath. Tecumseh planted himself in front of Tom, anger in his eyes. "I know you, Toom-She-chi-Kwa!" He growled. "And I think you know me as well! Now you have one chance to save your miserable life. That is by only telling the truth! Are you not the white-lover who acted as interpreter at the Greenville Treaty?" He had drawn his small skinning knife and was holding it mere inches from Tom's belly. "Lie and you die!" he said. His words were punctuated by jabs in Tom's midsection. The knife remained steady in his right hand.

"I . . .I can't hardly . . .breathe . . .great chief! Let me loose . . ." Owl Nest loosened his grip a little, but kept Tom secure. "Yes, Tecumseh it is . . ." he coughed and struggled to continue. "It is true. I know you now. But you did not speak at the . . .at the . . .Greenville conference, so for that reason I was unsure at first . . .but as you say . . ." A searing pain suddenly ripped through Tom's left ear. He cried out in pain as Tecumseh held up a fingernail-sized piece of flesh.

"I have marked you!" the larger Indian said angrily. "You are mine. You will do as I say without question. The moment you attempt to escape or defy me in any way, you will die. And," he shot a piercing glance at Simon who was watching open-mouthed nearby, "he will die also. Do not forget. Do not cause me to carry out this threat! Here." He thrust a scrap of trade cloth into Tom's hands and stalked away.

Tom fell to his knees, clutching the rag to his bleeding ear. "Oh Toomie, Toomie, why did that Indian cut you like that? And why did he look at me so mean like he done?" Simon whispered, casting a fearful glance at the silent Indians watching them. "Should I do a little dancin' for 'em, Tom? Do you think that would make them happier? What do you think, Tom?"

"It won't work this time. Forget that for now," Tom said through clenched teeth. "Tecumseh is too smart to fall for that. He only lets you get away with it because the other five enjoy it. He said he'd kill us if we disobey him."Looks like," Tom grimaced as the blood ran down his cheek, "yes, looks like we're stuck with them for a while! Can you find a piece of cloth to tie around my head? I've got to try to get this bleeding stopped."

*   *   *

"Two double-hands men, some women, some children," Owl Nest and Wader reported. "Kan- Ton is there! They boil for salt." The two Shawnees had returned at moonrise to report on their spying mission.

"Have they erected a barricade?" Tecumseh asked as the exhausted scouts prepared to sleep.

"No but their rifles are stacked, and the men never get far from them."

"Aho!" Tecumseh said quietly, "Now we sleep. Tomorrow we will enter their camp. Leave your weapons behind. There are too many of them for only the six of us to fight. Let us test their intentions. Perhaps we can somehow persuade the big Shemanese to leave his companions long enough that we can kill him. If this can be done, than we must flee, find our canoes, and get back to the north shore of the Ohieeo."

Tom and Simon had been ordered to place their bedrolls beyond the fire's warmth, but little heat was needed in these late spring nights.

"Toom-She-chi-Kwa and Simon, come to my side," Tecumseh said, making room near the fire. "I would speak with you about tomorrow." The two men reluctantly left heir warm blankets and sat down by the leader. He fixed his eyes upon Tom and spoke in a low but menacing voice. "You will stay at my side. Interpret for me everything that the Shemanese say when we meet. If you give false witness I will know it because Wader also can speak the white man's tongue. If you change a word, or in any way try to get a warning to the big white man, Kan-Ton, I will kill you! Do you understand?" He turned to Simon and regarded him for a moment. "You, black man, will dance and sing at the salt-makers' camp. Your purpose will be to keep them occupied and also to make them think that our intentions are only friendly. If you attempt to escape, or do anything that would warn them, I will watch you die very slowly by fire! Toom-She-chi-Kwa, tell the dancer what I just said. Do not leave out a single word. It is my hope and desire that both of you will learn to trust me and my companions to the extent that you will at some point join me in my grand plan of uniting all our people. The goal then, is to stop the Shemanese' constant invasion of the lands which The Great Spirit, Washeo Moneto, has given us. Sleep now. We rise with the dawn."

Tom slept very little. A dozen plans passed through his mind as he tried to think of some way that he might get a warning to Simon Kenton without Tecumseh catching him at it. Simon, or "Dancer" as Tecumseh's men were now calling him, had no problem sleeping. His snores could be plainly heard most of the night! Finally Tom had an idea. He slipped into the forest, found a birch tree, and stripped off a small piece of bark. Pretending to stir up the fire, he slipped a charred stick under his arm. Lying down once more, he scratched the word "danger" with the charcoal.

The day dawned cloudy and overcast. A cold mist of rain had soaked Tecumseh's band, as well as everything else. "Dancer" was up first. Singing softly, he hurried about gathering bark-covered sticks. These he would scrape down until they were dry enough to start a fire. Having washed the dried blood off the kettle, he heated water for a morning meal. The braves gave the former slave no thanks of course, but they were secretly glad to see him doing the chores that would have been theirs. Perhaps even more than his work, they appreciated his happy, uncomplaining attitude. Simon was only doing what he had been trained to do!

Tecumseh halted them well before they had reached the salt lick. Knowing that Kenton would have sentries posted around their camp, he motioned Tom, Dancer, and Wader forward and indicated that they should show themselves. Despite his orders to leave all weapons behind, Tecumseh held his own bow with an arrow nocked.

"Hello the camp!" Tom shouted, taking a step into the clearing.

"Don't move redskin!" A frontiersman materialized from a nearby thicket where he'd apparently spent the night. "I see you talk our lingo, but don't try nothing." The click of his rifle's hammer was plainly audible in the morning quiet.

"Oh don't yawl shoot me with some bullets massa! I'se jest a little ol' darkey is all I am, Suh. Lemme come outn these here bushes if it please yawl, Suh!"

"Come on out then. How many's with you? Walk real slow and let me see your hands."

"Don't shoot sir. We're friendly. There's me, the black man, and one other Indian. We are not armed."

"Get up, all you'ns!" the guard yelled over his shoulder. "There's a couple Indians and a darkey out here that wants to come in. Better cover them till we see what they want. Somebody wake Kenton and get him out here."

The rest of the salt-makers came straggling out, several of the men pulling rifles from the stacks around the camp. There was no mistaking Simon Kenton. A big, rather homely man, he was obviously in charge.

"Who are ye and what do ye want here?" the big man bellowed.

"We are here to trade for salt and for other business," Tom replied, careful to follow Tecumseh's orders to the letter.

"Take up your guns men. See to the loads. There's more of 'em hidin' around here somewhere. These three wouldn't be out tradin' all by theirselves."

"You are correct Mr. Kenton," Tom said, taking a step closer. "Our companions wait in the forest until they are sure of a welcome here. May I call them in, Sir?"

"How many and what tribe?" Kenton demanded as the armed settlers formed a loose skirmish line behind him.

"Only five, sir. They are Shawnee from a village far to the northwest." Several women and children had now awakened, curious about the voices.

"Call them in then, but if there's any monkey bidness, you," and he pointed his rifle at Tom's middle, "will get the first shot!"

At Tom's piercing whistle Tecumseh and the others marched confidently into the camp, carrying no weapons.

For the first time Tom noticed a short, pudgy Indian woman moving to Kenton's side. "I help with talk for meeting," she said, glancing at Tom with an expression he could not understand.

"Wal, wal," Kenton cried. "ain't that you, Tecumsee?" He strode forward and offered his hand. If Tecumseh was surprised he showed no indication of it. The chief took the outstretched hand and pumped it once. "Shore, that's you all right. Last time I seen you, you was just a little shaver, runnin' around Blackfish's cabin. What are you doing way down here?"

Tecumseh was obviously confused. He looked at Tom for a translation. "And how's your little brother, Tekskwatawa? I heard he was up there next to the Auglaize River. Callin' hisself a prophet, I heard. Is that how it is? Hope he ain't plannin' no mischief. We've had enough fightin' to last me a lifetime!"

After translation the Shawnee replied. "My brother is only a holy man. He asks the Great Spirit to forgive his children and bring back our old ways before we knew the Shemanese. I see little of him these days. I too wish only for peace between white man and red. I plan to do all I can to bring this about." Tom didn't think Kenton was buying these statements at all, but the frontiersman did not say so aloud.

Tom and the woman both interpreted. Wader had given up long before. "Chief Tecumseh comes not only for salt but to search for land where a few Shawnee could settle. They wish to be far from the Treaty Lands," Tom said, once again following the plan decided upon the night before.

"What are <u>you</u> doing with them then?" Kenton demanded. "You ain't dressed like no Shawnee I ever saw."

"You are most observant," Tom said respectfully. "I am a Wyandot. I asked permission to accompany Chief Tecumseh in order to seek similar grounds for my tribe." Where did <u>that</u> come from, Tom thought, amazed at himself.

"You women," Kenton commanded, "better get some food ready. I reckon these redskins will expect to be fed. They always do! Now, Wyandot, what's your name and how'd you get to speak such good English?"

Tom told him his name and briefly described his early life with Eli Miller at Fort Pitt. Of course he did not mention his recent trial and escape!

"And what about him?"

"He is my slave. I bought him with money I earned working in Eli's grist mill. His name is Simon, like yours, but these Indians call him Dancer. Want to see what he can do?"

"Why shore! It'll take the women some time to get the vittles ready. It'll be good to have a little fun for onct!"

Dancer went into his act with gusto. Skipping, twirling, and clapping the rhythm, he soon had attracted all the children and most of the women. The Indians stood stoically by, pretending no interest, but anyone could see that they too were following the performance. The salt-makers watched, grinning. Two of them even joined in by clapping along.

Suddenly the slave stopped, almost in mid-stride. Eyes wide, he began backing away from something on the ground. It was a bone. But it was the largest bone anyone present had ever seen! "Oh Massa, <u>Massa</u>! Lookee dere! Oh, I'se undone for shore. That big old thing's got <u>haunts</u>, and no mistake! Oh Tom, Toomie, get us out of here before the spirits comes onto all of us! Let's get goin'! Tell them Indians we is all in peril right here! Yassuh! Oh, yassuh we sho is! Tell all of the Indians Tom. <u>Tell</u> <u>them</u>!"

Tom was astonished. Was this part of the act that Dancer was supposed to perform? The monstrous half-buried bone was only one of many protruding from the clay along the creek. They were the reason this site was called "Big Bone Lick." The Indians, even Tecumseh himself, looked on in alarm. They cast frightened glances at each other, and almost as one, began to back away from Dancer and the object of his terror.

"What says the slave?" Tecumseh demanded, not taking his eyes off the trembling black man.

"Bad medicine! This is the dwelling place of evil spirits and the source of much <u>witchcraft</u>! That's what he keeps saying. He says we must leave here right now!"

"Tobacco! I need some fine tobacco," Simon shouted. He had covered his eyes with his hands but still stood very near the ancient bone.

Kenton motioned to one of the women. She approached the black man, holding a twist of tobacco in her hand. He snatched it and began shredding a small portion. Afraid to get closer, he begged the woman to sprinkle it over the bone. She did so, trying to hide a big grin. "Tell them Tom," he cried. "Tell them all to leave this place. There must be no talking anymore. We got to cross running water before we say another word!"

Toom –She-chi-Kwa had no idea how to respond to all of this. Six years living with the white man, Eli Miller, had changed much of his thinking about evil spirits and "hauntings", but he was still a full-blooded Wyandot Indian. That primitive part of his nature sometimes broke free. "If that was an act, it was certainly an impressive one," he thought. Pretending to examine the bone, he let the birch bark message fall behind it.

"Tell me! Tell me what the black man says we should do," Tecumseh whispered, still watching the terrified former slave. Tom told him most of what Simon had implored them. "I believe that man has 'the sight'," the chief stated. "My brother, Tenskwatawa, has it also. He speaks much of the activities of Motshee Monitoo, the bad spirit, and the evil being done by that entity. Whether all of this is true I cannot tell, but I say, 'why tempt the Evil One'? let us leave here. Ask Dancer to lead us, in order that we do nothing that could cause a bad wind to follow us."

They left Kenton's salt-making camp without any salt. Actually they'd had nothing to trade anyway. Almost running, they followed Dancer as he finally led them across a tiny stream, hardly more than a trickle. "This be just right," Simon sighed, falling to his knees on some moss. "Them haunts can't cross running water! Leastaways that's what old Toby always told us chillun. I kin feel a powerful freedom floodin' my soul right now. Can't you all?"

The Indians, showing obvious signs of relief, were all talking at once. Even Tecumseh's lips curved in a smile.

Tom slipped down beside the slave. "I got to ask you something, Simon. Do you really <u>believe</u> all that stuff about evil spirits, tobacco, and everything you told all of us back there at the salt lick?"

"I shore do, Toomie. Yessir, I does indeed! And I'll tell you this too. Some of them what was boiling up that salt water is gonna be dead before three days is out."

[Tecumseh's group had no way of knowing that two days after their visit, a sudden outbreak of cholera had taken two children, two adults, including Kenton's uncle, and a newborn baby!]

"Yessir, I do believe all that talk about spirits and such, but just betwixt you and me, Tom, I think I scared <u>myself</u> more than I scairt you Indians! Of course," he continued, "I could see that your plan to warn the big man with the same name as me wasn't going to work. I had to get all of us <u>out</u> <u>of</u> <u>there</u>!"

"You are one amazing man, Simon. Thank you!" Tom figured the act was a way for a mere runaway slave to show power over so many free adults, both white and red.

Tecumseh's plan to kill Simon Kenton did not come about.

After two days' travel, Tom finally felt confident enough to ask Tecumseh the question that all of them had on their minds. "Chief Tecumseh," he began, "I would respectfully ask why we continue to travel southeast. Is it a secret mission?"

The Shawnee leader stopped walking and surprised them all by ordering that they make camp, even though it was only early afternoon. As Simon hurried about preparing a cookfire, Tecumseh indicated that Tom should sit beside him.

"I have been watching you, Toom-She-chi- Kwa," he began. "My heart tells me that you are a man who can be trusted. A man who wishes the best for all men, white, red, and yes, even black. Am I correct in this assumption?"

"I hope so, Chief Tecumseh. I hope so! Some have said as much about me, among them Anthony Wayne, 'The Mad General'."

"Pah! He of the long knives? The killer of women and children, destroyer of fields of standing corn? I would not call that man 'friend' if I were you."

"As you have been watching me I have been observing you, Tecumseh," Tom spoke up boldly. "I see before me a man troubled in spirit. A man very afraid for all our tribes. Afraid even for the very way of life we, 'The People', used to enjoy. Therefore I suspect that this journey upon which we find ourselves has to do with some attempt to change this entire scenario. Is that not correct?"

"Oha! You have rightly discerned the truth. I am troubled by all that has been happening. I clearly remember you at the Council Of Peace in Green Ville. Even Little Turtle endorsed your work as an interpreter there. Sadly, I have lost much respect for that Miami Chief, as he seems to be agreeing with much of what the Shemanese say should be our course of action at this time."

"Do you see coming yet another war with the whites then?"

"Perhaps. But with Gitchie Maneto as my witness, it is my endeavor to take steps that will make such a war unnecessary. If all tribes, and even all septs, will finally unite and speak with but one voice, the whites would be afraid to instigate another conflict with us. Do my words make sense to you, Toom-She-chi-Kwa?"

"Yes, great one. It is a noble plan, and could certainly be successful. But who would be the one with the most courage, the most strength, and the unbounding energy to convince the many different segments of our people to unite in this way?" Tom asked, hiding his grin.

Tecumseh's smile was not wasted on Tom. "You already know the answer to that question. It is I, 'Shooting Star', who has set for my goal this great quest. Now I must ask you, will you help me, and by so doing help all of our people?"

"I would be honored, but I cannot see how a man of no distinction, a Wyandot partly raised in the white man's world, could possibly be of any help with such a huge undertaking."

"You have much to offer, Bluefoot. But mainly I seek your services as an interpreter if and when I encounter situations which involve the Shemanese. But far more important than all of which we have been speaking, I must ask you a final question, perhaps the most important one of all."

"And that is?"

"Do you believe that I, and others of like mind, am right in making this attempt? I demand an honest answer!"

"I do believe that you are on the right course. I will be at your side wherever your plans take you, but I must tell you that I am afraid your work is doomed to failure. It has been tried before, never with complete success."

"So it has been!" Tecumseh exploded. "But not by me!"

Simon brought them food he had prepared and asked what had been going on.

"Well Simon, or Dancer, I have just committed myself to what may be years of the hardest work any of us has ever undertaken. I would count it a favor and a privilege if you would come with us. Are you willing?"

"Oh Yassuh! Yassuh boss, I sho nuff shorely would. Yawl kin count on old Simon. I'se jest a-hopin' yawl'd ask this here darkey to go 'long with yawl. Yassuh, I shorely . . ."

"Cut it out, Simon! No more of this 'humble slave-man act. That's all over now. And thank you my friend for agreeing to be a part of this. Someday maybe I can repay you for it."

*   *   *

The year 1805 had crept up on all of them. Tecumseh, now officially Chief Tecumseh, Tom, his lieutenant and closest friend, and Dancer, Sachem of the Willow Springs sept, had once again established themselves in the vicinity of Greenville, near the Scioto River.

"I've been thinking about you, Tom," Tecumseh said. He was comfortably seated against the woven willow back rest beside the hearth. "Come and sit with me. How do you like my cabin?"

"Nice! Much like those of the Shemanese. A good place for you to rest after our long travels among the southern tribes. But what will become of this place when we travel again?"

"My wife, Mohnetosee, will care for it. She and her sister will live here while we're gone. Perhaps I will be able to return some time." A look of somber concern crossed his face as he prepared a seat for his friend. "There will be war. Of that I am sure. And I am also sure that I will be much involved in it. Our friends from north of the border have twice sent emissaries, hoping to enlist me in their plans. I have not yet given them an answer, but I will join them when war is inevitable. But . . . that is not why I summoned you."

"So then why do I find myself here, enjoying the parched corn and sweetened tea prepared by your woman?"

"I have decided," Shooting Star continued, "that it is time for Toomie to take a wife. Too long you have made your own fire, heated your water, cleaned your blankets, and prepared your food. Doing these things is not the role of a warrior, especially one who is a close friend of a Shawnee Chief! My woman does all such work and enjoys doing it. At least she says she does!" Mohnetosee smiled but said nothing.

"A wife? How could I ever afford a wife? I am not skilled in the hunt, even though you have tried to teach me the use of the bow and the musket. I know nothing of maintaining a garden, and I have no money to buy goods from a trading post. No, I'm afraid I would make a very poor husband, even if some maiden would be foolish enough to wed with me. She would soon be disappointed!"

"As usual, you are wrong! A good wife will do all of these things for you. Your role is to be that of a warrior."

"But I am not _that_ either! I have spent much of my life trying to promote peace, not war. Some warrior I would make! Waashaa Moneto help the man foolish enough to fight by the side of this skinny Wyandot, who is but twenty-four winters."

"During those last five years I have come to know you and trust you. Many battles have been lost, not for lack of troops, or ineffective leadership, but because of poor planning and insufficient knowledge of the enemy's intent. Here is where you, my friend, are worth more than ten double hands of fighting men! This I know, and this is why I must have you near me when the great battles are being planned. Is this ability of yours the result of your years in the Shemanese world? Perhaps. But never underestimate what you can contribute as we attempt to finally achieve our goal of equal status for all our red brothers. But now back to getting you a wife."

"There is a maiden living in the village of Long Robe. She is a Wyandot like you. Her husband died one year past. Long Robe seeks a husband for her, and has approached me about it. You and I will go and meet her to determine whether or not she would be an adequate companion and keeper of your lodge."

Tom was shocked! Of course he had often thought of marriage, but as he had expressed to Tecumseh, he really had nothing to offer a woman. The whole idea was preposterous. "When will this meeting take place?"

"Tomorrow!"

"Tomorrow? But I am not ready. I have nothing to offer her. My clothes are dirty and worn. See here, one toe peeks from my left moccasin. Another thing . ."

"Speak no more of this. In the morning Mohnetosee will do what is necessary to prepare you. We will leave for Long Robe's village at noon."

It was evening when they arrived. Tecumseh was uncharacteristically chattering away, but Tom was mainly silent. The lodge was small and very warm. At least it seemed very warm to Tom!

"Aho!" Tecumseh said formally. Much to Tom's surprise there were three persons present; a woman, a man, and a boy of about five years. There was not a smile among them!

"Aho!" said Tecumseh again, a little louder this time.

"I seek permission to speak in this dwelling," Toom-She-chi-Kwa said softly, remembering the instruction given him by Tecumseh's wife that morning.

"I am Flat Lance of Long Robe's sept," the man stated, standing with arms folded. He did not look friendly.

"And I am Chief Tecumseh, here to sponsor this man. Our purpose is to consider the joining of him and this woman. Who speaks for her?"

"Flat Lance speaks for them. As you already know she is

called Menseeta, Tadpole. Her son's name is Tolahaa, Red Gopher. We will eat, then speak with the suitor."

The evening meal was strained. Menseeta's brother didn't speak at all, nor did the boy. The woman served each one in the approved fashion, acknowledging their thanks with a few words.

"Now!"Flat Lance began, so loudly that Tom jumped, nearly spilling his plate of beans. "I ask you, Toom-She-chi-Kwa, how you would support my sister and her son. Do you hunt?" Not waiting for an answer he continued with the questions. "Do you have horses? Cattle? Furs? How do you make your living?"

"Within a few days I will be working at the French trader's post." Tom said staunchly. Tecumseh looked at him in surprise. Tom was pretty surprised himself! Once again whenever he was confused or in peril, answers seemed to come to him almost unbidden. "Since I am able to read the Shemanese writing, and can do acceptable work with numbers I will be of real help at the trading post. I have had dealings with the Frenchman before."

"You did not answer my question," Flat Lance said harshly.

"My pardon. I do not hunt, and I have neither horses nor cattle. None of these will stand in the way of making a living, however."

"As I thought! Working at the trading post is but a dream of yours. This boy," he pointed at the lad who was peeping fearfully from behind his mother, "is now nearly six winters. It is time for him to learn the bow, the tomahawk, and soon, the rifle. You have admitted that you are not a hunter. Who then will see that Tolahaa learns the way of the warrior?"

"You have spoken well Flat Lance. Let me propose a solution. That very problem has been on my mind since I entered here and learned that a child was involved in the proceedings."

Tecumseh cleared his throat and was about to speak but Tom silenced him with a raised hand. "It is evident that the boy loves his mother and his uncle. This is as it should be," he said smiling. "I would suggest Tolahaa spend every other moon with his uncle, Flat Lance, where he can be taught by one who is well versed in the way of the forest and the ways of war. He can then return every other moon to his mother and to . . . to . . . his stepfather."

Tecumseh did speak this time. "Toom-She-chi-Kwa you are too modest! You did not mention the two horses you have kept for a bride price. Since the woman has no living father, naturally they would go to her brother."

Tom shot an incredulous look at Chief Tecumseh. Two horses? What was that about? Shooting Star, his face showing no emotion at all, seemed preoccupied with the careful examination of a corncob "flutter fly" he had made from a corncob and three chicken feathers. Tom was both elated and humbled by such a gift from the Shawnee chief. Two horses were more than enough for a woman who had been previously married.

"Aho! It is well! It is well!" Flat Lance cried. "Take his hand, my sister. Touch his knee, nephew. All is settled. Toom-she-chi-Kwa you have a wife and a child as well. You will live here. Let us celebrate!"

Toom-She-chi-Kwa and Menseeta ["Tadpole"] spent most of their first weeks together getting to know each other. Talahaa ["Red Gopher"] tolerated his new stepfather, but there was no question that he much preferred spending time with his uncle. Both men worked at teaching the boy, but learning to read and do some figuring was no match for lessons regarding the bow and the hatchet!

"So what happened at Labeque's this morning husband?" Menseeta asked, not stopping her work of shelling corn into a basket.

"I believe that I finally convinced him that he needed me," Tom said proudly. "He was keeping very poor records, which was bad for his business. My white father wrote in his book, called a 'ledger', almost every night. He showed me the proper way to conduct a business. He was called a 'miller' since he ran machines which ground up grain to make flour."

"How does writing things on a paper help anyone make a better trade?"

"Give me a piece of that meat in the kettle and I'll tell you," Tom teased. "Yesterday he sold ten fishhooks to a Huron who was passing through the village. I remembered that he'd sold the same number to a friend of your brother for two pence less. So he lost money that he could have had. Also he does not weigh out things like powder and shot. He just guesses! Again he loses money."

"You are so smart, Toomie!" Tadpole smiled. "But what will this Frenchman pay you if you work for him?"

That question stopped Tom in his tracks! "He says that at first I will just be given food to take to our home. Later, maybe he will pay me with Spanish silver money. We shall see. We will talk no more about this," Tom said hurriedly.

As Labeque became more aware of the way Tom was helping his business he began to allow a few more favors. One of these was permitting the Wyandot to have a scrap of paper from time to time. These Tom put to good use trying to teach Gopher his letters. The boy was intelligent but not a good student. He hated sitting still, and found no use in making the "bird tracks" on paper. After three months Tom gave up, knowing that further attempts were only frustrating both teacher and pupil. Gopher was ecstatic and with his mother's permission began spending more and more time with her brother. Everyone was happier then!

*   *   *

The year 1809 found Toom-She-chi-Kwa and Monseeta doing very well. Two little girls had joined Gopher, their half-brother. Of course he paid them little notice. They were after all only <u>girls</u>!

Tom had taken over much of the trader's business, and was entrusted with almost complete freedom regarding the work there. His Quaker upbringing had instilled in him such absolute honesty that most of their customers preferred doing business with the Wyandot rather than the Frenchman. The proprietor didn't seem to care, as he plunged deeper and deeper into dependence on whiskey and rum.

Tecumseh's visit came as a complete surprise one winter morning. They had seen very little of him recently, as he was spending time either traveling to other tribes or negotiating with the Shemanese in Tippecanoe or Wapakoneta. Before he had spoken many words it was apparent that he was not a happy man.

"Aho! Toom-She chi-Kwa. You have prospered!" He paid little attention to Tadpole or the two little girls, but did accept a slab of cornbread with a dribble of molasses. "What is this you have on your body?" he demanded angrily, staring at Tom's linen shirt. "Have you then gone completely the way of the palefaces?"

"These clothes are part of my payment at the Frenchman's trading store. You can see that my wife has certain items like these as well. Are you displeased with these things?"

"I never thought you a fool, Bluefoot but now I begin to wonder. Have you not heard about my brother's visions? He is called 'The Prophet' and indeed as such he is. Washahaa Moneto has told him that we will never get our lands back unless we reject all the ways of the Shemanese. That shirt of bright colors and her dress the color of new grass is offensive to the deity. Go back to our mode of dress Tom, before it is too late. Only the white man's tools are to be tolerated. All else not of 'the people' is to be shunned. Tonight at sundown I shall return to your cabin. It may be that Tenskwatawa will accompany me. If so he will tell you in his own words what all red men must do in order to appease the Master Of Life. Should we fail to heed The Prophet's warnings our efforts to unite all the tribes will undoubtedly fail."

"I look forward to his visit. It would be good for my children to meet such a great man."

As promised, both Tecumseh and his brother Tenskwatawa arrived just before sundown. "Greet our visitors," Tom prompted, pushing his older daughter forward.

"Hello. Welcome!" the little girl said proudly in English.

"Pah!" Tecumseh growled. "I see you are teaching the little ones the language of the Shemanese! My brother and I will be leaving this dwelling. We cannot stay where the very things The Prophet teaches against are flaunted in our faces. I have spoken!" He headed toward the door flap, head back and shoulders braced.

"Enough!" Tom shouted angrily. "You are welcome guests in this home. However my wife and children will not tolerate such rude behavior from the two most esteemed leaders of the Shawnee. I will decide what manner of upbringing will be pursued under my roof. As you well know I am pledged to help you in your attempt to unite all the tribes. I am also prepared to be at your side in all the battles which are sure to come. I will not however, allow you or anyone else to dictate to me how I plan to raise my children. No one, except perhaps The Prophet himself, can know what the future will bring. I intend to see that my children benefit from a father who is of two worlds! Now, I have spoken!"

A tired smile creased the chief's lips. "Aho!" He said quietly. "I see the bear cub has grown claws! I beg your pardon. I have always admired your ability to cut to the heart of every matter. Why should I then be surprised at the way you run your own home? Again I say it. Please forgive me, Tom Bluefoot."

Tenskwatawa, who had as yet not spoken a word, surprised them all with an emphatic endorsement. "You have spoken well, Bluefoot. Sometimes my brother's zeal overcomes his usual proper demeanor."

"Thank you both," Tom said, feeling guilty at his own audacious behavior.

"I too ask forgiveness for my quick tongue. Let us begin again." He pulled his frightened daughter onto his lap, and placed one protective hand on the younger one's head. "Now we must eat. My woman has food prepared."

After their meal the early tension in the wegiwa dissolved like smoke. Tom's stepson, Gopher, did much to further appease the visitors by showing them the small, beautifully crafted bow made for him by his uncle. "Let us go outside and I will show you how Flat Lance has taught me to shoot!" the boy said eagerly. Even The Prophet smiled as Tom reminded the seven-year-old that it would be hard to hit a target in the dark!

Tenskwatawa seemed unable to relax. He sat stiffly erect on the empty ammunition box Tom had brought home from his work at the trading post. "I would inquire of the one with the red scalp lock," he said, his eye fixed upon Tom. "He who has but one eye as I do. Well I remember him at the healer's hut in Little Turtle's village. The medicine man took away his fever. Yes, I remember him well."

"He is married. As far as I know he is still a helper to the Captain who operates on the sick and wounded. All three live at Fort Pitt. That is all I know of him, as I had to flee from that place after stabbing a white man."

Tecumseh looked startled. "You never told me of this during any of our many travels. Why not?"

"The Shemanese may still be looking for me, so until today I have told no one. Simon, whom you call Dancer, ran away when I did. He wished to end his days as a slave to his white masters. I have heard that since Tecumseh freed him he has become a Sachem to a small tribe of Kickapoos who had relocated far from their homelands to a place south of the Ohieeo. I would very much like to see him again, but that may not be possible."

The Prophet then did a very strange thing. Reaching out to Tadpole he clamped one hand on her wrist and held on. "This 'Dancer' is a black man is he not? My brother has often spoken of him. Is it true that he has the power of a seer such as I have?"

"Yes that is what is told of him, and probably how he was able to become a Sachem." Tom had to grin as he imagined how the former slave had worked his way into the confidence of the small tribe's elders.

"And you say you wish to see him again?"

"Yes, Great One, but I know it will not happen."

Releasing the frightened Tadpole's wrist, he gave a command. "Give me half a handful of warm ashes," he told her. Then turning to Tom he asked for any item that had belonged to The Dancer.

"I have nothing of his," Tom said sadly, "but perhaps I could write his name on a bit of paper. Would that do?"

"If you mean to make his mark, it would probably work as well."

Tom quickly wrote Simon's name with a charred stick.

The Prophet held the ashes n his left hand. With the little finger of his right, he slowly traced the letters. As his finger ran across the first letter, The Prophet gave a sort of strangled cry. "The snake lies within this mark," he whispered. "You see it curves, then curves back again on itself! It will be so with whose name is in this mark!" Tenskwatawa closed his only eye and mumbled, "One double hands and one hand more and the black 'small king' will come. He seeks the great river and land far toward the setting sun."

"Fifteen days!" Tom thought. "It can't be!" But it was. In exactly that many days he would see his friend again!

"My brother and I have already given you our apologies for bad manners, but after you hear me it may be that you will better understand why we must speak as we do," Tenskwatawa said. He accepted a tin cup of sweetened tea, making no comment on the vessel's obvious connection to the trading post. As the tea grew cold he began to speak.

"The Great Spirit has spoken to me on three different occasions. The messages in every vision were the same. The white people are the offspring of the evil spirit which lives in the sea. Since the Shemanese came across the sea to our lands it is my belief that they were bewitched during the crossings and now cause much of the evil and mischief we must endure. Washaa Maneto has told me how our people can evade the bad medicine of the whites. We are to shun the use of 'devil drink', cloth of many colors, [he shot a look at Tom's shirt] Shemanese kinds of food, and everything made of hammered metal. Now Toom-she-chi-Kwa, maybe you can see why at first we nearly left your dwelling in anger."

"What should I do, Tenskwatawa?" Tom asked. "I have no desire to offend the Master Of Life."

"Leave the white man's store. It is full of things that are an abomination and things detrimental to the right way of life for our people."

"But I must get money to buy food for myself and for these." He indicated his wife and the children. "I was never taught the ways of the forest. I know nothing of raising cattle or horses, and of growing things I am totally ignorant! I am sure you cannot relate to such a sad state, but it is true nonetheless."

"Aho!" The Prophet said. "You have described the Holy Man who stands before you! Am I not correct, older brother?"

"You have spoken the truth," Tecumseh said, a sort of sad smile lurking about his lips. "With our father killed at the battle of Point Pleasant and our mother gone who knows where, it was not the best way for a son to learn to be a warrior. The Prophet had none of the other skills either, but the Master Of Life has sent him on a mission. Others, less gifted, see to his needs. Perhaps if you shun the things you must deal with at the trading post, the same will be true for you."

"I'm afraid not," Tom grinned. "There's only one Prophet, and it is he who shares his thoughts with us this night. But what are your plans now?"

Tenskwatawa emptied the last of his tea on the earthen floor. "I go," he said, standing, "to the north and west, to a place where two rivers meet and join. One is called Wabashia by the whites, but its proper name is Tippecanoe. We have begun to build a settlement there. A place where all 'The People' who are anxious for redemption from the Master Of Life can settle and learn how to live in such a way as to once again earn The Spirit's favor. They are," he said proudly, "calling it 'Prophetstown'."

"And you, Great Chief, what will you do now?"

"I go again to the Creeks and their allies to the south and east. I will invite them to make their way to Prophetstown, not only for spiritual renewal, but also to form a formidable army under my command and with the blessing of our own Tenskwatawa. By invoking the help and counsel of the Great Spirit, this time we cannot fail! And this time we will be assured that the untrustworthy British will actually join with us!" He stared at Tom with a fierce expression. "You must not divulge this to a single person!"

"Of course, my chief! The children are asleep and my woman can be trusted. Have no fear!"

"Then good night. May Washaa Maneto protect you and your family. We go."

*   *   *

It was the fifteenth day since Tecumseh and The Prophet's visit. Tom would have forgotten about The Prophet's prediction, but he had written the number fifteen on a page in the ledger. The afternoon was about over, and he grinned to himself, not surprised that Simon, The Dancer, had not appeared.

There was a gentle knock on the heavy door. At first he ignored it, thinking some mischievous child was playing a trick. But when it came again he left his stool behind the counter and went to investigate. Two Indian women were standing there, looking terrified. "Helaeeo," one said in broken English, looking at the ground. On her back was a cradleboard.

"Hello to you. What do you Kickapoo women want here? Do you wish to trade? Are you looking for someone? What is it?"

"Toom-She-chi-Kwa?" the second woman asked.

"Yes. That is who I am. Can I help you?"

"Simon say 'helaeeo'." They looked all around, even behind the counter. Then smiling, the smaller one stood in the doorway and whistled, doing a perfect imitation of a robin.

Simon slipped in, a huge grin on his face. "<u>Tom</u>! Oh Tom it's so good to see you again! Are you alone in here? Will anyone else come today?"

"Simon, my friend. How I've missed you! I'll lock the door, but why all the secrecy?"

"I got to be real careful Tom. Lucius has sent papers down the river offerin' <u>fifty</u> <u>dollars</u> to anybody who turns me in. You know I ain't worth no fifty dollars, but there's plenty of folks who'd sure like to get all that money!"

"Come on Simon. I'll close up here and you and . . . and . . . those women . . can all come to my house for supper. How does that sound to you? I know you're always hungry. At least you used to be."

"We can't Tom. Soon as it's full dark we got to be movin' on. We travel mostly at night. Our horse is tied up back in the woods a ways. Can't we just talk <u>here</u>?"

"Sure we can. Blow out that candle. We can sit on the floor. If anybody comes they'll think I closed up and went on home. The candle, Simon."

"Not yet. Got something to show you. Polly, come on over here." He reached into the cradleboard and gently drew out a little boy. "Ain't he something Tom? He's my son! Polly here's his momma and the other one, she's Beth, is Polly's sister. They're my wives!"

Like many men, Tom usually paid little attention to infants, but this child was the exception. The boy could only be described as "golden". His hair was curly and soft. Large eyes and long lashes made him appear older than his one year, but his skin color was what caught Tom's eye. It was neither the copper color of his mother nor the dark brown of the former slave. The child was beautiful!

"Simon you got yourself a really cute little son. What's his name?"

"I named him Lymon after my little brother, but his momma calls him Kwet-a-tek. It means . . ."

"Ripe Pumpkin," Tom said. "You forget that I speak their language. It fits the boy for sure. That's just his color. It's like gold."

Simon spoke softly to Beth, apparently the child's aunt, or perhaps his "second mother". She left quietly, peering this way and that as she eased out of the door. In a few minutes she was back, carrying a leather parfleche which she handed to her husband. Simon opened it and withdrew a spectacular headdress and several strands of beads. With an exaggerated flourish he put them on. "How do you like this, Tom Bluefoot?" he crowed, posing, arms folded and head thrown back.

Tom forced himself to keep from laughing. "What _is_ all this Simon?"

"Tom, old friend, you is a-lookin' at a genuine, full-bore Sachem of the Kick-a-Poo tribe. Yassuh, yassuh, yassuh. That's me! I reckon I fooled all them old Elders, and they just ups and makes me a Sachem. Lymon would be proud of me! Ha ha!"

The two men talked, Little Lymon slept, and the women dozed against one wall. Simon explained how he had fooled Tecumseh into setting him free. "I acted like I was getting messages from the 'Big Spirit' or somebody. Old Tecumseh figured there wasn't room for <u>two</u> 'prophets'! Ha ha." Too soon it was time to go.

"Did you say you've got a horse?" Tom asked as they prepared their few belongings. "How does that work with three of you? Your wives ride double and 'The Sachem' has to walk. Right?"

"Oh no! That ain't the way of it at all. I am their <u>Sachem</u>! I ride, they walk. Believe me they wouldn't have it any other way. Now Tom Bluefoot, we got to be going. My tribe released me from my duties so I could find land far to the west where they could all come and join me." He said a few words to the women and they slipped silently away into the night. The friends gripped hands, but could find no words to ease their sadness at what could be their last meeting ever. Both however felt that somehow their paths would cross again.

Tom handed him a pouch of cornmeal and a piece of dried venison, reminding himself to pay for the gifts out of his wages. "How will you go, Simon?"

"We're following your main trails now, but later on we'll just keep a-goin' on towards the settin' sun. We got to hit that big river sooner or later. Once we get across the 'Father of Waters' we'll be safe to travel in daylight. Beth and Polly has got relatives over there somewhere. We'll find them, Tom. Some time you got to come out that way too. Old Lucius and the law is lookin' for you too, so be careful. After all these wars everybody's jawin' about is over, you come out there to the West and look us up. As a Sachem, I might could find you a job! Haha!"

"You could get to the Ohio. It flows west and some say it runs right into the big river you're heading for."

"No, no, no! I got no idea of getting on any kind of water till we can get on a real boat across that big river. You know me better'n that Tom Bluefoot!" He hurried away in the moonlight.

Standing in the darkness, Tom thought, "I wish Tenskwatawa would come back. I'd ask him if I'd ever see my friend and his family again."

The Prophet did not come back. He had already left for the town that bore his name at Tippecanoe. Tecumseh also left for Prophetstown but after a short stay they left again, traveling far to the south on yet another attempt to convince more tribes to join his coalition.

After all their visitors had left, things returned to normal for Tom and his family. He was uneasy however. Simon's fear of capture and subsequent flight to the West was increasingly on his mind. He watched his little girls playing with the corncob dolls he'd made. Their mother was busy sewing beads on a buckskin jacket she'd made for him. "What would happen to them if someone from Pittsburgh would come by and see me?" he thought. "I'd be hustled back and sent to that prison up near Philadelphia. When I was single I didn't worry much, but things are different now. At least I'm glad Red Gopher has moved in with his uncle permanently." He knew this was not unusual. Most boys were encouraged to leave home in this way in order to be tutored by a relative or family friend.

Fear, Tom was finding out, feeds upon itself. More and more he found himself looking carefully at customers both white and red, who entered the post. Did that brave look at him longer than was necessary? Did those two Shemanese seem to linger over the merchandise and continue to glance his way?

Two weeks of this unease was enough! One evening he called Tadpoe to his side. "I have told you little of my life before you became my wife. As is proper, you did not ask. So now you must be told that the black man, Simon, and I ran from the Shemanese at Fort Pitt. He to escape from his master and I to avoid a life in the white man's jail!" If Tadpole was surprised she gave no indication of it so he continued, telling the entire story of his false accusation, the verdict of guilty, and finally Simon's recent warning.

"What will you do my husband?"

"I must leave here. You have made our home a happy place. Our girls have captured my heart. Although your son, Red Gopher, only tolerated me, he is happy with your brother where he can learn the skills a boy should know. You and our children will also go back to your brother until I can return. May Washaa Maneto protect you."

"But where will <u>you</u> go?"

"I will follow the path of our great chief, Tecumseh and his brother The Prophet. They have begun building a village where two rivers meet. It is for men and women of many tribes. There they will be taught how to return to the old ways , the life that was lived before the invasion of the white man."

"But how will you find this place, Husband? It must be far, far from Green Ville where we now live."

"Many of our kind are traveling that way. I see such travelers at the trading post nearly every day. I will choose a group and ask to travel with them."

"But how will you live once you arrive at this gathering place? There will be no job in a trading post for you there!"

"I plan to find The Prophet whom you have met here in our home, and offer to act as his interpreter. He will need one, as he has told me that many Shemanese are also arriving there, afraid that our people may be preparing for another war. I am sure he will welcome my services in the conferences sure to follow."

"What of the Frenchman and his post? And what of your work there?" Tadpole said with a frown. A tear could be seen shining on one cheek.

"I will work there a few more days. At the end of that time I will count out my wages. I will leave the Frenchman a letter, written in his ledger book. I will tell him I am moving west, and that's <u>all</u> I will tell him! As you know, I am an honest man. I will not steal from him, only take what is due to me. Half of the silver money I will give to you for your brother. The other half will help me on my journey."

Although tears were flowing, Tadpole did not complain or attempt to change his mind. He was the husband. Men of "The People" often left their homes and villages for a variety of reasons. It was to be expected.

"I will miss you very, very, much! The little ones will miss you even more! I shall ask The Great Spirit to go with you and . . . and . . ." she continued, "I will also ask Him to bring you back here to us some time!"

Two days later Tom had just finished counting the day's receipts when the door opened and two men entered. "Where's the owner of this dump?" the first man yelled, ignoring Tom completely. "I need some terbaccy, and I need it <u>now</u>!" He punched his companion with an elbow. "How long's it been, Hal? Gotta be a couple weeks since we had anything to smoke or chew either. Well Injun, where's your boss? We need stuff. We got no money, but these pelts are prime. Throw 'em up on that counter, Joe."

Tom was about to serve them when luck, the white man's God, Washaa Maneto, or <u>something,</u> made him pause. "If anybody knows anything about them two runaways," Joe said, "it'd be here in this trading post. Just about everybody has to come in here sooner or later. Is this here redskin the only one in here? Maybe he speaks enough English to tell us where the propierator is."

"<u>Where's</u> <u>the</u> <u>owner</u>?" Hal asked Tom. "The man, . . . big chief of post. Where? He come?"

"Look at that!" Joe guffawed. The redskin is starin' at the ledger book. He's probably tryin' to figger out what kind of a animal made them little tracks on the paper! Hawhaw!"

"Me not know. White man . . ." Here Tom lifted his right hand, thumb at his mouth, and pantomimed drinking. "Not know he come."

"Listen Injun. Have you seen a black man, a darkey, in here lately? He run away . . ."

"Aw save your breath. Look at him. He ain't understandin' a thing you're saying. I think he means the owner is drinking or drunk somewhere. Probably in that tavern we saw down that way."

"I reckon so. The owner must have left this Injun here to keep an eye out for people stealing the goods," Joe grumbled. "He shoulda sent somebody to keep an eye on <u>him</u>!" He jerked a thumb in Tom's direction. "Well it looks like we'll have to ask at the tavern. Better take our pelts along or that thievin' varmint will run off with 'em before we get back! Come on."

Heart pounding, Toom-She-chi- Kwa scribbled a note on the day's ledger page. He counted out the exact amount of the wages he had coming, including what he'd earned but not been paid for in the past. The task could have been confusing, but Tom had had much experience dealing with the various types of coinage then in use. He counted them out in a hurry; King George half pennies, British pence, Wellington half cents, Hibernia coppers, and even a few of the new American one cent "Libertys". He glanced around to make sure all was well in the post, blew out the candle, and locked the door. He ran full speed the three miles to his cabin.

Luckily the children, having been playing outside, were warmly dressed. Few words were spoken and in a matter of minutes Tadpole and the girls were on their way to her brother, Flat Lance, several coins jingling in her pocket. Tom was off in the opposite direction, heading into the deep forest.

*   *   *

BOOK TWO

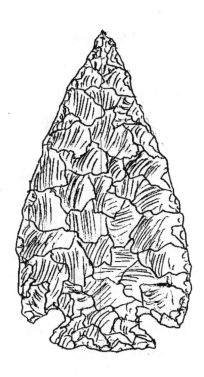

The trip had taken the better part of two weeks, but the weather had been good. The nine Kickapoos had welcomed Tom, especially when he offered them a few coins in payment. The far-flung influence of Tenskwatawa was much in evidence, as Tom's traveling companions had been quiet and composed during the entire trip. They hunted with bows and snares only. No guns were in evidence, and even their cooking utensils were of the old style. Tom was impressed. He'd had no idea of how far The Prophet's teaching had spread by this year of 1809.

Prophetstown was a beehive of activity. Located at the Tippecanoe River near the Wabash, there were perhaps two thousand warriors from at least twelve different tribes assembled there. Former enemies sat peacefully together, listening eagerly to the speeches Tenskwatawa gave nearly every evening. Tom sat and listened, but stayed well back out of sight. He was as enthralled as anyone. There was much merit in The Prophet's words. All Indians, regardless of tribe or traditional location, were to band together in order have enough strength to stop the sale of Indian lands and the encroachment of settlers. In order to ensure the blessing of the Great Spirit, all were to abstain from alcohol, shun Shemanese goods, and return to the old ways. Even the young braves seemed to be embracing the movement!

"Oho! The man of two raisings has come to his senses and joined us!" Tecumseh said, giving Tom a searching look. "Someone said you have silver money. Did you steal it from the Frenchman?"

"No, Great Chief. That man paid me for my work. It is the way of the Shemanese. Of course he tried to cheat me, but because he was often drunk, the fool was unsuccessful at it!"

Tecumseh chuckled, well aware of the Wyandot's clever mind. "And how are you managing to eat, now that you are here among these many tribes? Do you have any of the Shemanese money left?"

"My Kickapoo traveling companions ordered me to throw the metal money away, so I threw it into the bushes. When they were all asleep I went out and got it again!"

This time, Tecumseh laughed aloud. "Just as I would have suspected," he said, still grinning. "You are welcome at my lodge. My brother and I have more food than we can eat. All the braves bring gifts to us, but some have said that game is becoming scarce. Of this I have no doubt. Too many hunters in the forest. Enough talk! Now I must prepare for another journey."

"Where is your destination this time, Chief Tecumseh?"

"I go to the tribes in the West. Unfortunately I have had little success in the South, but I will try again later. Most of those tribes are too much entwined with the whites. They are also cowards! Perhaps Waasha Maneto will act favorably with me as I meet with the western tribes."

"I would be honored to accompany you," Tom said respectfully.

"No my son. Your place is here. More and more my brother's words encourage war with the whites. He will be much in need of a trustworthy interpreter when he encounters such men as the treacherous one of three names who calls himself 'Governor'".

"Three names?"

"William Henry Harrison! There is no doubt that some time soon we must fight with him and his soldiers, but we are as yet not ready. More tribes must join with us. Stay close to Tenskwatawa. My brother has the gift of prophecy and many are eager to follow him. However he is sometimes impulsive and acts before he thinks. You can help him, for I have come to admire the quick mind that resides in your skinny body!" He was smiling again but it was plain that Tecumseh meant every word. "I have ordered him not to attack yet."

Nearly a week after the Shawnee chief had left, eight braves with him, Tenskwatawa, The Prophet, deigned to notice the young Wyandot who was to be his principal interpreter.

"So you are still here. Did your black friend appear as I had foretold?"

"<u>Exactly so</u>! On the <u>very day</u> you had prophesied! So far as I know, by now he has gone beyond the Great River." Tom was not sure exactly how he should respond to The Prophet. The man was obviously revered by the great majority of those in the camp. Dressed in the finest beaded buckskins, he had adorned his body with an abundance of beads and feathers. What Toom-She-chi-Kwa found puzzling was that in spite of the man's contempt for anything manufactured by the Shemanese, the Seer sported a gold nose ring, huge German silver earbobs, thick copper bracelets on each arm, a silver crescent moon shaped chest ornament, and other such baubles. "It appears that the great man can excuse <u>himself</u> for such banned adornments!" Tom thought. Of course he was not foolish enough to say anything about it aloud!

"Why do you stare at me, Wyandot pup?" Tecumseh snapped.

"Please excuse me Great Prophet. I am overcome with wonder in the presence of one so renowned!" Tom lied. "I would consider it a great privilege if I were to be allowed to hear one of your speeches. Of course that would require your specific permission."

The Prophet sniffed, but seemed mollified by the flattery. "Tomorrow at the walnut grove you will hear me. A crier will pass through the camps announcing the gathering. You will sit near me."

"But I am not worthy of that honor," Tom said,

truly surprised.

"Of course you are not! You have been totally corrupted by your work in the Frenchman's trading post. You have lived in a wegiwa made in the fashion of the Shemanese, and you have attempted to teach your offspring the language of the hated Americans. Yes you are correct in saying you are not worthy, even to attend the gathering. However my brother has insisted that you be told to stay close by my side. He is a great warrior but also a fool! He does not trust me. I have tried to convince him that I speak the words of the Master of Life. Therefore I cannot be wrong. My steps are assured. When we meet the army of the one called Harrison, The Great Spirit will fight for us. We cannot lose!"

Tenskwatawa stopped suddenly, aware that he had said more than he intended, but his pride caused him to go even further. "Tecumseh assures me that you are to be trusted. Come with me now. I will show you how The Deity has further provided for his chosen children."

"What now?" Tom thought as they threaded their way through the hundreds of wegiwas and simple shelters that made up the temporary village of Prophets Town. The Prophet was greeted with respect that bordered on reverence by all they met. He acknowledged the adulation with a modest nod.

The log structure was not large, but constructed in a way meant to protect its contents. Two braves armed with lances stood beside the heavy log door. They raised a hand in greeting the celebrity, but cast suspicious glances at his Wyandot companion. The Prophet motioned grandly at the guards. With difficulty they dragged the door open far enough for the two men to enter. Tom caught his breath in surprise. He counted eight open crates, each crammed with shiny new muskets! Smaller boxes, as yet unopened, certainly contained powder and lead. The crown of King George was burned into each container. "Does this mean the British actually plan to be of help if there is a war?" Tom gasped.

"Of course! What else could this shipment mean? We expect more cases very soon."

"But I thought you were telling our people to forego the use of guns. Are these to be distributed to the warriors?"

"Some have questioned me about the use of firearms. Those who feel that such weapons should also be forbidden are misled. Hear what the Great Spirit has told me about the 'firesticks'. The Ruler of Life is well aware that in order to drive the evil ones back into the eastern sea we must fight him with the same weapons he will use against us. You have now seen the first cache of muskets given to us by our brothers, the British and the Canadians. Since they were the property of our allies these weapons are not tainted. They also strive for the defeat of the evil Americans . For those who have not thrown away their guns I tell them that they can be purified. They should hold them over running water for ten heartbeats, then sprinkle the barrel with tobacco. They will then be clean!"

Tenskwatawa qave Tom a look of pity. "My brother says you are very wise. I find you one who is slow to comprehend what is obvious. It is true that the British betrayed us in the battle with the Mad General at Fallen Timbers but they have assured us that this time they will be our brothers."

"Are they on the way? I've heard nothing from the scouts who often enter the lodge which you and your brother share," Tom stated, keeping a cautious eye on Tenskwatawa.

"No they are not. Had I summoned them they would be here already. Although their help will be appreciated, we who trust in the Master of Life require no assistance by white soldiers, be they British or not," he stated proudly. "Now," he went on, "here is something you do not know. The Shemanese general whom we call 'Three Names' is preparing an army to do battle with us. He is assembling them northwest of here on what the whites call St. Mary's River. Their headquarters are called Fort Wayne."

"Are you <u>sure</u>?" Tom blurted, greatly alarmed. "Do you expect an attack soon?"

"I cannot be sure. Waasha Maneto has not yet revealed it to me. We may know soon enough however. That General has asked for a parlay in two weeks' time.

You will interpret for me there. We must leave in time to arrive at Tippecanoe for the council meeting."

"What will be your position Great Chief? Do you think he will demand that you give up your weapons and stay here in the town that bears you name?"

"Yes. He will try to avoid a fight. He will also try to determine whether the British and Canadians are here with us. We will not surrender, nor will we accept any terms of peace. Our warriors are ready for war! With me as their leader we will wipe Three Names' godless army from the earth!"

"Are you expecting your brother to return in time for the attack? Tecumseh has expressed to me his wish that no action be taken until his return, so I thought . . ."

"Insolent Wyandot pup!" Tenskwatawa exploded. "What do you know of war? How can you dare advise me, a great warrior who lost an eye fighting for The People?"

"My most sincere apology Great One!" Toom-She-chi-Kwa said. He did not mention that it was common knowledge that The Prophet had lost his eye in a childhood accident. It was also whispered that the "Great Warrior" had disappeared when the battle with Mad Anthony Wayne at the FallenTrees grew intense!

Tom could think of no way to discourage The Seer from his determination to fight, whether Tecumseh was back or not.

"Perhaps I can find a way to delay the conflict when Harrison comes to negotiate," Tom thought, but he was far from optimistic.

"Come now! Come all! Come to the walnut grove!" The crier's voice interrupted Tom's thoughts. The faithful were being summoned, and already many could be seen hurrying to the gathering place. Tom was reluctant to go, but he had been ordered to stay close to The Prophet. Some he knew would resent this. Still he was curious about what was actually being said at these meetings. Quickly he checked his clothing to be sure he had nothing of the Shemanese world showing. Satisfied, he slipped off his moccasins as he had been told was the custom at such pretentious gatherings, and joined the others.

"Why does The Prophet allow this Shemanese-loving Wyandot to stand by his side?" Close Hunter hissed to those nearby. "It is said that he even worked in a Frenchman's trading post!" There was a general angry muttering of agreement.

"Why doesn't Tenskwatawa shut them up?" Tom thought. "I sure don't want to be here, but I've been ordered to do so by Tecumseh himself. The Prophet could tell them that, before somebody decides to put an arrow in my belly!"

The Holy Man, however, was not about to say anything to anybody. Standing slightly hunched over, he appeared to be deep in prayer or perhaps in a trance.

Twice his entire body twitched so hard he nearly fell forward. He began to mumble, but Tom could not understand a word of what The Prophet was saying. The many hundreds in attendance sat unmoving, making not a sound. Their anticipation was so great it could almost be felt! Was all this merely a deceptive performance by a talented actor? The entire proceeding certainly appeared to be legitimate. For the first time, Tom could see for himself the power that the Shawnee spiritual leader could command.

"Oh Master of Life," the small man suddenly cried out, his only eye turned to the heavens, "hear me now! Your children are in need. We humbly request your presence here on this night as we plan for a battle with that spawn of Satan who dares to oppose us." He went on in this way for several more minutes, the listeners mesmerized by the power of his oratory. After a short pause he turned to exhortation. "My brothers you have seen fit to honor me with your attention. Hear my commands. Not only hear, but obey! Put away anything and everything that speaks of the white people. Do not use the steel fire-strikers you have traded for. They are contaminated! Make your blaze with a fire drill, as has been done for more generations than we can number. Shun the soft food of the Shemanese. Spit out bread, beef, pig meat, and other such vile fare. Pray twice daily. Do not even touch the brown firewater. Above all, do not try to gain much wealth and personal possessions. Share what the Great Spirit has given you, and in like manner expect the same when you are in need."

Five Moravian missionaries seated near the front continually nodded in agreement, as Tom interpreted quietly.

Tenskwatawa went on for some time. Basically beseeching his followers to return to the old ways, the ways of their forefathers before the white Americans invaded the country they saw as exclusively theirs. Tom had to admit that there was much good in what The Prophet was saying. He returned to Tecumseh's dwelling deep in thought.

*   *   *

Tenskwatawa was not in a happy mood. The winter of 1809 had not been to his liking. For some reason, perhaps he thought, because of the evil intentions of witches, The Great Spirit had not provided the growing numbers of warriors with adequate food. Because of his accusations several innocent old women had been burned to death.

The growing village was indeed impressive. The Americans under Governor William Henry Harrison called it Tippecanoe, but The Prophet insisted on calling it "Prophetstown".

Tom was becoming bored. Of course the chiefs'

wegiwa was always well-supplied with food and fuel, but the warriors and their wives and children were deeply in want. Moravians and even some Quakers had done what they could to bring relief to the still expanding village, but they had been warned away by Harrison and his officers.

"When do you expect the return of you brother?" Tom Bluefoot asked The Prophet.

"Who can say?" The Seer growled. "He tells me nothing these days. He goes. He comes. He goes again! Always he insists that there be no battle without his presence. What has he seen of <u>conditions</u> here?" he shouted. "My warriors are <u>ready</u>. The British and Canadians send encouraging messages. They too wonder why we wait. Well . . ." his one eye fastened upon Tom Bluefoot, "what do <u>you</u> have to say? My brother always brags about your wisdom. So tell me, what do you think of our situation here, Wyandot?"

"As you well know, Great Chief, I am not a warrior, nor do I have the gift of 'second sight' as you do. Therefore my words can be of little use to one such as yourself. However . . ."

"<u>However</u>!" The Prophet snapped. "Always with you there is a 'however'!"

"Shall I not speak then, Great One?"

The Prophet said nothing for several minutes, then finally grumbled an answer. "Speak. <u>Speak</u>! Even though I can have little confidence in one raised by a Shemanese. Anything would be better than the eternal waiting in this cursed wegiwa. Say what you will!"

"I do not wish to offend. You have provided for me and allowed me the privilege of hearing many of your wonderful speeches. Because of your influence, if not honored, I am at least tolerated here in Prophetstown. I am in your debt. I will offer some remarks but please understand that I do so only to help you clarify your own thinking." Tom hated to grovel so, but he had soon learned that it was the only way to get the man to listen.

"I have the greatest respect for your brother, Tecumseh! He is well aware of your gifts and your eagerness to defeat the enemies of our people. Believe me, he is of the same mind. However . . ." Tenskwatawa sniffed at the word. "However, your older brother strives for more than just a victory. It is his desire that all tribes be united, with one voice, in war and in peace. He tries to stop the constant selling of our lands to the Shemanese. Often this has been done by so-called 'chiefs' who do not even rule the land being sold. Sold for worthless trinkets and promises! He desires that any land being sold must meet the conditions of all tribes everywhere."

The Prophet sat against one wall smoking a long pipe. He had assured his followers that tobacco use was not to be shunned. After all, the weed had been cultivated by The People for all time. In fact the Seer had in one of his speeches expressed that The Master of Life <u>encouraged</u> its use!

Tom waited for a time. Hearing no objection, he continued. "It is true also that braves from many tribes, some far from here, have heard of your leadership. More are coming all the time. By waiting patiently your ranks will increase. You can never tell if the British and Canadians will actually support your cause when war comes. The more fighters in your army, the better!"

The Prophet grunted something then motioned for Tom to continue. "Tecumseh, 'Shooting Star' knows the value of superior numbers. He is a patient man, as can be proven by his repeated trips to the various tribes, seeking their support. Also his ability as a commander in battle is well known. With him at your side, victory would almost be assured."

"Are you saying that I am not capable of leading warriors into battle?" Tenskwatawa's words were soft but held a deadly ring.

"Oh no! Not at all!" Tom gasped. "I merely point out that your giftedness and his are quite different. Blended together they will make a formidable force. That I believe is why your brother has asked that you wait until he can join you in the assault. Is it not true that two braves might be given different skills, one with a bow, the other with the lance? Apart they might be successful, but <u>together</u> they will be <u>victorious</u>!"

"Has the insolent young pup finally run out of

words?" The Prophet asked, but Tom could detect no real malice in the question. He could only hope that Tenskwatawa would take his advice.

Prophetstown was continuing to grow. Lodges and shelters were springing up everywhere. Toom-she-chi-Kwa was especially impressed with the beautiful "tipees" being erected by the women of the western Wisconsin tribes. These dwellings boasted double interior walls, movable flaps at the smoke hole, and of most interest to Tom, fine drawings and paintings decorating their outsides. Wisconsin was not alone. Groups from what would one day be called Michigan, Illinois, and even further west came trickling in.

Encouraging as the added numbers were, they created a serious problem for The Prophet and his fellow leaders. Game was nearly eliminated as the many hunters scoured the nearby forests. Having neglected their gardens in order to attach themselves to Tenskwatawa's teaching, there was little fodder for the horses tethered everywhere in the surrounding area.

Both Tecumseh and his brother knew that something drastic must be done before their followers, understandably, began to leave Prophetstown. Tenskwatawa, albeit reluctantly, once again sought advice from "the insolent Wyandot pup".

"If you were me, and thank The Great Spirit you are <u>not</u>!" the Seer began, not meeting Tom's eyes, "how would you go about feeding the numberless hoards that come to hear me, and to join in our cause?"

Tom Bluefoot chewed quietly on a piece of smoked venison and pretended to be thinking about the problem. In fact he was very sure that The Prophet already knew what must be done, but he was looking for someone to blame, should the action go wrong. "I speak only to answer the direct question of my highly esteemed leader," he began, hating himself for yet another such cowardly approach, "but perhaps my words will simply help you clarify your own thinking on this matter."

"Well, what do you think then, Bluefoot? Speak now or hold your tongue here in my lodge."

"To me it seems that two brothers, both clever and wise, could easily fool the one who calls himself 'Governor' of this area. Harrison, from what I have heard is a vain and pompous man. That kind is most easily misled. Were I you, I would go to him. Appear to be humble and contrite. Promise peace from all the brothers who gather here. In return ask for corn and other essentials. Perhaps my words do not mirror your thinking on this matter, but I can see that you are troubled about how to feed this multitude ."

"Aho! You have interpreted my very thoughts exactly! Or did I tell you all of this before? At any rate Tecumseh has promised to return in two days' time. I will send him to the British beyond Detroit, and I myself will seek a conference with him of 'Three Names'. We will fool him into providing us corn and perhaps even some of their horrible salted cow's meat. Aho! Once again I have solved the problem!"

Tom paid no attention to the slight. He was more concerned with keeping the man from beginning hostilities without the support of his brother, Tecumseh. Thankfully it would take time for the conferences to be arranged and if successful, time for delivery of the needed food. For the moment, Tom could relax, knowing that the crisis was over. Still he had a feeling that The Prophet would attack Harrison's forces whenever he felt like it, whether Tecumseh was present or not.

Governor Harrison was not the easily duped fool that the Indian leaders thought him to be. He was a soldier, and one well aware of the wiles of his enemy. His main concern was the lack of reliable information regarding the Shawnee leaders' immediate plans for an attack. He sent several of his soldiers into Prophetstown disguised as traders or even missionaries, to gain information, but most of them were easily found out and were lucky to escape with their scalps intact. The gifts of food and a little powder and shot had not had the desired effect.

Following the meager gifts, Harrison thought that the Indians were subdued enough that another purchase of treaty land could be successful. The acreage he coveted was a huge tract along the Wabash. Harrison had no doubt that the land sale, being called "The Treaty

Of Fort Wayne" flew in the faces of Tecumseh and The Prophet. The fact that Little Turtle of the Miami, long an enemy of the Shawnees, was one of the principal signers of the land sale, angered the brothers even more! They accused the Miami Chief of siding with the Americans.

The Indians were angry and did little to disguise their feelings. When ever larger numbers of western tribesmen began to arrive, the Shawnee Holy Man was greatly encouraged.

* *

"You seem to be of two minds, my Chief," Tom stated, handing Tecumseh a burning twig.

"It is so, Toomie. I suppose you have heard how my meeting with him of three names nearly resulted in bloodshed. His soldiers had drawn swords and my braves' bows had arrows nocked. It was a close thing, but there was no fighting. The next day talks went better." He lighted his pipe and seemed to relax a little.

"Did the governor listen to your requests then?"

"He pretended to, but he relies on those cowardly chiefs who teach bowing to the Americans. They tell their young men that they should get along with the whites. Plow the soil! Plant corn and beans! Wait for the great 'Father George Warsh Ington' to tell his people to send food and presents! <u>Páh</u>!"

"And who are these chiefs who would side with the enemies of our people?"

"There are many. Most have little influence but there are three who carry much weight. One of them is whom we call 'the old woman'. He is Little Turtle of the Miami. Another is his friend at Wapagonettia, Chief Black Hoof. Can you believe it? He is a <u>Shawnee</u>!" He spat angrily and stopped speaking for several minutes.

"Isn't there something that can be done to change their minds?" the Wyandot asked, peering at his chief.

"Ha! We have tried. Oh how we have tried! Both my brother and I have parlayed with them. Many of their young men would join with us, but without the sanction of their chiefs they will not act as their hearts tell them. There are others like these chiefs. The Shemanese have blinded them with gifts and promises. They are fools to listen!"

"I feel you have not told me all that makes your heart be troubled. Perhaps I could help you in some way," Tom Bluefoot said quietly, aware that he was treading on dangerous grounds!

Shooting Star turned toward his young companion and regarded him with surprise. "Perhaps you can," he said, frowning in the firelight. "You are one of the few I can really trust. What I say now is for you only. Should you even <u>whisper</u> what I'm about to say, I will kill you myself!" These last words were said so matter-of-factly that Tom believed them implicitly. Tecumseh did not make idle threats!

"Do not doubt me my chief. I would not have survived this long were I unable to control my tongue. Tell me your thoughts. They will remain with me alone."

"Among my many concerns is my brother, known everywhere as a prophet, and he certainly is. That he has the gift of 'second sight' there can be no doubt. He speaks powerful words that can excite many. Yes he can <u>speak</u>! Perhaps it might be said that he talks <u>too</u> <u>much</u>! Did you know that he was once called Lalawethica, 'The Rattler'? Indeed to this day he rattles on! I do not condemn him. He is my brother, and has done much for our people. His orations bring back our pride. Once again I warn you, Toom-she-chi-Kwa, if you repeat these words you are as good as dead! Yes The Prophet claims that The Master of Life speaks to him directly, giving advice and instruction. Perhaps that is true. I cannot be his judge. Such is his power and vision that more tribesmen than can be numbered eagerly follow his every word." Tecumseh paused to relight his pipe, glancing at Tom to see if the young man was still listening.

Tom was not sure if the Chief had said all that he was going to. He waited for some time, then risked a response. "Your pardon Chief Tecumseh, but from what you have said and from what I myself have observed, I can see little reason for your concern. Has it not been his teaching alone that has filled Prophetstown to overflowing?"

"Yes, that is true. However it seems he has never learned the value of patience. He excites his listeners to the extent that they want to attack the Americans now! As I have told you many times before, he must wait until we are completely ready to fight, and that the British are truly with us. I am afraid he will begin too soon." Of course Tom had heard all of this before, but he hoped hearing it all again would help the troubled leader.

"You must stay close by his side. You can then prevent him from a quick, premature strike," Tom said.

"How can I? I must continue my travels, as I still have hopes for a coalition of all tribes . It is the only way to stop the continued selling of our lands, and to convince the Americans that we are too strong for another war with them."

With a sudden complete change of expression, The Chief asked Tom a question. "And you. Where is your heart, Tom Bluefoot? In the coming war would you prefer that our people or the Americans be victorious? You have lived in both worlds, and as much as anyone, can be the judge of what would be best for all."

Tom had feared that sooner or later this question

would come up. Most of the important member of the tribe knew him, or knew of him. As an interpreter and sort of advisor to an army major in 1895, he had traveled to most of their villages, urging the chiefs to attend the Council of Peace at Greenville. Then when the tribes were assembled to sign the great treaty he had acted as principal interpreter for General "Mad Anthony" Wayne. Yes, he was known by most of the many chiefs! It was a thought that frightened him. He was well aware that back in those times many did not trust him. They thought he was slanting his translations in favor of the Americans. "How?" he thought, "will they look upon me if I am there when the battle begins?" He decided to forge ahead.

"Chief Tecumseh," he began hesitantly, "I hope you are not planning to ask me to watch The Prophet again while you are traveling. He doesn't have confidence in me or in my opinions. Perhaps you could order one of your sub-chiefs to help your brother with his decision making. If it were not for . . ."

"Be quiet!" Shooting Star did not raise his voice. Tom was shocked. "Let me remind you of something, Toom-She-chi-Kwa. You gave me your life and the life of the black man in exchange for the lives of the settlers on the Ohieeo River. Although I have since given the black man his freedom, you are still my slave! You will do as you are told. Can you not see that I dare not reveal my concerns about my brother's shortcomings?" After this outbreak the chief softened a little. "The Prophet <u>does</u>

listen to you. At least as much as he listens to anybody! You are a calming influence on him. He has told me as much. Hear my words!"

"I did not mean to forget my place as a slave. You have treated me so well that it has temporarily escaped me. What would you have me do?"

"The same as before. Speak to him, reassure him, advise him as much as you can. I leave in three days for the southern tribes I will be gone one double hand and one hand. I am afraid of what may happen during that time. As always the young braves are eager for battle. I am not afraid of conflict and plan to lead our people when the war begins. However, as one who has much experience on the warpath I say 'not yet'! We are not ready!"

"Tadpole and I have been living with three Kickapoos lately, but I will move back to The Prophet's lodge immediately. I will obey your orders."

"It has already been arranged. I need to be gone for the fifteen days. May Waasha Maneto grant that nothing happen during that time! Now I must confer with my traveling companions. You may not see me in the next three days, as I have much to do."

*   *   *

"But why do you wish to make that five day journey all the way back from Prophetstown? Are you unhappy here? Your brother may not even welcome us," Tom Bluefoot said petulantly. He felt sure that Flat Lance held him in contempt, and that he was undoubtedly fostering that attitude in Red Gopher, Tadpole's nine year old son. "Even though Tecumseh has given me permission to go, I feel I should stay here with him and The Prophet." His wife said nothing but by the set of her jaw it was obvious that they would be making the visit back to see her brother in Greenville.

"I wish for the girls to get to know their brother," Tadpole said, putting a few items in a buckskin bag.

The following morning they set out, the girls and their mother singing a happy tune about a dancing badger. Toom-She-chi-Kwa sulked for the entire five day journey.

"Aho! My sister!" Flat Lance exclaimed. He had been away on a hunt but had just returned when Tom and his family arrived. "Red gopher, here are your sisters. They have grown almost as tall as you, don't you think?"

"No! They are not <u>nearly</u> as big as me. They are but little girls! You promised to take me on a fox hunt today. Now I suppose I will not be permitted." He was angry and it showed.

"You can see that my sister and . . and . . .this man have come to us. I wish to spend time with her and her girls." Tom noticed that he was not mentioned in the welcome. "The fox will not fly away! Another time we will take up his trail."

Tom had an inspiration. "Flat Lance, my brother-in-law," he began politely, "perhaps I could accompany the boy. Then he would not be disappointed and you could spend much time with your sister . . . and with my daughters." He had made no attempt to soften his words and Tadpole's uncle was well aware of it.

"I don't want him to go with me! He knows nothing about calling foxes. He spent too much time in the Frenchman's smelly store. I will go alone!"

"No my son, that would be unwise. You know as well as I that a party of Eel River renegades has been seen in the area. They would like nothing better than to kidnap such a handsome youth as yourself. Tom Bluefoot will go with you, or you will not go at all."

The boy gave Tom a sullen look. "Do you know how to sit without moving for a long time?" he demanded. "Do you even know what a fox looks like? I doubt it! Come on then, it grows late."

They squatted down behind a screen of berry bushes overlooking a small open glade. Tom had to admit that his step-son was right. He knew nothing about calling in a fox! Still he was determined to avoid making a fool of himself in front of this boy. They sat, neither one moving a muscle. Red Gopher kept an eye on his step-father, probably hoping the man would make some mistake.

After quite a long time, the young hunter placed the back of his left hand against his lips and made a soft squealing sound. It was done to mimic the cry of a small animal in distress. He did it again, then waited.

Tom would not have seen the animal at all had the lad not given an almost imperceptible nod. It was not a fox, but a full-grown bobcat! Moving one hand very slowly, the boy picked up a stone he had placed on his knee. Keeping his hand below the bushes, he flipped the rock beyond the animal. The tawny cat turned quickly to the right, trying to see what had caused the noise. In a smooth, well-practiced motion, the bow came up and an arrow flew.

The bobcat gave an angry yowl and limped away, blood dripping from an arrow wound in its foot. Tadpole's son was mortified! He had done everything right, then missed by taking a too hasty shot. He pretended to examine his small bow, keeping his eyes down.

"Aho! Very clever! Very clever indeed! You are a hunter young man!" The boy gave Tom an angry look. He did not relish being made fun of!

"I certainly would not have known what to do when that bobcat appeared. But you did! Obviously you wounded him on purpose. We came for a fox, not some smelly cat. Your well-placed arrow will make him run far from here before his scent can scare away any red foxes in the area. Well done my lad! I can see that you will very soon bag a beautiful red fox, or perhaps even two. I can hardly wait to tell your mother and you uncle what a hunter you have become!"

"You did well too," the boy said magnanimously. "I think I could train you to become successful in the forest. But . . . it would take a long time!" Tom Bluefoot pretended not to notice when the boy placed a hand on his shoulder.

Both smiling happily, they headed for Flat Lance's wegiwa.

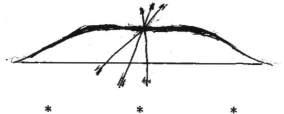

*   *   *

Tenskwatawa did not seem happy that Tom had joined him once again. By giving the young Wyandot many undignified duties he hoped to get him to leave, but this did not happen. Things appeared to be proceeding as normal, although there seemed to be a constant stream of warriors coming and going from The Prophet's lodge. "Are you planning to attend my meeting tomorrow night?" he asked abruptly on the tenth day after Tecumseh's leaving.

"Yes. I am looking forward to your words. Many warriors have been asking for you while you were secluded in your prayer lodge. I told them you were conferring with The Master Of Life. They too are anxious to attend the meeting tonight. Some have told me they expect to hear an important announcement. Why not wait until your brother, Tecumseh, returns? Whatever is in your mind to do can be shared by both great leaders. All who hear your words can then be assured that there is total agreement between the two of you."

"Pah! Shut your mouth, white-lover! I know what you are attempting to do. You are in league with my brother in this. I am no fool. You forget that The Great Spirit confers with me. It is He who will dictate what I say and what I do! You, Toom-She-chi-Kwa, are not to attend tonight's meeting! If I see you there I will order you killed. I have heard enough from you. I perceive the echo of Tecumseh's words in your voice. He who is never quite ready. Always he seeks more and more tribes to join with us. I say, and The Master of Life concurs, that the time to strike is at hand! Leave me, Wyandot pup! I do not wish to see your face for two days. Go!"

Tom gathered his few things and stood at the door for a moment. He was about to plead with Tenskwatawa, but when he saw The Prophet's murderous look, thought better of it.

The nights were still fairly warm in the fall of 1810, so Tom rolled up in his blanket under an ash tree. He made no effort to move back with the Kickapoos, nor with his own wife and children.

A small stone bounced off Tom's head, waking him with a start. "Why do you sleep like that when he who speaks with the gods is about to tell us what comes next? Get up and join us. Hurry up or we'll have to sit so far back we won't be able to hear what is being said!"

Tom sat up, blinking in the moonlight. "Who are you?" he asked.

"We are two brothers and a cousin. Our chief, Makes The Sign, is here at Prophetstown with us. We wish to hear the words of The Prophet. We will follow him wherever he leads us. We hope it is to <u>war</u>!"

Tom made up his mind in an instant. "Do you plan to paint your faces then?" he asked. "It would seem to be the proper thing to do, since your inclination is to fight."

"You are <u>right</u> Wyandot!" one of the brothers cried. "We should have thought of it. There's a fire over there. I have much vermillion that the British gave away. Let's hurry!"

It was stroke of fortune for Tom Bluefoot. He could blend in with the other three, and with a liberal use of face paint, be almost unrecognizable. He had given up attending the meeting, knowing that The Prophet would not hesitate to have him killed, but here was the solution. After streaking his cheeks and forehead, he threw his blanket over his head in such a way as to nearly cover his eyes. He felt safe.

"You won't need that blanket," one of the brothers laughed. "Tenskwatawa's words will soon warm your heart as well as your body. Take it off."

"I know I should, but an old woman of my tribe once told me, 'a bare head honors no one'. I never forgot those words," Tom lied glibly.

The three impatient braves looked at each other in alarm. "Go back!" the oldest one hissed. "Get anything we can use to cover our heads!"

Tom hid a grin behind one hand.

"Brothers! Hear the words of the Master Of Life," Tenskwatawa began after a lengthy pause. "While as you must realize I am not permitted to tell you all of the Great One's words I can give you my own. Be assured that what I say now is exactly what The Deity would have me impart to you."

Tom, listening intently from far to the rear of the vast assembly, could not help a sardonic smile. He well remembered that during his years with the Quaker Eli Miller, whenever a Shemanese tried to mimic the Indians, they had them saying such things as "ugh", or "me go", as if the red men were incapable of any sort of civilized speech. "If only," Tom thought, "they could hear this Shawnee now they would never again consider the Indians' speech primitive or crude!" The Prophet was indeed an orator of uncommon ability. His words continued.

"Now brave ones, you no doubt are expecting me to raise the bloody hatchet. I too would be happy to do that very thing. But this is where communing with Washaa Maneto provides direction far beyond our mere human wants and desires. Just last evening as I was in a trance-like state, I was told by the Entity that as of this moment we are not to participate in an attack! From my own personal observations I must concur. We are not yet ready. More warriors join us every day, but this is also true of the whites. Our spies have informed me that 'farmer-soldiers' from Kain-Tuck-Kee are coming to join Governor Three Names' forces. Do not fear. When the time is exactly right The Great Spirit will tell me and <u>then</u> the bloody hatchet will be raised high above my head!"

A roar of approval rocked the clearing. There were even a few war cries from those assembled there.

The Prophet silenced them with a simple gesture from his right hand. "But be it known to you all," he continued, "when the actual conflict begins I will not be there to lead you into battle."

"No! <u>No</u>!" growled the assembly. Some stood and raised both hands, begging the Holy Man to take back these words. There was a murmur of uncertainty throughout the throng.

Tom was astonished! What was happening was almost unbelievable. Relief flooded his mind as he realized he had no need to fear a fight before Tecumseh's return.

"<u>Hold</u>! <u>Hold</u>!" the Prophet shouted. "I do not mean to abandon you! May Washaa Maneto strike me with a lightning bolt if such a thing ever entered my mind! No, my brothers, the one to lead against the hated whites will be Tecumseh, 'The Shooting Star'. I will not lead <u>in body</u> but be assured that in spirit your Prophet will be present in every engagement!"

The roar of approval surpassed anything that had been heard before. Tenskwatawa was not finished yet, but Tom slipped away filled with joyous relief. He rolled up in his blanket and this time slept soundly until dawn.

*　　　　*　　　　*

Two years slid by in what seemed only a few weeks. Tom's wife, Tadpole, and their two growing daughters had come back to Prophetstown, having been summoned by Tecumseh himself. The chief claimed that he wanted the family to come for Tom's comfort, but the truth was that he planned to include women and children in his delegations with the Americans. Their presence would help give the impression that all was well and that the Indians only wanted peace. A small but adequate lodge had been erected for them, but Tom still spent most of his time in the dwelling of Tecumseh and Tenskwatawa.

Tippecanoe, now almost universally referred to as Prophetstown, had spread out to such an extent that it covered all of the nearby meadowland as well as the much of the forests along the Tippecanoe river. Feeding the thousands of warriors, as well as a considerable number of women and children became an intermittent problem.

Both Tecumseh and The Prophet received repeated invitations to meet in Vincennes with Governor William Henry Harrison or his subordinates. Sometimes the chiefs agreed to attend, making sure to appear peaceful, submissive, and even desperate. The results were usually gifts of adequate food from the Governor. Tom Bluefoot earned the respect of both sides as he continued to serve as principal interpreter.

During these years the Indians loyal to The Prophet made frequent trips to the north, engaging with both the British and with Hull, the American General at Fort Detroit. More food and supplies resulted from these visits. Tecumseh and Tenskwatawa were often seen with smiles on their faces, proud to have convinced the Americans that their desires were only peaceful, while at the same time reassuring the British of their loyalty to the king!

With tensions between the Americans and the Indians receding, many of Tenskwatawa's followers left the area to hunt or to tend the gardens they had abandoned in their home villages. This was encouraged and soon resulted in enough food to see them through another winter. It was mute testimony to the charismatic power of The Prophet that nearly every one returned to Prophetstown after their journey home!

Still not all was well during these intervening years. Several leaders, derisively called "government chiefs" such as Little Turtle, Black Hoof, and others, did not agree with those who secretly favored another conflict with the Americans. A notable exception, Main Poc, himself a Shaman of considerable note, was able to convince his Potawatomis that they should side with The Prophet. Unfortunately the Holy Man was invited to visit Washington and was greatly impressed with the white man's world.

 Following his excursion his loyalties began to falter.

Tecumseh and Tenskwatawa continued their duplicity, vowing friendship with Governor Harrison at every opportunity, and there were many. The Prophet could see that these meetings were favorable to his cause, and finally was in complete agreement with Tecumseh's advice that no attack be instigated until the natives were completely ready.

That patience was sorely tested when Harrison managed to "buy" a huge section of land from 'Government Chiefs' of the Miami, Potawatomi, and Delaware. The transaction was called "The Treaty Of Fort Wayne". The Indians of Prophetstown and elsewhere were <u>furious</u>!

Tom Bluefoot was possibly the best informed non-chief in Prophetstown. The evenings in Tenskwatawa's lodge and his work as the interpreter gave him ample news of each happening. Both brothers now seemed to trust him to the extent that he was included in every gathering. He learned much, and he <u>worried</u> more! Tadpole and the girls however, seemed happy enough in the growing village.

Tom was able to keep them well-supplied with food, since the two chiefs' followers tried to out-do each other with gifts for their leaders. For the present all was well with his little family, but Toom-She-chi-Kwa feared for their future. What would become of them when the war, which he was convinced was inevitable, swept through the land?

Concern for his family was not the only thing that was troubling the Wyandot's mind. "What should be my role when the shooting starts?" he often asked himself. Tadpole, always the typical Indian wife and mother, did not hesitate to give advice.

"Stay close to Shooting Star," she said calmly. "As for the one-eyed chief, I do not trust him. He is very much full of himself. He is like the coyote. They snarl and bare their teeth, but when even a young lad gets close they turn and run away!"

Tom Bluefoot smiled at Menseeta, his wife. He appreciated her wisdom and common sense. "Like a coyote, you say? Yes, I see that side of him too. Tell me, do you really believe he has powers from the Master Of Life?"

"I believe he has powers, sure enough, but from <u>whom</u> I would not venture to say!" They both laughed at her insight.

"It is coming!" Tom whispered to his wife, assuming that the little girls were asleep.

"What's coming?" the voice of Tethica, the older child, asked from her pallet near the wall.

"Nothing!" Tadpole whispered quickly. "Go back to sleep before you wake your sister."

After a time, Tom began again. "There will be war very soon. 'Governor Three Names' is even now leading an army north from Vincennes. Of course The Prophet's scouts are watching them. It is inevitable that when the two armies meet it will be war. We must make plans! <u>Now</u>!"

"But I thought Tenskwatawa was ordered not to fight unless Tecumseh was with him," Menseeta whipered. "Is he not far to the south once again? Perhaps there will not be any fighting now. Maybe not at all."

"No, my wife. The Prophet will have no choice. The American army is growing larger every day. The militia from Kain-Tuck-Kee has arrived and Harrison is eager to confront our people. There is little doubt that the Governor is aware that Tecumseh is far away and will not be here to command our forces. He will attack! Of this I am sure!"

"Then we will win!" Tadpole said excitedly. "Never have I seen so many warriors in one place. Shawnee, Miami. Kickapoo, Wyandot, Eel River, even a few Iroquois from far to the east. A vast army, all ready to raise the hatchet! My heart tells me that a great victory is in store for our people!"

Tom did not reply for so long that she finally jabbed him with an elbow. "Well, don't you agree, husband?"

"Ouch!" Tom complained. "Ah, as Tecumseh often says, 'If women were chiefs there would probably be no wars. The enemies would only talk each other to death!'"

She poked him again, harder this time. "Be serious, Tom Bluefoot. Don't we have so many warriors that we will overwhelm the white soldiers?"

"I hope so, but how I wish Tecumseh was here with us. Tenskwatawa has the braves eager to fight. He inspires everyone, even me. But he is not a War Chief."

"Maybe not, but why do we need a war chief, when The Prophet has the words and assurances of The Great Spirit?"

"You are right, and we all are depending on the intervention of the Master Of Life. But no-one can be sure of God's favor. Do you know what that man is telling our braves these days? He is saying that they need not fear the Shemanese guns. 'Their bullets will simply bounce off you bodies,' he tells them. I cannot help being skeptical. Remember I was much involved with General Anthony Wayne in the battle at the Fallen Timbers. I saw what American muskets and their shiny bayonets can do! Please understand, little Tadpole, that because of my years living in the white man's world, it is not easy for me to see the spiritual side of things."

"I know," she murmured. "Let us sleep now. The sun will rise tomorrow. We will talk again."

"One more thing. What will you and the girls do while I am at The Prophet's side in the fighting?"

"Our daughters and I will <u>be</u> <u>there</u>!" she stated stoutly. "I will see that they stay out of danger, but I will join the other women and children who will be helping with the wounded and bringing food and water to the warriors. I know my place, and nothing you say will change my mind in this matter! Now we <u>must</u> get to sleep!"

   *   *   *

The weather remained almost balmy in the early fall of 1811. Tom had barely been home during the last two months. His work as the interpreter for both chiefs had kept him traveling almost constantly. When he did arrive back at his small lodge he was often so tired that most of the time he slept.

This was not the case on November sixth, 1811 however. "What <u>is</u> <u>it</u> Toomie?" Tadpole asked for the third time. "You look exhausted!

Why do you pace about like a caged raccoon? You sit down then jump up again. You may as well tell me. I will find out sooner or later anyway!"

"Put the girls to bed. We must talk, little Tadpole. What I have to say must not be heard by them."

"I will not, husband. I know what is on your mind. It is on my mind as well. The girls have heard the talk. Everyone in Prophetstown knows that the Shemanese troops are making camp very close to us. Do you think an attack will come tomorrow?"

"We are not afraid, Cheswiga," the older girl shyly told her father, calling him by the term of endearment he loved so much. "Our mother will keep us safe if there is a war. My little sister and I will help carry water to our brave warriors. When we go to play in the middle of the village we pretend we are helping in the battle!"

Tom Bluefoot was appalled! "How do you know all of this?" he growled. "What have you been telling them, wife? They should not be planning such things."

"I have told them nothing! As they said, everyone is talking about the coming battle. It would not be possible to not know what is happening here in Prophetstown! All the children will help. Ours will do the same."

"I don't care what the other children . . ."

"Why are you so worried, Toomie? As soon as the bullets start to bounce off our warriors' chests the Long Knives will turn and run away. The Prophet has told us as much," she said, trying hard to convince herself of the truth of these words.

What could he say? His wife was merely stating what every Native American believed to be true. The mood in Prophetstown was almost festive. All assumed that the sooner the Americans attacked, the sooner there would be a great victory for the Indians. Tom desperately wished that he could feel such confidence, but he could not. Tecumseh was again far away. The Prophet at times seemed confused and unsure.

As the little family prepared for bed, Tom uncharacteristically drew his daughters close and hugged them almost desperately. Tadpole saw this of course, and did all she could to reassure her Wyandot husband, but it did little good.

"<u>Get</u> <u>up</u>! <u>Get</u> <u>up</u>!" a young brave shouted, sticking his head inside their door flap. "The Prophet needs you immediately. He has sent me to fetch you!"

Tom had not slept at all and suspected that Tadpole hadn't either. He dressed quickly as Menseeta woke the girls. He knew that there was no time, nor any point in trying to persuade his wife to keep the little girls from the conflict. She was a Native American wife and mother. She would do her duty as she saw it!

Tom glanced at the moon as he hurried to The Prophet's lodge. Perhaps two hours until daylight. He heard no shooting, so it was clear that the action had not yet started. "Do we attack first?" he whispered, almost running to keep up with Tenskwatawa.

"Of course! I have been conferring with The Master Of Life and that is His message. Stay close to me, Tom Bluefoot. I still do not completely trust you. It seems to me that sometimes your loyalties lie with the whites."

Tom did not reply. Tenskwatawa was right

in this. It was true that as Tecumseh had guessed, he had mixed emotions regarding which side should emerge victorious. Perhaps the battle itself would help him decide once and for all.

There was little need for talk. Tenskwatawa and two war chiefs had made the battle plans several days before. Using the element of surprise, an especially chosen few were to break through to the center of the Americans' camp and kill the hated Governor Harrison. Unlit torches had been prepared and made ready for the precise moment of attack. The British had kept their promises. A great many muskets were in the Indians' hands, and of powder and lead there was plenty. The natives of Prophetstown were well prepared.

Tom was impressed. With over a thousand warriors gathered within a quarter of a mile of the American army, few sounds could be heard. Only the soft clicks of the musket pans broke the silence as the Indians saw to their priming. Even the wives and children, hidden on the far side of the creek, made not a sound.

No command was given, but the simultaneous lighting of the torches gave ample evidence of the battle's beginning. Tenskwatawa and Tom were stationed far back from the action, The Prophet kneeling in prayer before a tiny fire of sticks. Uncertain of his duties, Tom was saying a quick prayer to the white man's God when he heard a shot. A sentry had spotted the five special assassins crawling through the undergrowth toward Harrison's tent. The alarm was given and shooting began from both sides. Harrison was not killed, and the advantage of surprise was lost.

Far from unprepared, the American soldiers had been ordered to sleep in their clothes, keeping one hand on their muskets. They rose in an instant, lighted torches of their own, and formed a series of skirmish lines. This development was the farthest thing from The Prophet's hopes and plans. Still the Indians fought valiantly, using muskets and tomahawks with deadly effect.

The battle raged on for nearly two hours. The soldiers were unable to make good use of their bayonets since the natives had spread out and were firing from cover. Although the numbers of dead and wounded was not large for either side, the Indians, outnumbered nearly two to one, could not afford to lose many warriors. As the sun's first rays came peeping over the land it was apparent that The Prophet's braves were losing heart.

"What are you doing this far from the fighting?" Big Drum shouted, nearly in Tenskwatawa's ear. "You must be seen! Our people feel you have abandoned them. Observe Three Names! He rides to and fro, very near to the front lines of battle. He waves his great curved knife and shouts encouragement. His soldiers fight harder. You just sit back here . . ."

"He makes medicine!" Tom shouted. "He invokes the help of The Great Spirit. He works hard at the task he feels is his! Go back to . . ."

"Get him up! I would see him standing before our troops or so help me I will shoot him where he sits!"

There was no question that Big Drum meant every word! "Get up! I will help you. We must go to the battle. Here, take my arm. We will run!" Tom shouted, almost dragging the Seer along. Shouts of joy greeted them as they staggered forward, The Prophet's feet dragging more with every step. "Now!" Tom hissed. "Tell the braves to fight on and fight harder!"

Still half pulling the terrified Shaman, Tom Bluefoot suddenly found the two of them actually in front of a double hand of Indian braves. He jabbed The Prophet hard in the ribs, trying to get him to do something to rally his troops. The Shawnee was shaking so hard he could hardly speak. Finally he tried. "Fight on, brave ones! The victory will be ours. The Master Of Life has told me . . ." Whap! Whap! Two bullets passed directly between Tom and Tenskwatawa's head. The Prophet froze, his one eye wide open and staring. He was unable to move.

Tom gave the man a vicious slap across the face and pushed him so hard he nearly fell. The Prophet seemed to wake up then. He turned and dashed into the trees. Tom started to run after him in the same direction when something like a mighty hand clutched at his left arm and sent him reeling into the bushes.

"Cheswiga! Cheswiga!" Half conscious and sick with pain from his wound, Tom turned his head toward the sound. Was that his little daughter's voice? It was! She was darting

toward him! "<u>No! No! Go back!</u>" he screamed,
but the little girl kept on running, her slim legs
flashing in the morning sun. "<u>Stop!</u>" Tom
screamed again, but the noise of the battle
snatched his words away.

The next thing he saw would remain in his
mind for all of his next fifty winters of life. Tethica
was suddenly hurled forward, arms flying upward
and head thrown back. She landed in a tangled
heap, her spine shattered by the American's
musket ball. She did not move. Tom forced
himself to his knees, fighting nausea and vertigo.
He clutched his bleeding arm, trying to staunch
the flow. After staggering a few steps toward his
fallen daughter he saw Tadpole splashing through
the creek at a dead run. She gathered up her
daughter and sped back into the safety of the
timber.

Rage! Never before in his life had Toom-
She-chi-Kwa felt such a towering emotion. There
was no <u>reason</u> for this atrocity! Standing in full
view of the enemy he shouted a curse at them.
Ignoring the crack of a musket's near miss, he
raced back to the Indians' battle lines. Snatching
a tomahawk from a fallen warrior he roared at
his comrades. "Fight you <u>cowards</u>! Kill the

Shemanese! Kill these beasts who would murder an innocent child who was simply trying to help her wounded father. <u>Follow me</u>!" He took two steps toward the enemy and nearly collapsed. Big Drum grabbed him around the waist and dragged him out of danger.

After another hour the battle was over. Neither side could claim a decisive victory, but for the Native Americans it spelled defeat, and virtually the end of The Prophet's influence.

Tadpole had placed Tethica's body on a bed of moss beside the very rivulet both had forded during the battle. There they mourned the innocent little one's death.

Despite their almost overwhelming grief, for the sake of their only remaining child, Tom and Tadpole did all they could to maintain some semblance of normalcy. The weather had turned cold. Their hastily constructed wegiwa provided little comfort, but they hardly noticed. The once proud village was gone. Small dwellings, temporary shelters, many beautiful tepees erected by the Winnebagos, even the great council lodge, nothing but ashes. Smoke still rose from what had once been Prophetstown.

Governor William Henry Harrison had ordered the village burned to the ground, even going so far as to search out the hidden caches of corn and beans, and adding these vital stores to the raging flames.

Tadpole's simple care of Tom's wound had saved his arm, but the muscles were all shot away. Never would it be the same again. He paid little attention. Grief for his daughter and disappointment about the lost battle filled all his thoughts. "One thing," he told Tadpole one night as they shivered before the shelter's small fire, "I am no longer of two minds. From this day forward I am Wyandot! The white man's world no longer draws me. I am of The People!"

His wife mumbled a reply but it was obvious that she little cared what Toom-She-chi-Kwa had decided. She was grieving. She was not alone. Of those who remained in the forests near what had been Tippecanoe, hardly a family had been spared a dead or severely wounded member.

*   *   *

"Who is out there?" Tom asked, rising from

the buffalo robe that all three had to share.

"It is I, Tenskwatawa. May I enter your lodge?"

"Send him away!" Tadpole hissed angrily. "Has he not caused us enough trouble?"

"You may come in," Tom answered, not sounding very friendly.

"I have brought kindling for your lodge," The Prophet announced, throwing a pitifully small bundle of sticks by the fire pit. "I am hungry. Do you have any food to share? I well remember giving you much corn, beans and venison when you lived near my lodge before the battle."

"We have only a little parched corn. It is soiled and gritty. My woman scraped it up from the ashes. It is what we have been living on these last weeks." He turned to Tadpole and told her to build up the fire and prepare some of the gritty mush.

"Why do you lie under your robe when it is hardly past sundown?" he asked rudely.

"We must keep warm. Also sleeping helps

us forget our empty bellies. Where have you been since the battle, Tenskwatawa? Have you been well?" Tom could tell that Tadpole was disgusted at her husband's polite greeting of this charlatan. Had she been able she would have thrown him out! Being a good wife, of course she said nothing.

"I have been far away. In the north there are those who continue to respect me for my powers."

Stirring a fire-blackened kettle, Menseeta sniffed derisively. She made no effort to hide her disgust at the man's continual attempts to promote himself.

"Do you feel that The Master Of Life deserted us during the battle?" Tom asked, handing The Prophet a burning twig.

Lighting his pipe with exaggerated care, he finally replied. "The Great Spirit was angry because so many of our braves refused to give up whiskey, Shemanese clothing, and white man's bread. I tried as hard as I could to seek forgiveness, but too much damage had already been done. That is why I left the battle early. I needed to find a place of solitude in order to seek

His forgiveness and offer prayers of repentance. My supplications were not enough." He concluded sadly.

Tom had all he could do to keep from lashing out at this fool whose pride had caused the loss of so many lives, including that of his beloved little daughter. Finally under control he regarded the shrunken old man before him. Changing the subject he asked a question. "I understand that Tecumseh has returned from the South. Have you seen him?"

"Yes, I have seen him!" Tenskwatawa snapped. "He struck me in the face and ordered me to go north. He says there are many who seek my life. This I do not believe. I am their spiritual leader! It is only I who stand between the unbelievers and Waasha Maneto. I am not afraid! It is only because the sunlight hurts my only eye that I travel at night. Also . . ."

"Have some more mush," Tom rudely interrupted him. He could not stand to hear any more ridiculous excuses.

Wisely, The Prophet made a hasty exit!

Two days later Tom and Menseeta had

another visitor. Tecumseh and his six travelling
companions arrived at midday. "Are you well? Is
your wound healing?" The chief asked, glancing
around at their pathetic dwelling. "Come to my
lodge. We have some food and warm robes.
Some of the food, such as wheat bread, is of the
Shemanese. My brother would not approve," he
remarked wryly. "but I no longer hold with his
restrictions."

"He has been to visit with us," Tom said,
following the chief. "I believe he is afraid,
although he says he is not. I think he hides during
the day and travels only at night."

"So he has come back here. I sent him north
where they have heard little of the battle. He
should have stayed there!"

"He told us that his medicine failed because
too many did not follow his teaching. Perhaps he
is right."

"I fought with him when I first returned.
Since then I have learned more details about
Harrison's army's advance. I suppose my brother
felt he had no choice but to strike first. Maybe
that was right. Had I been here I might have
reached the same conclusion. It is in the past and

cannot be changed. What is important now is planning for the next step in our struggle."

"The next step?" Toom-She-chi-Kwa asked.

"Yes! The whites are now in a war with the British. We will go to Detroit and join forces with those of the Great King. We are not through fighting yet!"

"May I be of service in some way?" Tom asked, trying to hide his useless arm under his shirt.

"Yes. Again I will be much in need of a trusted interpreter, since there will be many discussions with the British and the Canadians."

As they seated themselves in Tecumseh's newly-constructed lodge the chief turned to Menseeta. "Let me tell you, little mother, that a great sadness lies within my heart at the loss of your oldest girl. I hope you have had time to mourn for her. Several have told me of her attempt to comfort her fallen father, and of your brave action to recover her body. You are a fine example of a courageous wife and mother,"

"Thank you, Chief Shooting Star. Much joy has gone out of our lives, but we carry on in spite of this."

Tecumseh nodded sadly and placed one big hand on their younger daughter's head. "Now Tadpole, your man has told me of your son and brother in Greenville. You are to go to them and stay until the war is over and your husband can return."

"But Chief," Tom cried. "I do not . . ."

"You have already given one child and a shattered arm to our cause. I will not be responsible for any other. I Have spoken!"

"Is it true that an American army is marching toward us here in Detroit?"

"Aho! Bluefoot, I must say that many times you are better informed than the chiefs!" Tecumseh laughed. "Yes it is true enough. They are mostly volunteers from north of the Ohieeo. The one in charge is named Hull. Our spies tell us he is an old man, perhaps too old for the defense of Fort Detroit. But who can say for sure? Is your arm giving you much pain these days?"

"No, it is nearly healed, but useless. That reminds me my chief, I have a request."

"Of course. What is it?"

"Could you assign someone to teach me to load and shoot? Living so long with the Quaker, I was never taught the use of such weapons."

"But why do you ask this? I have always known you to be a man of peace. What has changed your mind?"

"I would like to be of greater service when our people meet the enemy. For too long I have been like the baby otter, unable to decide which side of the river is best. Much as I admire many aspects of the Shemanese world, my mind was made up the instant my little girl was shot down during the Battle of Tippecanoe. From that day forward my allegiance lies with The People alone."

"I am glad, Toomie. Wait here for a moment." He left the fireside then returned shortly, carrying a new British musket.

"Oh no, my chief, you do not have time to waste teaching an untrained person such as me!"

Tecumseh made no reply. Instead he suddenly thrust the heavy weapon at Tom's chest. "Take this," he commanded. "Aim the gun at that big birch tree."

Only able to use his good right arm, Tom struggled to hold the long barrel steady.

"Your intentions are good, my son," Tecumseh said kindly, "but it is plain that you would be of no use when the shooting is heavy." He took the musket back. "As my translator you are worth more than many braves who can lift one of these heavy weapons. Stay with me. I need your ability to change my words into the silly-sounding language of both the Americans and the British."

"I will do my best," Tom said. "Do you plan to cross the Detroit River soon?"

"Within a week. I must be in Amherstburg for yet another conference with the Redcoats. Now that war has been declared, I assume our warriors will be used to help in the capture of Fort Detroit, There may be many deaths on both sides of the fight!"

"Why do we wait? It would seem that by not attacking the Americans at Detroit it will allow even more time for the one you call Hull to march his army north to defend the fort."

"You are right, Toomie. Sometimes I feel that you would have made a good chief, except for one thing."

Surprised and amused, Tom Bluefoot asked, "and what thing is that?"

"The fact that you are a <u>Wyandot</u>!" he growled. "Even now your tribe fills the village called Brown Stone, just across the river from where we sit. They say they cannot make up their minds as to which troops they should join, in this war. Everyone knows they are simply waiting to see which side is stronger. Then they will attach themselves to the winner! <u>Pah</u>!"

"What can be done?"

"I have arranged to parlay with Walk-In-The-Water and Roundhead, principal chiefs of your tribe in the north. I will try to persuade them to side with The People and the British against the Americans. Do you have any influence with the Wyandot nation?"

"Hardly!" Tom murmured wryly. "Many think I am a traitor! It would probably serve your purpose best if I didn't even accompany you to this meeting. You would not need an interpreter there."

"You will be with me!" Tecumseh stated. "Why do your own people feel this way? Is it because of your work at the Greenville Treaty? Probably they have forgotten about that by now. After all, that took place sixteen years ago. Yes, you will be at my side as usual. We will speak of this no more."

Brigadier General William Hull, Governor of Michigan Territory, arrived at Detroit without incident, nearly two thousand militia with him. Emboldened by his successful march, he soon decided to make an excursion into Canada as a sort of attempt to "test the waters" regarding the British defenses.

"Help me with this blasted Shemanese abomination!" Chief Tecumseh demanded, struggling with the striking military jacket he had been given by the British command. It was bright red, like those of the other officers.

"Hold still," Tom said, grinning. He managed to slip the new garment over the chief's shoulders and guide his arms into the sleeves. He stood back then, watching Tecumseh struggle with the many brass buttons.

"Do these things up for me!" he snapped. "Remember that you are still my slave. Do it!"

Tom Bluefoot was careful to avoid a smile as he began working the shiny buttons down the front.

"Pah!" Tecumseh roared. Yanking mightily, he managed to rip the jacket from his back. He threw it into a corner. "How can anyone fight a war wearing anything like that?" he grumbled. "I will dress as a warrior, the same as I always have. I do not need a fancy coat to lead our brothers in battle. Get rid of that thing!"

At that moment a runner burst into the temporary shelter and shouted, "We are winning! The enemy retreats as we advance. The Master Of Life is with us!"

The chief seemed unimpressed. "These are but minor skirmishes," he said as the runner dashed away to spread the news. "Before anyone can claim victory we must strengthen our hold on forts Malden and Detroit. This may mean a further excursion into Canada."

Tom helped his chief prepare to join his warriors. "But it would seem that these small triumphs would do much to encourage our people when the major conflicts begin, would it not?"

"Let me tell you something that once again, if you ever repeat it you are a dead man!"

"You know I can be trusted, Chief Tecumseh. You need not degrade my allegiance with such threats!" Toom-She-chi-Kwa amazed himself with his own bravado.

"Aho! You are right. Sometimes I treat you as the young man you once were. My apologies! You have been a loyal helper and a trusted advisor for these many years, especially now that you have given your complete loyalty to your own people! How many winters are you now?"

"Thirty-eight, my chief. As you can see my braids are now streaked with silver, but they are still on my head!"

Both men laughed as they hurried toward the sounds of battle. The fighting had virtually stopped. Nothing seemed to be happening, so Tecumseh took advantage of the time to encourage his fighters. Tom accompanied him, but stood in the background unless the chief wanted to talk with one of the few British regulars, most of whom seemed to stay well behind the front lines!

At twilight Tom and Tecumseh bivouacked near a number of Shawnees. "I have never heard you say what happened at the siege of Fort Meigs. Several have told me that you showed compassion on some American soldiers. What happened?"

"Aho! You were one very sick interpreter at that time. I could have used you in my consultations with the British, but your wound had become infected again. Is that not correct?"

"Yes, Chief. I was told that for a time I raved and shouted for my dead daughter. Our healer cured me of the fever, but I was too weak to walk for several days after that. So as I said, I have never heard the truth of the engagement at the fort on the Maumee River."

"I am ashamed to say that I did have compassion on the many 'long knives' we captured. Although we fought well we could not breach the ramparts of that great fort, nor could we continue to face the cannon on its walls. He of three names had sent messengers for reinforcements but the fools blundered into our ambush. We took many, many prisoners. Understandably, our young braves, excited by the fighting, began to massacre the captive American soldiers. Scalps were taken, and the defenseless militia were being chopped to pieces. So I ordered the senseless slaughter to stop."

"I am glad you did that, my chief."

"Perhaps I am getting too old for this war," he sighed. "Or it may be that I have spent too much time listening to my slave, whose heart is like that of the Quakers." He glowered over the fire at the Wyandot but Tom knew it was just banter.

"What is your age, Chief Tecumseh?"

"I am not really sure, but my sister keeps track of such things. According to her I am four double hands and one hand more. This is probably about right. You are fortunate that the white man who raised you saw to it that you could read and do the work of many numbers. Would that I could have had such training!"

"Yes, Eli Miller did teach me those things that all Shemanese children must learn, but now I wish that I had been taught 'the way of the warrior'. Then I could be of greater help to our cause here in the north."

Tecumseh made no reply. Whether he agreed could not be determined. "We will sleep now. In two days our forces must prepare for an attack on the fort at Dee-Troyt."

"Will it be a major assault? Do you anticipate much help from the British and Canadians? Will we have cannon to blast the stockade walls?"

"Be quiet! Too many questions. Only hungry magpies gabble away like you. The only answer I can give you now is that it could be a long, hard-fought battle with much loss of life. The Canadians plan to fire their cannon from ships on the river if needed. However, I have a plan which if successful could see the fort surrendered to us without any bloodshed!"

Amazed, Tom asked still another question. "How do you plan to accomplish that?"

"I have told you how much I admire the British Commander, General Isaac Brock. Since you were our interpreter at several meetings, I'm sure you too can see what a great soldier he is. He is a man! What you don't know is that he brought his own interpreter to two of our recent meetings which were held late at night in his tent. You were sleeping!"

"Ah so Chief Shooting Star, had I known of it I would have immediately joined with you. Please accept my apologies. It will never . . ."

"It is of no importance. I have learned that General Brock loves to trick the enemy, just as 'The People' do! Now you will see if our ruse will work on General Hull and his soldiers at Fort Dee-Troyt!"

Tecumseh chuckled as he rolled up in his blanket. "Now we must sleep. There is much to do!"

*　　　　　*　　　　　*

"What do you know of this man?" General Brock asked, handing Tecumseh a cup of sweetened tea.

"Our enemy, Governor of the Mishiganican Territory, has been given the title of Brigadier General in the American army. He fought well against your people in the War of the revolution," Tom Bluefoot translated rapidly. "He is old and some bad birds say he is sick. Still, we must face him and his troops with caution. He knows how to fight, and he finds comfort behind the great walls of his fortress." Tom paused for a moment to readjust the sling which supported his useless left arm.

General Brock looked over his pipe at the Wyandot. "And what of you, young man?" he asked, puffing away.

"Me?"

"Yes, you. Where did you learn such excellent English?" Surprised by the attention, Tom explained how he had been raised by a Quaker. He then had to change these words into the Shawnee tongue for his chief!

"And your arm, were you wounded in battle?"

"Yes sir. I took a musket ball at Tippecanoe. It has healed well, but is of little use anymore."

"I can see that you are of great value to Chief Tecumseh in such deliberations as these in which we are now engaged. Much damage has been done over the centuries by simple misunderstandings. Please know that I and my associates do appreciate your services!"

Tom's face reddened as he interpreted these words to a grinning Tecumseh.

As Tom rapidly kept up the translations, Brock continued conferring with Tecumseh over the strategy needed to take Detroit. "I'm sure your scouts have confirmed the rumor that reinforcements are on the way from the Ohio country. Hull had asked for them, but the fools made the mistake of trying to march men and even some cannon through 'The Great Black Swamp', which lies some seventy mile south of Detroit."

"Aho! Your spies agree with ours. Walk-in-The-Water of the undecided <u>Wyandots</u> [he cast a disapproving eye on his interpreter] has told Small Sayer, my advisor, that they have abandoned that fruitless route and are now sending men and supplies across the lake of the Eries."

"Yes, that is also true. All of this simply means that we must move quickly if we expect to capture that important fort. But first we must defend our garrison at Amhertsburg. Do you agree Chief Tecumseh?"

"Of course! My warriors will be there, ready to fight!"

They continued to discuss strategy well into the night. Subsequent meetings and planning sessions over the coming days proved to be successful, as Fort Maldon at Amhertsburg held against the American attacks.

"Great news! <u>Great news</u>!" Tecumseh shouted.

"Our allies, The British, have taken Michilimackinac Island and taken the fort there without firing a single shot!" Tecumseh cried, pounding Tom on the back. "It has been said that the entire garrison surrendered and have agreed under oath to never take up arms against us again. They were put on ships and sent south on the lake of the Hurons. What great news! Find General Brock, Toomie. We must make plans immediately."

"The word is," Brock exulted, "those at Michilimackinac had never been informed that war had been declared. Our warriors scaled the steep and forbidding hill on the island's north shore during the night. At dawn the Americans were greeted by cannon and hundreds of armed troops looking directly down into the fortification. Their commander had no choice but unconditional surrender!"

"I seek the translator, Tom Bluefoot," a very young Wyandot messenger called out, looking about at the cluster of makeshift dwellings.

"I am the interpreter you seek," Tom replied, eyeing the lad curiously.

"You are to come with me immediately," he said importantly. "Chief Walk-In-The-Water requests your presence."

Tom shot a look at Tecumseh, but the chief motioned for Tom to go on. It would take two hours to reach the Wyandot area.

The big Wyandot chief was talking with half a dozen braves when Tom finally walked up. "I am Toom-She-chi-Kwa, interpreter for the Shawnee war chief, Shooting Star. I believe you sent for me?"

"We already know who you are!" one of the braves snarled, making no attempt to soften his words.

There was no mistaking Chief Walk-In-The-Water. He strode up to the small interpreter and punched him in the chest with a finger. "You are known to stay very close to Shooting Star. Is that not correct?"

"It is, Chief," Tom said stoutly, not backing up a single step. "Unfortunately I am not a warrior, but my heart is in this fight as well as the next man. I do what I can to keep the talking going correctly between The People and our Shemanese allies. Now what is it you want?" Tom had surprised himself at his angry reply. To his amazement the chief chuckled and glanced at his companions.

"Aho! The young badger has spunk! That is good. What happened to your arm?"

Tom told the details of how he had been wounded during the recent battle of Tippecanoe. Slyly he added some heroic, but completely fictitious details to his account. They seemed impressed. After all, who could argue with a withered arm tied up in a sling?

Walk-In-The-Water cast a glance at the others standing by. "I see we have a <u>hero</u> in our midst! We should pay homage to this man." The irony was somewhat overdrawn. "Now Toom-She-chi-Kwa, we have a mission for you."

"I am at your service, Chief."

"You can tell Tecumseh that he can count on the Wyandots' allegiance in this war with the Americans. We await his commands."

Tom was disgusted by this cowardly approach. He was sure that announcing such an important decision was given to him because Chiefs Roundhead and Walk-In-The-Water were too embarrassed to meet face-to-face with Tecumseh, the principal warrior chief. He did not mention his conclusions, but merely nodded his head and replied, "I shall tell him immediately. He will be greatly pleased. And," Tom continued, twisting the knife, "I am sure he would expect you to meet with him in person very soon!"

Naturally, Brock <u>was</u> elated to learn that the vacillating Wyandots had finally given up their neutrality stand and were joining in the war. Further encouragement for the Shawnee war chief came when he learned about the arrival of a significant number of warriors from Michilimackinac, which was now in British hands.

It was time to begin the assault on Detroit. His plan was both risky and audacious. Even though many of the British officers thought it a mistake, he set out to trick the Americans into surrendering Fort Detroit without the need for a long and bitter siege.

"Toomie," Tecumseh said, "you will accompany me and Major General Brock as we approach the fort under a flag of truce. Today go back to your Wyandots and tell them to have all their braves here tomorrow, painted for war! They are to assemble behind you, the Major, and me as we near the walls with the white flag. Those of Roundhead and Walk-In-the-Water are to use war cries, screams, and everything they can do to appear eager to get into the fort and massacre everyone in it! Yes, they are to appear anxious to fight, whether they really are or not! Now go. We will approach the stockade at noon tomorrow."

Tom noticed an uncharacteristic lopsided grin on Chief Tecumseh's face. Like many Native Americans, he liked nothing better than deceiving the enemy!

Some time after dawn the drums began. The Wyandots, led by none other than Roundhead himself, were marching through the forest to assemble at Brock's headquarters. Tecumseh watched their approach, his face showing no emotion. There could be no doubt that they made an impressive sight. Bare to the waist and daubed with blue and vermillion, They kept their muskets or bows proudly in hand. They milled around, waiting for orders. Tom noted that there were more than Wyandots in the gathering. Hearing the drums and anxious to take part, there were Kickapoo, Ottawa from Michilimackinac, and Winnebago. Most had applied war paint.

With Tom interpreting, Major General Isaac Brock addressed the crowd. "We have done much to deceive this one called General Hull, who cowers behind the wooden walls of the fort. We arranged to have one of our runners 'lose' a dispatch in which we wrote that no more of The People were to arrive here, as we have too many already!" He grinned at the painted listeners and many smiled in return.

Tom had to admire the trickery about to be fostered on the officers and soldiers in the fort. He continued translating as Brock further explained the plan. "All drummers, position yourselves close behind those of us with the white flag. Half of you warriors come next, screaming the war cry and brandishing your weapons as if you cannot wait to scale the walls and take many scalps!" He motioned for Tecumseh to come forward and explain the rest of the ruse.

Shooting Star graciously indicated that Roundhead and Walk-In-The-Water should join him. "Those who do not follow the white flag are to begin marching, one hand abreast. Be sure to move across any openings in the forest so the sentries on the walls can see you. Then circle around out of sight and march through again. Keep doing this until you are ordered to stop. Many British regulars will be joining you in this charade. Those watching will be convinced that there are many times more warriors opposing them!"

Roundhead now spoke briefly, relieved that Tecumseh bore him no ill will. "Brothers," he began, "our spies have confirmed the rumor that Hull, he who commands at the fort, is old and sick,He has little heart for the battle and has said as much to his fellow officers. Not only that, but our scouts have seen many women and children entering the fort, seeking safety behind the log walls. Surely the one in charge is fearful of their fate, should the battle go against them. The time is now right to deceive the Americans. Aho! Let us begin!"

Tom experienced moments of *déjà vu*. The present scene eerily mimicked his part in the 1794 surrender at the battle of Fallen Timbers. He stayed directly behind Tecumseh and Major General Brock, who were marching side-by-side. Roundhead and Walk-In-the-Water came next. A squad of six red-coated British regulars brought up the rear.

As the delegation crossed the cleared area surrounding the fort's south gate, they stared in puzzlement at the loopholes near the top of the palisade. Not a soul was to be seen! Had the stronghold been abandoned? After a few more steps the question was dramatically answered. There was a roll of drums and instantly at least one hundred splendidly dressed regulars popped up, rifles aimed point blank at the delegation.

"Stop! Not one more step or I give the order to fire!" the officer shouted. "As of now my troops are commanded to honor the flag of truce . Who speaks for this rabble?"

"I do. I am Major General Isaac Brock of His Majesty's Provincial Army. With me here are Chiefs Roundhead and Walk-In-The-Water of the Wyandot Nation, an honor guard of six British regulars, and my interpreter, Mr. Tom Bluefoot. Now I would request that you order your sentinels to stand down before something unfortunate happens."

The order was promptly given. Although every soldier remained very much in evidence, they did at least shoulder their rifles. "Now," the American officer growled, "state your business here at Fort Detroit."

"I have two more requests," Brock shouted. "First you will please speak slowly, in order to allow time for your English words to be translated for our two Native American Chiefs." The officer nodded but did not reply. "Secondly, this parlay must be between this delegation and the supreme commander of your fortification, whom I am told is General William Hull. We will not continue until he is present on the wall, or we are invited inside the fort."

Again the officer did not reply, but stepped back to make room for a portly older officer dressed in a too-small uniform. It was obvious that Hull had been present all along, probably watching through a loophole in the wall.

Toom-She-chi-Kwa was shocked at the sight of the American General. Even at this distance his sunken eyes and unhealthy pallor indicated a very sick old man. His voice was strong however as he addressed the British delegation. "State your business," he said, making an effort to square his sagging shoulders.

"We are here, General Hull, on a purely humanitarian endeavor. As you can see, these Chiefs and I command a vast force of militia and Indian warriors. Look if you will at the forest beyond you. There you will see but a small fraction of the fighters available for an assault on your fortification. I offer you generous terms for the complete surrender of Fort Detroit. Should you agree, I will withhold the troops for enough time to allow the safe removal of all non-combatants. Your soldiers will either be taken prisoner or placed under a ban of honor to cease all hostilities against our nation and our king."

Tom translated rapidly, both chiefs crowding close to hear the words in their language.

"Should you deny this offer," Brock continued, "I cannot guarantee the behavior of our Indian allies. As you undoubtedly know, they can become <u>ruthless</u> in the extreme! What is your answer?"

There was not a word from Hull or the other officers. They remained standing, staring angrily down at those under the white flag.

"Very well! My offer will stand until nine o'clock tomorrow morning. I would suggest that you spend much of the coming night conferring with your staff and considering the future of the women and children who have sought safety behind your walls. It is within your power to prevent the needless slaughter of so many! I wish you good day."

As Tom finished the final translation he noticed Walk-In-The-Water scowling at General Brock. The chief made no attempt to disguise his displeasure. Roundhead, however, showed no emotion at all. The General ignored both, as he and Tecumseh headed back into the forest.

"Well Toomie, what do you think? Will Hull surrender or fight?"

"I think if the decision were left up to the officer who first spoke to us, there would be no question. That man has eyes for battle! The commander though, I think may accept your offer and surrender. I will ask Chief Tecumseh what he thinks of General Hull and his prediction of what may happen."

Tecumseh seemed relaxed as the delegation entered the trees and joined the waiting forces. He answered Tom's question with but a few words. "I see in that old man a picture of myself was I to live another two double hands of years. His body is sick and his will is sicker! Yes, he will probably surrender unless his officers can convince him otherwise."

"Aho! My Chief! You will live much longer than two double hands of years. You are a long way from the plight of the General of Fort Detroit. Your body and your spirit are strong! The British General, Brock, seated over there with a pan of food has told me of his great respect for you as a man and for your leadership ability. I can tell you that such praise for one of The People by a British man is rare indeed!"

"Pah! You will help provide me with food, then all of us must rest and sleep until nightfall. Tell Brock to order double sentries all around our camp, and keep half the warriors awake and armed during the night."

"Of course! Sit over there until I can get your food ready. May I ask you a question?"

"Always with the questions! This trait of yours must come from your years living in the Shemanese world. All they seem to do is <u>talk</u>! And when they are not talking they are <u>going</u> <u>somewhere</u>! What is your question, Wyandot?"

"I would ask the reason for such heightened security. It would seem to me that both sides are bound by the truce. At least until morning."

"Toom-She-chi-Kwa, sometimes I despair for your sanity! It was you yourself who told me that Black Pipe, your uncle, had told you that one must always imagine himself in the place of his enemy. That was very good advice. Were I the Commander of fort Dee-Troiyt on this night, I would dishonor the truce and attack before dawn. Of course I am not that man, and I doubt if he has the will. Still, we must be alert. We are not the only ones who know how to play tricks!"

"Tom Bluefoot," General Brock called. "Eat and rest until dusk, then you will accompany me through the camp to encourage both your people and mine. I'm ordering that each one make his own fire. To those on the walls it will appear that our forces are much greater than they really are. Then when the moon is high they are to await my signal to begin drumming. Larger fires are to be kindled at various locations and all should make as much noise as possible. War cries, firing in the air, drums, everything!"

At evening they moved through the camp, General Brock giving encouragement. Tom translated the General's words as well as his orders for the night. Tecumseh's suggestions were followed as well, and the encampment was made secure.

At midnight Tom nearly leaped from beneath a piece of moose hide when the racket suddenly began. There was no doubt that further sleep was impossible for combatants on either side. He could not help feeling sorry for the women and children behind the log walls of Fort Detroit. Undoubtedly most had heard of the savagery perpetrated on those defeated by victorious Indians. Their terror would be increased by the ominous sounds echoing from the forest. It was a cruel trick, but Tom hoped it would be effective enough to force Hull to surrender.

At nine o'clock in the morning the August sun was hot already. General Brock snapped his watch closed and assembled the truce delegation. The white flag hung limp in the stillness as they neared the walls. Tom was surprised to see General Hull standing alone on the catwalk near the southwestern corner of the fort. His face was a study in dejection and despair.

"Good morning, General," Brock shouted. "We await your decision."

Without hesitation the American general replied, his voice sounding weak and tragic. "In view of the fact that we are greatly outnumbered, and in consideration for the lives of the many women and children inside our walls, I agree to surrender this fortification . . . with one condition."

"What is it?"

"We require three days to make a proper and orderly abandonment. My junior officers, who do not agree with surrender, and I, feel that this is but a reasonable request."

General Brock, with Chief Roundhead, Walk-In-The-Water, and Tecumseh, by his side, shouted, "You have three <u>hours</u>! He saluted smartly, did a very proper about-face, and the delegation marched back to their encampment.

Tom was overjoyed at this surprising development. He knew that Brock had shortened the evacuation time because he did not know how long he could contain the Indians. Tom was completely sympathetic to the Indian cause, but he hated the thought of the butchery of innocent people which often followed an Indian victory. The delegation had hardly reached the forest when shouts and clashing sounds signaled that the evacuation of Fort Detroit was already in progress!

Brock had all he could do to keep the Indians from storming the fort before the three hour truce had ended. By forcing such a rapid evacuation, the general had seen to it that much plunder would remain for the victors. Even so there was not much celebrating during the three hours. The natives would have preferred a fight!

"What will happen to the American soldiers in the fort?" Tom asked as they followed the chiefs toward the open gate.

"I will see that the Ohio militia is paroled, and all have safe passage back to Ohio Territory, where they will be banned from any further action against our king. The American regulars will be taken to Quebec City as prisoners of war. Now you must help me and the chiefs keep a careful eye on the savages . . .excuse me! I meant on the natives! to be sure there is an orderly distribution of the spoils of war."

Tom kept Roundhead and Tecumseh informed of everything the General was saying. Walk-In-The-Water had gone back to his people. It took all Brock and the chiefs could do to avoid a mad melee when the Indians were allowed to enter. There was good reason! The

People were shocked at what lay before them: twenty cannon, more than two thousand rifles and muskets, kegs of powder, bags of bullets, cases of rum, food, and all kinds of tools and household goods! Thanks to General Brock's foresight, distribution of the booty was carried out with very few problems.

General Hull, Commander of Fort Detroit, was treated fairly , and provided with a wagon and team for his ignominious trip back to Ohio. Once there he would certainly face a court martial for being duped by such an age-old trick!

Brock made a slight motion to Tom Bluefoot. Tecumseh and Roundhead had each taken an elaborate sword from the officers' chambers, and were moving on to see what else might be "liberated". Tom hurried up to see what his General wanted.

"Here. Take this case Tom. You have earned this and more!"

"Thank you General, but there's nothing I really need here. Maybe . . ."

"You <u>may</u> need what's in this box some time. Go ahead, open it."

Toom-She-chi-Kwa worked the clasp and lifted the mahogany lid. His eyes popped open in surprise. Nestled neatly on their bed of blue velvet lay a brace of the most beautiful small pistols he had ever seen. "But . . .General these must be . . . be worth . . .I mean thank you sir!"

"You are welcome. I found them in a hidden drawer under the Commandant's desk. Do you know how to shoot a pistol?"

"No sir, I don't, but I intend to learn as quick as I can!"

"Find Sarah Willow Tree among the Potawatomi and ask her to meet us at my command tent," Brock said, grinning at his stunned interpreter.

Late that evening the Potawatomi chief arrived, the Indian woman with him. "Ah so, Toom- She-chi-Kwa, the General has told me of your gift. Willow Tree here will build you holsters for them. You can wear them on your waist. All will then see a man well-armed and proud. One arm is enough for a pistol!"

Sarah Willow Tree said hardly a word as she stretched a thong around his waist to determine his size. She bit a small notch in the leather to mark the length. Next she lifted one of the pistols, placed it on a scrap of deerskin and by scratching around the weapon, made a pattern. Still silent, she put the pistol back in its nest and walked into the forest.

Tom was elated. He planned to soon find someone to teach him to load and shoot. He knew that being virtually one-armed, there was little chance he would ever be able to hold and aim a heavy rifle. The pistols were exactly what he needed! Whether he would ever actually wear them remained to be seen.

With little translation necessary, Tom gained Brock's permission to offer his help with the Americans' evacuation. Ignoring the hateful looks of the hurrying soldiers, he carried supplies, uniforms, foodstuffs, and anything else that was being stacked on a street in the Detroit village. The three hour truce was ending. He returned to Tecumseh as the chief prepared to leave. "What is to happen now?" he asked, almost shouting to be heard over the hubbub of evacuation.

"All chiefs are to keep careful control over our victorious warriors. We are pledged to avoid any massacre of citizens or soldiers. It is a stupid mandate, and one that may cause problems for the British in the future. We shall see. While you were foolishly helping the fleeing troops, did you see a Shemanese healer among them?"

"No, but there was much confusion. I think I was lucky that one of the Ottawa braves didn't club me to death! I could see the hate in his eyes!"

Tecumseh nodded, apparently not surprised. "You were a fool to venture among the defeated enemy as you did. Still it is said that Waasha Maneto watches over children and fools, so you were lucky. Now there is little time remaining. Go among the enemy once more. I have been informed that Three Dogs, a Shawnee never noted for much intelligence, accidentally shot himself in the leg during the noise-making last night. I am told the doctor has only one eye, but has some skill in treating such wounds."

Tom nearly fainted. "What . . .what . . .was that you said . . was . . ."

"You were not listening as usual. I said you were lucky."

"No! No. About the <u>healer</u>. He has only one eye?"

"That is what I have been told. Yes . . ."

Tom was off at a dead run, nearly bowling over soldiers, Indians, and women, in a mad dash through the fort. He saw him then, heading out of the gate, carrying a small child in his arms.

"Sean! <u>Sean</u>!" Tom shouted, shoving people aside. "Sean, it's me, Tom Bluefoot! Stop for a minute."

To his surprise, Doctor Sean O'Casey gave him an angry look and kept on walking.

"I saw you running around in the fort a few minutes ago. What do you want? This little girl got trampled in the rush. She has a broken leg which must be set immediately."

Tom was astonished. Why was he being treated like this, he wondered.

"Well hurry up! I have no time to waste on a <u>traitor</u>!"

So <u>that</u> was it. "Sean, please let me explain," he pleaded. "After you finish with the child come to General Brock's headquarters. We have a gunshot wound that needs your services. We can talk then. We <u>need</u> to talk, Sean!"

The doctor was gone, carrying the small Indian child into a house near Fort Detroit. Tom walked slowly away, deeply distressed.

Several hours later doctor O'Casey appeared carrying his medical kit, a scowl in his face. "How did one of your rebels get wounded anyway?" he demanded, facing General Brock. "As far as I could tell there was no shooting from either side during this fiasco!"

Tecumseh waited for Tom to translate, then asked him to explain to the doctor the careless self-inflicted wound. The chief was not particularly rude, which surprised Tom Bluefoot. A messenger was sent to find the wounded brave and get men to carry him to Brock's command tent.

"Sean! Sean!" Tom pleaded. "Sit down here and let me tell you what has happened since my escape from the jail at Fort Pitt."

Sean did not respond so Tom continued. "First tell me what has been happening in your life. Is Chloe well? Do you have children? How did you end up in the American army?"

Sean softened somewhat, but did not belabor his answers. "Chloe is fine. We have two boys. She and a young doctor-in-training tend the sick in Captain Friederich's old Pittsburgh office. The Captain no longer practices medicine. He is old, and has trouble remembering anything. He even forgets to eat. Chloe takes care of him." There was a moment of silence. Belatedly, Sean finally asked, "What happened to your arm?"

"I want to hear more, Sean. A lot of time has passed since Simon and I escaped. You did not say how you became attached to the army. Is Chloe with you?"

"I was 'conscripted'!" Sean growled. "No, Chloe and the boys had to stay in Pittsburgh. Although I miss them terribly, I am glad they're not here. I suppose I will be going back to them soon, the same as the soldiers. I am pledged to no longer take part in the war. We leave tomorrow. Now tell me of your life. I see that you have taken to wearing your Indian clothes again."

"Oh Sean, I wish you would try to understand. I had no choice. For a while I worked in a Frenchman's trading post near Greenville, but I had to leave when I learned that the authorities were still looking for Simon and me. I had married a Wyandot widow, but when I left the trading post job I had no a way to support her. We had two daughters. Tecumseh and his brother, Tenskwatawa took care of us in return for my interpreting for them. There was a battle at . . ."

Four braves entered the area, carrying the injured man on a blanket. Sean took over immediately, the very epitome of confidence and skill. "Continue, Tom. I'm still listening," he said, busy at his work.

"I can stop talking if it will distract you," Tom said as Sean probed for the musket ball. "But I must ask about Eli Miller and the grist mill. What happened there?"

"Go Ahead. This man hasn't uttered a peep yet! I've never seen such courage as the Native Americans show, no matter which side they are on! I'm sorry to tell you that the Quaker died after you escaped. He never regained consciousness. The mill was sold and all the relations returned to Virginia."

"I have never actually <u>fought</u> in any of these battles," said Tom, "but I was helping The Prophet when I took a bullet in the arm. The impact knocked me down. My wife, Tadpole, and our two daughters were camp followers at that time. When my seven-year-old saw me fall, she broke free from her mother and came running toward me. An American soldier shot her in the back. There was no need for that! She was only a child, afraid for her father. From that time on I have aligned myself with Tecumseh and his brother, called 'The Prophet', against the Americans and the British who fight with them. If you cannot understand my feelings then I am sorry, but that is how it is!"

The wounded man flinched as the doctor prized a fifty caliber musket ball from deep behind his shin bone. The Indian still did not cry out, but a pitiful agonized moan escaped his lips just before he fainted. "I can see how you feel, Tom. I'm sorry for my attitude toward the best friend I ever had, but such atrocities happen from your braves too." He turned to General Brock, who was talking to two American lieutenants about evacuation details. "My compliments, sir. By restraining your Indian allies after our surrender, you have saved countless lives and avoided unimaginable mutilations! Would that all officers would show such compassion."

Toom-She-chi-Kwa was well aware that Doctor O'Casey had said these words for his benefit as well. Yes, terrible things happen in war, no matter where your sympathies lie.

"And what happened to the black man who escaped with you? I forget his name," Sean said, bandaging the leg wound.

Tom laughed for the first time. "I don't know how well you knew the slave, but he and his little brother were two of the cleverest men I've ever come across! Would you believe that now he calls himself a <u>king</u>? He has two wives, a son, a crown, and a growing following of 'subjects'! He really beats everything, Sean!"

Sean grinned too. "Where is he now? Do you know?"

"He and his wives were heading west to avoid capture by the 'slave catchers'. I think he planned to cross the Mississippi. I'm sure that wherever he is, that rascal will be <u>doing fine</u>!"

Both men were beginning to feel comfortable with each other again. "What will happen now?" Tom asked as Sean re-packed his equipment.

"I'll be heading back to Ohio with the troops. I plan to stay out of sight, lest I get 'conscripted' again, regardless of the ban. And you?"

"After this victory I'm sure General Brock, our Indians, and the British will be marching into Canada to continue the fighting. I will be going with them."

"I wish you luck, Tom. Promise me one thing: when all of this craziness is finally over, come to Pittsburgh and visit Chloe and me. Bring your wife and child."

"I promise, Sean. Now remember, there may be bounty hunters still looking for me back there. If you talk of our meeting here in Detroit don't use my name. When we do get together we should always stand side-by-side. That way I can be your other eye and you can be my left arm!"

"I won't forget, my friend. Goodbye, God go with you."

"May Waasha Maneto protect you, Doctor O'Casey! Goodbye."

*   *   *

"Do you see that big man moving among the Kentucky militia?"

"Yes General, I see him and I <u>know</u> him! That man with the coonskin hat is none other than Simon Kenton, the Indian fighter!" Tom said, handing the telescope back to General Brock. "Blue Jacket and Tecumseh had ordered a squad of warrior to kill him as soon as war seemed imminent. But, as they had learned earlier, he is a hard man to kill!"

Brock handed the telescope over to Tecumseh who spent several moments studying the enemy. They were hidden in a bit of swampy ground very close, almost too close, to the enemy at a Canadian village called Moraviantown. The place had been named for a religious group which had brought some Lenape there because of their fear of the Iroquois.

"This <u>Proctor</u>!" Tecumseh growled. "He has no desire to fight! Why else did he abandon Fort Malden? Our red brothers west of Detroit will now be unprotected. We have no choice but to follow this cowardly Shemanese! <u>Pah</u>!"

General Brock left soon after this, much to Tecumseh's disappointment. Tom did his best to reassure his chief by pointing out that Procter, whatever they thought of his leadership, had had no choice but to retreat north up the Thames River. Commodore Oliver Hazard Perry's ships had kept British supplies from Amhertsburgh, causing near starvation there. Few details of the situation were available, but it made little difference. Tecumseh and most of his warriors wanted a <u>fight</u>!

"What are you doing?" Tecumseh asked rudely as Major General Henry Proctor was hurrying to load a large bateau with sacks of foodstuffs. Tom diplomatically softened the question as he translated, but one look at Tecumseh's face told the British General more than his words!

"Tell him I must see to the safety of my wife and children! Harrison's troops are not far behind. I have ordered Colonel Warburton to take command. Tell your chief that he is welcome to accompany me as we head north. Further, tell him that this is not a retreat, but is in fact a 'strategic withdrawal.'"

Tom did his best , but Tecumseh was furious. "Much more of this sort of 'leaderrship'," the chief used the term with heavy derision, "and his natives will dessert to the west. Who could blame them?"

Two hours later Colonel Warburton took charge, but wisely included Chief Tecumseh in every important decision. Both leaders were well aware that they were badly outnumbered. William Henry Harrison was in command of at least five thousand regulars and militia, while the British and Indian warriors totaled less than two thousand. This imbalance did not deter Chief Shooting Star however.

The Americans came relentlessly forward. Their mounted regulars had no trouble advancing, since foolishly, Proctor had not taken time to block the trail behind his retreat. He had at least seen to the placing of a cannon in the road facing back toward the Americans, but with the sight of the charging mounted troops, the British emulated their officers, abandoned the field piece, and ran away! Most of Proctor's men surrendered.

"Here they come again!" Tecumseh shouted as a small number of horses pounded forward, some skirting the swamp and a few splashing through. Led by their fighting War Chief, the Indians managed a volley of fire which took a heavy toll on the cavalry. A further set-back occurred as the invading army lost Major James Johnson, shot in the chest.

"Toomie! Toom-she-chi-Kwa! Are you here?"

"Right here, Shooting Star! I'm trying to stop the bleeding on this man's leg. What do you need?"

Tecumseh paid little attention to the wounded Canadian. He spoke rapidly but calmly. "Tom Bluefoot, I must ask you for a pledge of obedience."

"Yes, Chief Tecumseh. Anything!"

"It is apparent to me that we cannot win this battle, nor probably the war either. Last night I heard the owl calling. I believe that bird heralds my spirit. Tomorrow may be my last day upon this earth. Now! Promise me this: you have not chosen to fight, as you have not worn your fine new pistols. Stay close beside me. When I fall, drag my body away from the conflict. Make it appear that I was not even in the battle. I will

<u>not</u> allow the Shemanese or their treacherous Indian allies to savage my dead body. <u>Swear it</u>!"

"I swear it will be done, <u>if necessary</u>, but I do not believe that Waasha Maneto has any intention of calling you yet!"

"Take these things," he said urgently. He had put all of his medals, arm bands, and even his prized gold earrings [which Tom instantly recognized] into a small pouch. "If I fall I wish to be just like any one of our brave warrior, not as the chief that I am."

"Please, my chief, do not talk in this manner. You will live to fight on for a long time! I know . . ."

"Take this! Do not let it depart from your hand!" The pipe tomahawk felt unusually heavy in Tom's good right hand. "Now, one more pledge from one who is still my <u>slave</u>!" Tecumseh managed a tired smile, then continued. "If I fall, badly wounded, but the spirit has not left my body I am trusting you to bury this hatchet in my skull. Send me to the Happy Land before any of The People, who have chosen to fight against us can cut my body to pieces. Put your hand in my armpit. Now <u>swear it</u>!"

Tom could hardly believe what he was hearing. Tecumseh, Shawnee War Chief, diplomat, one always working toward the future good of his race, had never spoken in such a way. Toom-she-chi-Kwa was crushed. What if it were true? Could he deliver such a stroke to this noble warrior? He hoped desperately that Shooting

Star would not come to such an inglorious end, and that he, Tom Bluefoot, would not have to be a part of it!

"Swear it!" Tecumseh repeated, checking the load in his rifle.

"I swear my chief, and my friend!"

Firing became sporadic as Tecumseh and his warriors fought valiantly to slow the American advance. Tom felt a seething hatred for the retreating General Proctor.

"This Warburton," one of Tecumseh's lieutenants asked, "is he a warrior worth our final hour?"

"He seems to be a good officer, but he has been given an almost impossible assignment," Tom replied, looking around for Tecumseh. "I do not believe our chief knows the man, but he certainly does know Proctor! Pah!"

The Americans came steadily on, fixed bayonets aimed directly at the forest on the banks of the Thames. While most of the American troops had been told that "the redskins can't shoot straight", they saw their comrades double up and fall, shot dead by a hidden Indian whose marksmanship was superior to that of most of the attackers!

"Get back further in the trees, Toomie," Tecumseh ordered. "Remember you pledge! If you fall or even take a bullet in your good arm, you will be unable to fulfill your vows to me."

Tom was greatly encouraged when he saw his chief hurrying from one group of fighters to another, rallying them to keep covering for Proctor and his family's retreat. His encouragement did not last however.

Suddenly shooting Star could be seen with a group of six warriors, obviously preparing for a rally against their pursuers. A squad of some twenty mounted cavalry was attempting to flank the defenders by galloping along the sandy shallows of the Thames River. Before Tecumseh could get his men into favorable firing position, Chief Roundhead [Stayeghtha] led a small force out of the forest, intending to stop the cavalry's flanking maneuver.

Tom could see Tecumseh's expression of approval and respect for the Wyandot chief. Hesitant though he and his braves had been, they were now acquitting themselves with great honor. Then tragedy struck!

Roundhead went down, a sabre nearly decapitating him. His fighting ax went flying from his fingers. His companions drove the horsemen back enough to drag their leader's body into the forest. Tom could not believe what he was seeing. Roundhead had done all he could to live in peace with the Shemanese. Now, here beside the Thames River in Canada he lay dead from a white man's sword. Toom-She-chi-Kwa was reminded once again of his long dead uncle, Black Pipe, who often said, *"Sooner or later in a man's life will come the time to fight. Then that man must show his courage."*

Tom had no time for reflection. Leading an attack eerily like that of the fallen Wyandot, Tecumseh rushed directly into a rank of four mounted militia. He managed to thrust his short lance into the thigh of the sergeant who was leading the charge, but one of the troop fired his pistol point blank into Tecumseh's chest. The chief went down hard. The riders skirted his motionless body and kept on galloping north, having no idea that the man they had brought down was perhaps the most famous and respected American Indian leader in all of America and Canada!

Tom, still gripping Tecumseh's tomahawk, fought down the urge to run to his fallen leader. He knew that if he should be wounded he would be unable to fulfill his vow. He waited, hidden in a dense willow thicket, until even the slogging foot soldiers had marched on past the few hidden warriors. At last, tears nearly blinding him, he knelt beside the man whose life blood was soaking the Canadian sand. The few remaining Indians, busy seeing to their own dead and wounded paid little attention, since even they had been fooled by their chief's deliberate lack of regalia.

Tecumseh was still alive! His chest rose and fell as he struggled to breathe. That the wound was lethal Tom had no doubt. "Can you hear me, my chief?" Tom spoke into he man's ear. Tecumseh's eyes opened slightly, but he showed no other indication of life.

Tom gently shook Shooting Star's shoulder but this only made more blood flow from the wound exactly in the center of his chest. The Wyandot spoke to him again but still there was no response. A decision must now be made. Was the great warrior suffering with pain? Did he have any awareness of Tom's presence? Toom-She-chi-Kwa had been given a terrible assignment but as his "white father", Eli Miller often quoted, *"A promise made is a debt unpaid!"*

Tom Bluefoot, interpreter and friend of the fallen hero, sat quietly at the edge of the Thames. No longer young, Tom remembered so much of what the dying man had meant to him. Tears no longer streaked his copper-colored cheeks but a great sadness was evidence enough of the depth of his feelings. He stared in horror at Tecumseh's tomahawk, but finally hefted it in his good right hand. He stood then, eyes lifted to the heavens. His prayers were a mingling of those to Waasha Maneto and to the Shemanese "Three Part God". Trying hard to keep from seeing Shooting Star's serene-looking face, he knelt on one knee and raised the ax over his head. He was in the very act of striking when he heard something like a long-drawn-out sigh.

Tecumseh was dead

Tom had a difficult time dragging the body far into the forest. It was almost impossible with only one functioning arm, but finally he succeeded. There were no other bodies in the little glade Tom had chosen for the Shawnee leader's final resting place. Tom thought it would be what Tecumseh would have wanted.

Using the great chief's own tomahawk he chopped and scraped a trench beside the fallen hero's body and slid him gently into it, placing the man's favorite ax by his side. He covered the grave with a scattering of leaves and moss, then brushed the sand to hide the burial from any accidental discovery by one of the braves from Harrison's army.

Throughout the history of the American and Canadian nations, Tecumseh's burial site would be endlessly discussed and argued about, but it would never be found!

A great sense of sadness and lethargy gripped the interpreter. For several hours he sat at the edge of the Wyandot camp and thought about his life. Where should he go from here? It was obvious to everyone that despite the battles and skirmishes still being fought near fort Niagara, the war was lost to the British and Indian coalition.

Tom was suddenly startled by a shout from beyond the camp. "Hello the fire! It is I, The Prophet, seeking permission to rest by your side. With me are seven comrades, each of whom showed uncommon courage and valor in the conflict."

"Come in, Tenskwatawa," Grey Stone replied. "We have been wondering where you were during the battle at the Thames."

"So!" The Prophet snapped. "I have not yet been offered food or a place by your fire, and already you question my activities during the fighting." He sat down, glowering at the Wyandots, especially Tom Bluefoot. "This is what occupied my time and energy as we moved up the river, when that British fool, Proctor, was running away with his family and a cartload of goods. I told him to ready the great gun. "Aim it" I told him, "behind us to stop Harrison's army before they could catch up with us. Then I said . . ."

"Yes, we saw the cannon abandoned at the side of the road. What happened to it?"

"Those who were to make the gun shoot became scared and ran on north. Pah!"

"And where was your brother, our War Chief, during all of this?" Grey Stone demanded.

"He was at my side, just as he should have been! My medicine was strong and he relied on me to keep him safe. I then had to travel north toward Moraviantown. Shooting Star told all the women and children to go with Proctor for their safety."

"But what of Tecumseh?" one of the braves asked again.

"I have been told that he and a small war party remained behind to destroy the bridges and hold the Longknives back. I had planned to help in that rearguard action but I was needed elsewhere. As for my brother's whereabouts, I do not know and the Great Spirit has not seen fit to tell me."

"Tecumseh is <u>dead</u>!" Tom said bitterly.

Shocked, Tenskwatawa looked from one to another, his one eye wide open. "It cannot be," he wailed, falling to his knees. "The Master Of Life assured me that no harm would come to him! My medicine is <u>strong</u>! I don't believe that Shooting Star has gone to the 'Happy Place'. Take me to his body immediately!"

"He is probably buried by now," Tom said sadly, "but no one knows where." This was true in a sense, but Tom had no choice. He had to honor the great chief's last request.

"But . . . but . . . my medicine! It has never failed before! I will . . ."

"Do not speak to <u>me</u> of 'your medicine'!" Grey Stone snarled. "You told us that your prayers to The Great Spirit would make the American bullets bounce off our bodies with no harm! Pah! Look at my shoulder." He pulled his tunic open to show a ragged gash, still not completely healed. "Many of our brave warriors had similar wounds. Some of them are dead. Do not speak to me of your magical powers!"

The Prophet stomped away from the camp, motioning for Tom Bluefoot to follow. As Tenskwatawa had expected, they were welcomed at a small camp of

Wyandots. It was a very subdued meeting, as the camp was still mourning the death of their revered leader, Chief Roundhead. Tom noticed that although The Prophet was treated politely, the adoration the man had come to expect did not materialize.

Suddenly the quiet was shattered by a mounted messenger riding pell-mell through the camp. "Mount your horses!" he screamed. "The Americans have overtaken our fleeing women and children. Proctor's wagon load of supplies has been seized. Leave everything! Flee for your lives!" He pounded into the forest to warn other encampments.

With no thought for the safety of those who still believed in him, Tenskwatawa seized a horse, threw a blanket over its back and galloped away, not to stop until he had found safety in the village of Dundas, nearly forty miles to the east. Offered a battered old nag, Tom plodded along, soon far behind.

Bluefoot's companions were certainly not alone in the Canadian village of Dundas. Refugees, both warriors and civilians, were arriving there by the hour. All were hungry and few had clothing adequate for the coming winter. While the British had compassion for the more than two thousand refugees, there was not enough food and clothing for half that many.

Once again The People must spend a miserable winter, freezing and hungry.

Tom was kept busy much of the time, serving as

an interpreter for the British officers who often visited the camp. The Prophet had also moved into the same large longhouse where Toom-She-chi- Kwa had been invited to stay.

"Pah!" The Prophet growled at a small group of Potawatomi huddled near the central fire. "I am sure you have heard what the treacherous Redcoats are planning now." Tom and the others did not respond, as at this time the holy man was merely tolerated by most. Hearing no response, he answered his own question. "They fear that many braves will begin leaving when spring comes. They try to bolster our courage by inviting some of our chiefs to their great city of Quebec."

"Will you be leaving soon?" Tom asked innocently as some hid their smiles.

"I will not be going. They urged me, and promised many presents, but my duty is here with those in dire need." He looked around the circle to see what effect such noble words had on the listeners. No one looked at him, and no one said a word. Even the youngest knew that it was all a lie. Tenskwatawa had not been invited!

No one having challenged him, he continued his angry diatribe. "Would I associate with such rabble? Also attending this delegation will be Packeeta, my nephew, Tecumseh's son. He is no more than a boy! No! I declined their urgings and will do all I can to get us food from the British. I have spoken!"

In the days and months that followed, only the

high-ranking officers, both British and American were kept informed of the peace negotiations taking place across the ocean in Ghent, Belgium. Had word of the progress gone out, nearly all of the Indians would have immediately deserted the cause and headed for their homelands.

Although most of the other chiefs paid little attention to The Prophet, the British continued to give him honor, hoping that he would be able to assist them when the war finally ended. This, of course, merely increased the vain man's delusions of his own importance. For those forced to live in the same longhouse, his behavior became almost unbearable.

"What is to happen now that we find ourselves in this village with all these warriors, as well as women and children?" Tom asked, scraping the last crumbs of corn from his bowl.

"Now that I have been named 'Principal Chief Of All Western Tribes', my advice and opinions are much in demand," The Prophet replied grandly. "A vast army of The People, as well as some Redcoats will soon engage the Americans at the river above the great waterfall they call Nia-grrie."

"Will you then lead us in this coming conflict?" Tom asked.

"Of course! You sometimes seem to be without much sense, Tom Bluefoot. Who else but I would be in charge? Of course one of my importance may not be permitted to be in the very front of the attack. My position will be to stay back and plan each segment of the engagement."

Tom experienced a strange combination of disgust and pity as he absorbed these latest declarations. He knew he must continue to support the man, but if even a part of this was true The Prophet would be in dire need of an unbiased interpreter. He held his tongue.

*   *   *

There were several attempts at major battles during the following year-and-a-half, but The Prophet always managed to arrive with his warriors a little too late to engage in any serious fighting!

"Will all this fighting and bickering ever be <u>over</u>?" Tom Bluefoot sighed, hanging his dripping moccasins on a stick beside the fire.

"The Master Of Life has told me . . ." Tenskwatawa began, but seeing the looks of disgust on the others nearby, he changed his tune. "It is the belief of all the chiefs and officers that there will be no more fighting in the spring," he concluded lamely.

"And what are your plans then?" Tom asked.

"There are many who beg me to return to the Wabash and rebuild our villages there. If Harrison or some other foolish American makes this impossible, I plan to lead a great number of our people far west beyond The Father Of Waters to the land of the Kansans. There we will live in peace, following the ways of our ancestors."

"And you will be this great gathering's religious leader, I presume?" Main Poc, chief of the Potawatomi asked, turning the slab of pork the British had finally provided.

The seer turned an angry eye on the speaker, not sure if the question was meant as a compliment or an insult.

"I believe," he answered grandly, "it is now time for me to inform all of you that I have been in secret meetings with the Americans. They are anxious to bring us back to our homelands, where all can live in peace."

"Aho!" someone said, but most remained silent. The 'secret meetings' he alluded to were not secret to most of the chiefs. They too had been contacted, but so far none had seen fit to leave Canada. The British had provided food and some clothing, and even though neither was enough, most felt it was more than they would have back in the Northwest Territory. They were, after all, losers in the war.

Due to his many sessions as an interpreter Tom was known to most of the Indians. As they waited for a clear indication that it would be safe and prudent to travel south, all were becoming restless and bored. The Redcoats had continued to encourage hunting and trapping excursions, but welcome as fresh meat would have been, it was a foolish dream. Only a few braves had decent guns, and those who did had no way to get powder and lead. To make matters worse, the best hunters knew that there was no game to hunt! So they remained by their smoky fires, shared the meager food rations, and grumbled.

"You seem very quiet tonight," Knee Bell stated, handing Tom a sliver of hard beef. A Chippewa from Michigan Territory, he and Tom had become friends. Although he was much younger than Tom Bluefoot, they had often worked together during the many conferences. Knee Bell was fluent in the language of the Winnebago, Sac Fox, and of course his own Chippewa tongue. He had learned English while working for the British soldiers in Fort Michilimackinac.

"It is because there is nothing to do," Tom replied gloomily. "We sit by the fire and hear stories of great deeds done by those who love to tell them. My guess is that half of what they brag about never happened!"

"More than half!" the Chippewa chuckled. "You are missing your wife and daughter aren't you? How long has it been since you have seen them?"

"Perhaps seven or eight years. My little girl must be a woman now. She may have married. I hope she and Tadpole are happy. When I left they had gone to the lodge of her brother. He seemed a good man who would care for them. I hope so."

"That does not appear to explain all of your low spirits," Tom's friend noted shrewdly.

"Strange as it may seem I also grieve for the two great men I have been privileged to know as friends. One an American; General Anthony Wayne, and the other whom you also knew; Chief Tecumseh of the Shawnee. I have no skill in the forest, I can hardly stay on a horse's back, and I am so small I often go unnoticed. Despite all of this I have been closely involved with major happenings in many places. I have traveled further than most in my tribe, and the words of important persons which I have translated have been written down in books. I should be happy and proud, but I am not."

"How many years are you?" Knee Bell asked, tossing a pine cone on the fire.

"That is another thing!" Tom groaned. "I don't think of myself as _old_, but my bones speak the word. Aho! I must stop this useless talk before I have dragged you down with me! Let's go to sleep now. Things always look better in the morning."

"Let me give some advice to such an _old_, _old_ man!" the Chippewa grinned as they prepared their sleeping robes. "You need to go home to your wife and daughter. A warm lodge, food prepared by loving hands, and the proud looks of a loving daughter are all the medicine you need!"

"You are right of course. But how will I be able to care for them once I return? In addition to all my other failings, now I have only one arm that works at all. I can't just show up and expect my brother-in-law to take me into his home. He has already done that for his sister, her son, and the child we had together."

"Aho!" Knee bell said quietly. "Like me you have only one skill to offer. Take your wife and daughter and head west. Join with one of those white families who are beginning to cross The Father Of Waters. You told me earlier you once worked in a trading post. Any trader, be he British, French, or American, would be a fool not to take you on as his interpreter, Think about it!"

"What a <u>great</u> <u>idea</u>! You may have given me a plan for the rest of my life! But I would need some silver money for provisions until I could be ready to take my wife and daughtern on such a journey. I have nothing now. I depend upon the British for food, such as it is, and even the occasional piece of cast-off clothing they bring us. No, without some money it would be impossible."

"Get money then!"

"Of course, but how?"

"Although we have not known each other long, I have watched your dealings with the whites. You are not very big, and you have some other problems, but never have I known one quite as clever as you! When do you next interpret for The Prophet and the Redcoat Major Bidwell?"

"In two days' time. But what does that have to do with . . ."

"Listen to me, Toom-She-chi-Kwa. Have you noticed all the necklaces, bracelets, arm bands, and other such ornaments The Prophet puts on himself lately?"

"Who could not notice?" Tom laughed. "I sometimes wonder how he can walk with all that silver and copper hanging on his body."

"Let me tell you my friend, those baubles are not all that he has been given! Surely you have noticed the moosehide money pouch he wears on his belt. It is full of British silver, and I suspect, even a few gold sovereigns! He has been paid well for his service to the Great King. You have done him much good, even to the extent of making him look impressive in the eyes of others. It is time you were paid for your labors. Think about it!" Saying no more, Knee bell settled himself to sleep.

Tom Bluefoot lay awake half the night, planning, plotting, and considering. When the conference began at Running Springs two days hence, he would be ready!

The gathering was not large. Not only The

Prophet was there but also three other major chiefs. Representing the British, two majors and several lieutenants had arrived. After the obligatory smoking and the sharing of food, The Prophet motioned for Tom to come to his side. "Prepare to interpret the words of The Principal Chief Of All The Western Tribes," he said grandly, his eye sweeping the gathering. The other chiefs exchanged thinly disguised glances of disgust, but there was nothing they could do about such bragging. Unfortunately for them, The Redcoats had <u>agreed</u> to that title! "Tom Bluefoot," he continued, nudging the Wyandot with an elbow, "see that you translate without fail every word I say. Today's conference could mean that I am free to go back to the Wabash and rule over all the tribes!"

"Yes, a few wrong words or even a phrase left out could mean disaster. All your plans would be in ruins. It is even possible that the officers could get the idea that you are threatening them! Yes, my chief, a proper translation is critical at this point," Tom said, smiling kindly.

Tenskwatawa was a charlatan and a coward, but he was no fool. "What are you babbling about?" he hissed. "The conference is about to begin. I am the principal speaker."

"As well you should be!" Tom exclaimed. "It is my expectation that as Principal Chief Of All The Western Tribes, you should be willing and even <u>anxious</u> to pay well for a proper and indeed elegant translation."

"Aho! So you expect to be paid do you?" The Chief's voice was rising with anger. "Let me tell you . . ."

"I would suggest that you lower your voice," Tom said calmly, "All are listening and watching. Would you have them believe that you are unable to pay for my services? You, 'The Principal Chief Of All The Western Tribes'? Would you have them see you as merely a minor chief who does not even have three silver coins with which to pay his underlings?"

"I see your plan, Toom-She-chi-Kwa. I <u>will</u> <u>not</u> <u>pay</u>!"

"Very well, you have spoken. I will be leaving in the morning. It has been far too long since I have seen my family. May I wish you much success at this conference. It is unfortunate that your fine words will seem to be nothing but gibberish to the British. Now I must . . ."

"All right. All <u>right</u>! You have me at a disadvantage." Trying to make the best of the public display, he opened his money bag with a flourish, counted out three silver dollars and dropped them into Tom's outstretched hand. The conference was a great success.

At every subsequent occasion, Tom demanded and received three silver pieces. In six weeks' time he had accumulated enough money to head back to Ohio and attempt to be re-united with his small family.

*   *   *

Tom simply stood and stared. The circle of ashes gave mute testimony to what had happened. The small house where he and his wife and daughters had once lived was gone, obviously burned to the ground. Nothing was left. He approached the nearest dwelling and called out, "Aho! The camp! I ask permission to be seen." He stood respectfully, not moving until the tattered door flap opened. A very old man stood peering uncertainly at his visitor. "Hello, Grandfather," Tom said, using the greeting of respect.

"What? I do not hear well. Come closer."

"I am Toom-She-chi-Kwa. That fire ring over there is where our wegiwa once stood. Do you know where the woman and child have gone? They are no longer with Flat Lance, her brother."

"Aho! I know you now. You are Wooden Nail, ain't you? My eyes have the dimming affliction. Too many years in the smoke of the lodge fires. Too many years doing <u>anything</u>! Don't just stand there, Wooden Nail. Come closer. Do you have vegetables to sell? Any whiskey? I am out of firewood. Can you help me gather some? I fall down when I go into the forest."

Tom was perplexed. "I am not Wooden Nail," he said, nearly shouting. "I have been gone for seven years.

I once lived here with my wife and little girls. I worked as a clerk in the French trading post. As you can see I was badly wounded in the war. Now that the fighting is over I have returned. Do you . . . know where the woman, named Tadpole . . .<u>has</u> <u>gone</u>?" He spaced the words out and said each one loudly and as plainly as he could.

"<u>Tadpole</u>! Yes! A girl with her. They went away to live with her brother. Someone said they all went away. They said . . .said . . . to Prophetstown."

Tom was stricken. Prophetstown again? Why would they have left Greenville for that fire-ravaged, war-torn village?

The old man was shivering. "I am cold now. I will go in and get under my robe. I have no kindling for a fire."

"Wait, Grandfather. May I enter your lodge? I will see what can be done for you, then I will gather firewood enough for many days. Do you have flint and steel for fire-making?"

"Come in. Come in, Wooden Nail. I would offer you food if I had very much. Do you plan to live here with me? You are a cousin of mine, you know. Why are you here? What happened to your arm? Do you have any white man's bread? Don't just stand there. Come in, come in, whoever you are."

It was a pitiful situation which unfortunately was being re-enacted very often throughout the Northwest

Territory. Liquor, soft foods, inadequate wages, all had contributed to such a sad state of affairs as Tom was seeing before him. He was reminded again of why he had chosen to fight with The People against the invading Americans. He cleaned up the wegiwa as best he could, shook out the moldy, flea-infested buffalo robe and settled the old man under it. "I will be back soon, Grandfather," he said as he slipped out of the door opening. Even using only one arm, it was a matter of but a few minutes to gather a large bundle of sticks. He took all the kindling inside, checked to see if the smoke hole was clear, then lit a small fire. The old man was asleep when he left.

"What are you <u>doing here</u>?" The woman's sudden voice made Tom jump. "Did you intend to harm Lost Knife? Stay here until I bring my husband. He will deal with you!"

"Please, please! I am Toom-She-chi-Kwa. I used to live here with my wife, Tadpole. I have been away to war. I was asking the old man if he knew where Tadpole had gone. I gathered some kindling for the man. I meant him no harm. He seemed confused in his mind, but for a moment he remembered my wife and child. He thought she had gone to Prophetstown with her brother."

"Are you . . .are you the Wyandot who worked for Lebeque at the trading post? I think I remember you, but I was only a little girl then. I am sorry I was rude. Let me see to the old man, then you will come to my house for supper. You look like you haven't had much to eat lately!"

"Thank you! That would be wonderful. Perhaps you will be able to tell more about the whereabouts of my wife."

She did not answer, but before she ducked under the door flap she gave Tom a troubled look.

The venison was tough and stringy, having been "jerked" during the past fall. Carmen Slow River served it proudly however, complimenting her young husband for his skill on the hunt. She offered Tom a small bowl of hominy, cooked with bits of government beef. The food was good, especially to the Wyandot who had eaten little during his homeward journey.

Thanking her and the man, Tom quickly steered their conversation back to the whereabouts of his wife and daughter. "The old man said something about Tadpole moving to Prophetstown on the Wabash. Do you know if what he said is true? I know that many from various tribes are re-gathering there, even though the governor had burned the village and is now trying to discourage resettlement there," Tom prattled on, hoping to hear what Carmen Slow River knew about his wife.

Somewhat reluctantly, she did speak then. "Yes, what the old man told you is true, even though he often forgets. Sometimes his words wander along several paths and it is not easy to follow them. My man and I look out for him as best we can, but we have little to share. What he really wants is whiskey, which is what he shouldn't have! We feel that he is not long for this world, but sometimes these old ones surprise us. They hang onto life like climbing ivy grips an oak."

Still neither Carmen nor her husband said anything about Tadpole. Tom could wait no longer. "And my wife, is she well, there by the Wabash? Is my daughter still with her? What can you tell me?"

The young wife shot a look at her husband who shook his head sadly. "Toom-She-chi-Kwa," she began, "before leaving this place, your woman married a French trapper. He took her and the girl to the village that was, as you have said, being rebuilt on the site of old Prophetstown. She had . . ."

"Married? Married? But I am her husband! How could she marry another?" Tom cried.

"She had no choice," the man said. "You were gone for a long time. She thought you were either killed in the fighting, or had abandoned her. A good man, even though he was a Frenchman, offered to come and take care of her and her grown daughter. She had <u>no choice</u>!" the husband repeated angrily. "Would you have them starve? Pah!"

"But her brother, Flat Lance, was to see to . . ."

"Her brother, who is my cousin, is dead of the white man's spotted sickness. Of his son, Red Gopher, we know nothing. Many others also perished from that sickness two years ago. Be thankful that she and her girl were cared for. You were gone, your family abandoned."

Tom was in shock. "But what . . . what will I do now? I must go and find her! I will show her that she still belongs to <u>me</u>! Yes, I must go immediately. Perhaps . . ."

"Don't be a fool!" Carmen said stoutly. "Leave her alone. She has a new life now. Your presence would only cause much trouble and confusion. Do not try to find her. That part of your life is <u>over</u>! Stay away from Prophetstown."

"Another thing that you must remember," the man said, looking Tom in the eye, "is that she now lives as wife to a man of the forests. It is quite possible that they are no longer even in the new village. She must follow her man as he sets his traps along the rivers far to the west. His living and hers come from the pelts he can gather. You cannot trap the beaver in a place of many lodges!"

"We are sorry for what we had to tell you, but it is better that you learned this from us, rather than confront your woman and her man if they are indeed still in Prophetstown. Tadpole had told us how you were shot in the arm, and your older daughter killed in the battle. We are sorry but such is life sometimes. Find a new wife or do without one. The Great Spirit will guide you in the years to come. All will be well again. You will see."

Carmen's words almost did not penetrate Tom's

mind. Still angry and confused, he hardly knew what to do next. He thanked the couple and wandered outside, not knowing where he was going. It was so much to think about. He hadn't gone far when Carmen called to him.

"Come back Tom. You can sleep here until you decide what to do. We have room near the fireplace."

"No, but thank you. Now I must be alone to gather my thoughts. I will be well and an answer will come to me soon. Once more, my thanks." He turned and kept walking, heading for a maple grove where he planned to place his sleeping robe.

In spite of all the disturbing revelations, he slept quite well, but toward morning he had a vivid and compelling dream. Simon, the slave who had escaped with him those many years ago, appeared in his dream. It seemed that the runaway was standing at the edge of a mighty river, a wild crown of many feathers on his head. White teeth flashing in a huge grin, the former slave seemed to be calling and waving for Tom to come and join him. As the dream ended, there appeared the figure of a woman, burdened down under a huge back pack. For a moment she turned and looked sadly at Tom. It was his wife, Tadpole!

"Get out of here, redskin, before I cut off them braids and stuff 'em down your throat! You see them boys doin' the poling? They'd like nothing better than to practice takin' scalps offn the likes of you!"

"Might as well save your breath, Cole. He can't understand you anyway. Wonder if he's got any more money on him? Old man Kaser says the varmint paid for his passage down the Ohio on our flatboat with a genuine King George six pence! Wonder where he got that kind of money. Looks like his one arm's all busted up."

"Probably stole the money! Hey boys, what say we just sort of tackle that little Injun? One of us kin hold him while we jest see what he's got in that pack of hisn. He might have some more of that silver with him. Seems like it'd be only fair that he share his money with us, don't it?" Cole said, looking at the four other "boatmen" behind him.

"Redskin," Cole growled at Tom, "you give money us!" He pounded his chest and glowered at the Wyandot. "Give us!" he repeated, thrusting a copper coin in Tom's face. "Give, or . . . or. . ." He made fighting motions with both fists.

Tom rose from the box where he'd been sitting and calmly faced the ruffians. "For your information, gentlemen, I have no more money in my pack. And if I did I would certainly not give it to you!"

"Wal I'll be . . ." Cole said, "he kin shore talk our

lingo good! What do you think boys, is there any reason we shouldn't just grab him and go ahead with my plan?"

"Wait a minute," Toom She-chi-Kwa said with a smile. "There is something in my pack that might be of great interest to all of you boatmen." He opened his bundle and reached in. As they crowded closer he whipped out the remaining dueling pistol he'd been given at Fort Detroit. Sadly, the other pistol had been traded for food. Using only his good hand, he snapped the hammer back and brought the small weapon to bear directly in Cole's face. As they backed off in surprise, he further stated, "You should all know that I sleep with this pistol in my hand. I keep it loaded and primed. I will shoot the first man who takes a chance at stealing anything of mine! You have been warned, so back off and leave me alone!"

"What's going on here?" Kaser, the flatboat owner demanded, glaring at each one in turn. "Cole, and you others, get back to your posts. You are supposed to be watching for snags and sandbars. This Indian has paid good money for his passage. Leave him alone and get back to work!"

Tom sat back down, his heart still pounding. He had told the truth, as indeed there wasn't any money in his pack. His three remaining silver pieces were strapped securely on his upper thigh, undetectable under his buckskin trousers.

Three days later, Kaser called all the passengers to

the bow. The sun was just peeping over the river to the east as they released the lines that had secured the craft during the night. "Tomorrow we should make it to Chambers Landing, that is if we don't get another blasted headwind. We're gonna need supplies and fresh drinking water. Them two ladies we got along is complainin' agin! Haw haw. Anyways there might be another passenger or two. If there is, you're all to make room for them. Indian Tom, you're to keep on sleeping behind them crates like you been. Boatmen, sleep up on deck towards the bow. Any questions?"

Chambers Landing was about what Tom had expected. A collection of shacks, two wegiwas, and a rickety "store" made up the establishment. But what immediately caught all the passengers' eyes was a group of four Indian men seated beside a small fire. Tom was surprised that he recognized one of the seated braves. It was "Catecahassa", Chief Black Hoof! None of the natives moved as the boatmen secured the flatboat at a rickety wharf. Black Hoof, now in his late seventies, was still a striking figure of a man. Piercing black eyes, what might be called a "noble" hooked nose, and a strong chin, set him aside from most men of his age, Indian or white.

Tom stepped ashore and approached the four Indians still seated by their fire. "Aho! Chief Blackhoof," he began, "it is good to see you again after all these years. Are you well?"

"I am well. I know you. Are you not the small

Wyandot who helped convince many chiefs to attend the great Greenville Treaty?" He stood then, but Tom could not help noticing how long it took the man to gain his feet.

"I am indeed that very one," Tom replied, clasping Black Hoof's outstretched hand. "You have maintained the look of a leader of men! It is an honor to see you alive and well after these more than twenty years. Are you and your friends planning to join us on our journey down the Ohieeyo?"

"We are. We are returning from a long and tiring trip. Our bones tell us we are getting too old for this life!"

"You will have much time to rest while we float down the river. What is your plan to get back to your people at Waughpaughkonneta?"

"We will leave this large and clumsy craft at the entrance to the Great Miami River, buy canoes, then paddle north on the Mad River to Pickaway Town. If the smaller streams prove to be too shallow we will finish the journey to our village on foot."

"This appears to be an arduous trip after you leave this great western-flowing river, Chief Black Hoof."

"It is. It _is_! That is why I have brought these strong young men along on my journey. They will paddle, I will _ride_! Ha ha. But what of you, Toom-She-chi-Kwa? When I last saw you both of your arms were working well.

What happened?"

"I took a musket ball at the Battle of Tippecanoe. My left arm has been useless ever since."

The flatboat was becoming crowded, but each group kept to itself as Captain Kaser had ordered. The boatmen had little to do, since the river was running high, and sandbars were few. Tom had feared trouble between them and Chief Black Hoof's men, but the ruffians wisely kept their distance from the well-built and well-armed braves seated along the rails.

Tom enjoyed conversing with the famous Shawnee chief as the landscape rolled slowly by. When the conversation finally began to lag, Black Hoof asked for further information regarding Tom's association with The Prophet.

"So you spent almost twenty years with that old Charlatan? Do you have any proof of that statement?"

"None but my word, Chief Black Hoof. If you don't believe me, that is your affair, but it is true, nevertheless. I was also the principal translator for Tecumseh, The Prophet's older brother. I could tell you the details of nearly all the major battles, beginning in 1812. I was not a warrior, and after I could no longer use my left arm, I was not even a scout. But I did know the language of both the Americans and the British. I was useful in that way."

"What is Tenskwatawa doing now? Is he still

wheedling money and goods from the defeated British? Or is he doing that through the Americans now? I am sure he is hard at work looking out for <u>himself</u> these days!"

Toom-She-chi-Kwa did not answer for a moment. He had no real love for Tenskwatawa, but the seer had provided for him for many years. Some loyalty was therefore in order. "The Prophet was far from perfect, as are all men," Tom began, "but I will say this much in his behalf. He never ceased to urge The People, regardless of which tribe or Sept, to honor the old ways of life, to stop depending on Shemanese goods and practices, to avoid the white man's 'fire-water', and never to sell any part of our land! In this he is to be honored."

"Did he ever speak of someday traveling far to the west of the 'Father Of Waters'?"

"Yes. On more than one occasion I overheard him discussing the possibility. Whether he was sincere or not I could not say."

Black Hoof fixed a glittering eye on his companion and posed a final question. "You claim to have spent many years living with that one-eyed man. I believe you. Tell me then, <u>did he</u> have magical powers? Did the Master Of Life actually communicate with him? Did a great vision cure him of his love for strong drink? Please be truthful, Toom-She-chi-Kwa!"

"Aho! You have asked <u>three</u> questions, great chief. As to his actual powers, I can truthfully answer that <u>he</u>

<u>did</u>! On two occasions he demonstrated his ability in ways that cannot be doubted. I cannot, nor can anyone living, prove that he actually communicated with The Master Of Life, but I believe that he did. Furthermore, there can be no doubt that he was cured from the shackles of whiskey in a single day."

"What makes you so sure of these statements, Toom-she-chi-Kwa?"

"My Wyandot father was bound by the 'devil drink' for much of his life. I was able to help him escape this affliction but it took nearly a year to do so. For that reason I can only conclude that in but one day divine intervention brought about The Prophet's deliverance from his cravings. In all the years I was associated with him I never saw him touch strong drink!"

"You have answered well, Tom Bluefoot."

"Thank you."

"Now, Wyandot, I am inviting you to my village for a visit. I will show you how my people have prospered by learning to live as the Shemanese do. Our farms yield much corn and wheat. We have orchards. Many of our Shawnee raise cattle and horses, even hogs. I myself discourage pigs. They stink up the whole town! A group of people called something like 'Quaker Friends' spent much time with us. Do you know of them?"

" I <u>do</u>! A Quaker man raised me from about age six to twelve. He was wise and very kind. I miss him."

Tom, always the polite one, then broached the subject that both men knew was lurking just below the surface of all the easy talk. "Many chiefs, at least those actively engaged in fighting the Americans, were angry that you discouraged your warriors from joining in the wars. Did you know this?"

"Pah! Of course I knew it! They called me a 'government chief.' They made others believe I was afraid to fight. That is untrue! I knew that despite the bravery of our fighting men, we were destined to lose these battles. The Shemanese had better guns, more equipment, great cannons, and many more soldiers than we could ever put in the field. It would seem that The Prophet would have been told this by The Great Spirit. I ask you, what has all the fighting, noble as it was, left us? Our red brothers are dead, buried who knows where, their wives and children left hungry and cold. I knew it would be this way, so I chose to embrace the white man's way. As chief I was responsible for all who followed my leading. They may call me all the names they wish, but first they should visit Waughpaughkonneta and see for themselves what the way of peace has done for our Sept of the Shawnee!"

Softening somewhat, Black Hoof continued. "And you, Toom-She-chi-Kwa, what will you do now that Chief Tecumseh has gone to the Happy Place, and Tenskwatawa no longer has many followers?"

"I'm working my way west, Chief Black Hoof. I have a friend who is now a doctor in Pittsburgh. I had hoped that he might accompany me across the Mississippi, but he has a wife and children. He does not wish to leave his practice, and his wife has no desire for the hard life in the wilderness."

"So you go alone then. What will you do to keep yourself alive in that great unknown land? It would be hard enough for a younger man, and one with two good arms!"

Tom gave a long sigh. "You are right. It may be that my desire is nothing but a foolish dream, but I do have a plan."

"What is your plan?"

"My friend, a black man who had been a slave in the Shemanese world, met me again two years ago. He has the gift of 'second sight', as well as the gift of a devious tongue! A small Sept of a local tribe has proclaimed him a king!"

"Aho! I know of this man! He and his wives spent two nights in Pickaway town. I made the short trip there to see him. Everyone made much of the man, especially the young maidens! Luckily for him his two wives kept the women away! Ha ha!"

"So you know of him too. Did he tell you any of his plans? I need to try to follow his travels in order to meet him beyond the great river."

"I am sorry, but I had no chance to talk with him. He did several fine dances and great crowds surrounded him, clapping and singing. They showered him with gifts and urged him to stay right there in Pickaway, but he refused."

"He is afraid of his former master. As a runaway slave in the white man's world, he feels he must travel far to the west to avoid being caught, punished, and enslaved again." Tom did not mention that he too was a fugitive, and like Simon, would only feel safe in the West.

"You will have no trouble finding "The Dancer" as he calls himself, for he would be remembered wherever he goes. When you reach The Father Of Waters, travel along its banks and ask at every crossing site if they had transported a black man and his wives. When you find where they were taken across to the western shore, go over yourself and start your search there. His trail should be easy to follow from that point on. No one could forget The Dancer!"

"Thank you Chief Black Hoof. You have given me much good advice. I think I have enough silver money left to pay for my crossing. Then if I can find The Dancer before too long it should go well with me. He did not mention a secret thought that had never left his mind.

The dream had come again during a thunderstorm two nights before. Once again the plodding figure was burdened under a heavy pack. Beside her walked a tall, slim girl dressed in ragged Shemanese clothing. As before the woman turned, and in his dream, looked directly at him. There was no reason to doubt that the travelers were his wife and grown daughter!

Tom experienced a great feeling of relief. His plans were made. The future looked bright, and he was embarking on a <u>mission</u>! The Ohio River rolled on toward the West and new adventures for Toom-she-chi-Kwa, Tom Bluefoot.

THE END